I0663075

Alien Blood Wars

MATING DANCE

SAMANTHA CAYTO

Mating Dance
ISBN # 978-1-78686-003-3
©Copyright Samantha Cayto 2019
Cover Art by Cherith Vaughan ©Copyright March 2019
Interior text design by Claire Siemaszkiewicz
Pride Publishing

Published in 2019 by Pride Publishing, United Kingdom.

Pride Publishing is an imprint of Totally Entwined Group Limited.

MATING DANCE

Prologue

Barbary Coast, San Francisco
1901

Harry watched dispassionately as Alex snapped the neck of one of Dracul's human minions. The man had sealed his own fate the moment he'd volunteered to do his master's vicious bidding. Harry felt nothing but contempt for the vile criminal. As the corpse slunk to the floor, Harry eyed the back staircase leading to the third floor of the brothel.

"Alex, I will go up to see who is sequestered there and render what aid I can." He lifted the doctor's bag he held in emphasis. "Then I—or we, if the poor soul is willing—shall meet you out back."

His leader approached, his gaze roaming the narrow corridor in search of unexpected danger. "We'll go together."

Harry put his free hand on the hilt of the dagger sheathed on his belt. It had been a gift from an Ottoman prince and it was one of his most prized possessions. He knew well how to use it. "You have more important matters to attend to. It is still possible that Dracul's brat remains on the premises. He's stupid enough to grab his ill-gotten gold before fleeing."

"Val will see to that. And, I am curious as to what lies upstairs as much as you are."

Harry believed that claim. They'd been surveilling this place for weeks before attacking. The nature of the small third floor remained a mystery. Its use was sporadic compared to the rest of the saloon and whorehouse. Whoever lurked there was either dangerous or precious, perhaps both. The rest of the building was rife with all manner of enslaved women, drugs and alcohol, all visibly available without concern that the local police would bother to intervene. Dracul's business was hardly unique in the city, yet, because it was his, Alex felt compelled to shut it down. Anything they could do to strangle Dracul's sources of income was all to the good.

Harry also knew that Alex was not in a mood for discussion, so he simply replied, "Please allow me to go first. If there is a hurt human there, they will find me less…shall we say intimidating?"

Alex nodded once. "Very well. Have a care, though."

"Of course."

Harry didn't hesitate to proceed. While he'd chosen to adopt a care-taking role in their new life, he was still a trained warrior. He could fight and kill when necessary. Somehow, he doubted that it would be. As he climbed the steep, tight stairway, he felt a strange sense of what humans would call destiny. Something, or someone, called silently to him.

He paused only a second at the wooden door that he wasn't surprised to find padlocked on the outside. Whoever resided behind it was a prisoner more so than the other lost souls housed within Dracul's den of iniquities. Harry crushed the lock with a quick squeeze before he steeled himself to go in.

He stood on the threshold of a single, sparsely yet richly appointed bedroom. A thick oriental carpet and silk brocade wall hangings caught his attention first before a quick movement forced his gaze to the far end. An adolescent boy slid off the bed in a graceful movement to stand with head bowed. His curtain of dark hair hid his face, but Harry had seen enough in that quick moment to know he was the most exquisite thing in the room. And of course, that explained everything. Even in the notorious vice-ridden Barbary Coast, availing oneself of the pleasure of a boy prostitute would be a shameful thing. Only the richest, most daring of men would do so. And it would have to be well-hidden from prying eyes.

The inhabitant stood mutely, undoubtedly waiting for orders as he'd been trained to do. He wore only a long, red-silk robe that hung open. His slender and perfect body was on display. It was too much to see, especially given his young age. No longer a child, yet not quite full grown, he shouldn't be an object of sexual desire. Harry felt ashamed to have even glimpsed as much as he had.

He turned in a futile effort to block Alex from seeing. "Please, leave this to me, sir." He kept his voice low so as to not scare the boy any more than they had already.

Of course, Alex had viewed everything, being taller than Harry and more of a warrior. He would have taken in every detail with a single glance, and that's why he didn't argue about going. "I will leave this to you, Harry. We'll make sure the building is cleared. Don't worry about danger when you come to join us outside. Give me your bag, so that you'll be able to carry him with ease."

Harry didn't hesitate to do as ordered. There was no question in his mind that he would be bringing the boy with him. And as Alex had already surmised, there was likely nothing for the boy to wear other than his robe. Those delicate feet shouldn't be forced to walk in the cold muck of San Francisco's streets.

Once Alex had left, Harry turned back to the boy. He hadn't moved an inch, but he wasn't completely still. His fingers plucked nervously at the robe and his heart beat rapidly. Harry focused on that bird-like flutter, while he inhaled the boy's scent. Underneath the acrid smell of fear was a sweetness that caused Harry's own blood to heat. He tamped down the sexual reaction but vowed that he would patiently wait for the right time to show his instant devotion to this irresistible creature. In all the years they'd been marooned, no human had ever compelled him this way.

He took a slow step forward. "It's all right. No need to be afraid. I won't hurt you."

The boy flashed his dark eyes at him for a split second before lowering them again. In that moment, Harry saw the disbelief. This boy had no reason to trust. "How may I please you?" he offered.

That voice, so soft and melodious in perfect, clipped English, sent a shiver along Harry's nerves. He swallowed hard in reaction before whipping off his coat. "There'll be none of that. Put this on," he added, approaching the boy slowly so as not to scare him even more. "It's cold outside." He held the coat in front of the boy until he reached for it with his small, trembling hand. "I'm going to carry you to protect your feet and take you away from here. You are safe with me."

Again that flashing look that broke Harry's heart with its hopeless cynicism. The boy's reticence led to Harry helping him. Harry was careful to touch as little of the human as possible, buttoning the coat to provide some privacy. No one would ever again see anything the boy didn't freely show.

"What is your name?" he asked, determined to give this former slave of Dracul's as much dignity as he could. Thinking of him as merely a boy made him into an object, instead of a person.

There was an audible swallow. The pulse at the base of the human's throat pulsed rapidly. "L-Lucien, Master."

That brief hesitation, as if saying his own name was somehow foreign to him, sent Harry's heart tumbling even further. He knew in that instant that no matter what, he would dedicate his life to protecting Lucien and giving him everything he wanted.

First, though, he had to take him away to safety. Scooping him up in his arms, he said, "Master will do for now, but I'd prefer that you call me Harry."

Lucien gasped and stiffened for a second or two before relaxing into Harry's embrace. Then he did an extraordinary thing. He lay his head against Harry's shoulder and sighed. It was a sound of utter peace, and that simple and inexplicable show of trust sealed Harry's resolve.

Someday, he hoped Lucien would call him husband.

Chapter One

Boston, Club Lux
Present day

Trey entered the club with a sense of excitement and trepidation. The grand reopening was something he'd been looking forward to attending. After the intense rescue mission and final confrontation over in Wales, he relished the idea of life returning to normal. He didn't question how his definition of what that meant now included hanging out with aliens in an exclusive place with mostly naked go-go boys and rooms where a guy could get his freak on.

The club was packed, all its members apparently coming after months of renovations due to the kitchen fire. Although the whole event had been staged as a cover, the damage had been real. Alex had taken the opportunity to redo the entire first two floors. Trey was looking forward to seeing the results and enjoying being there without being on the clock as a cop.

He was, however, on *edge*. Earlier in the day, he'd received a short, polite text request from Harry to come and speak with him at Trey's convenience sometime that night. The alien doctor had rarely communicated directly with him before. It shouldn't cause any alarm, yet it did. There was a simple reason for that. Demi. Harry was the hybrid boy's father, and things had gotten pretty intense and weirdly intimate between them during the rescue. Not only had Demi continued to show his devotion to Trey, but Trey had also lost his own internal struggle to hide his feelings for Demi.

If he thought about it—and he did constantly—he could still feel Demi's fangs sunk deep in his wrist, sucking in his blood for life-saving nourishment. He didn't regret a thing that he'd done in Wales, would do it again in a heartbeat. It was the aftermath that haunted him. He hadn't known how to act or what to do once they'd been safely back, first at Malcolm's castle then in Boston. His conflicting feelings for the half-alien man-child hadn't gotten any easier to deal with. And now Harry wanted to talk. About what was the question that had plagued Trey for hours.

His brooding was disturbed by Karl smacking his arm. "Man, this place is hopping."

They'd come together because his partner had asked that of him. Straight as an arrow, Karl wasn't exactly comfortable in such an unabashedly gay space. But he was in deep with the club's bar manager, Kitty, and he welcomed any excuse to spend time with her. Trey figured they'd done a lot of that when they'd mutually held down the fort during the Wale's adventure. What, if anything, had transpired between the seemingly mismatched couple hadn't come up voluntarily from

Karl. Trey didn't feel comfortable raising the issue, either.

"Not surprising, given how long it's been closed. And there's nothing like it in Boston to take the clientele away."

There was a short line of men approaching, where they showed their membership cards to a pretty boy who managed to flirt and scrutinize with equal skill. Trey started to pull out his own wallet as his turn came, but Val materialized out of the shadows and intercepted him.

"No need for that, brother." The massive guy with the don't-fuck-with-me Mohawk greeted both Trey and Karl with surprising warmth.

They each went through the ritual of hand-clasping and back thumping of the typical modern American tough guy before Val led them past the checkpoint.

"We've got a VIP table set up for you right by the dance floor." Val glanced back at them. "It's permanently yours, actually. We, ah, hope you both come anytime you feel like it."

Although Alex had extended free membership to them both previously, Trey hadn't felt comfortable imposing on the generosity. Plus, he hadn't wanted to give Demi any wrong ideas. Now that he was muddled in his own thinking about the boy, he had more of an incentive to stay away. Still, the fact that the Stelalux clan thought well enough of both him and Karl to give them a reserved table was sweetly endearing. They weren't merely tolerated by the aliens or useful tools for them. They genuinely liked them, apparently.

"Thanks," he said over the din of the music. "We appreciate it. Don't we, Karl?"

"Yeah," his partner said, craning his neck around the room. "Although no offense, I'm more of a sit at the bar kind of guy."

Of course you are. "None taken. Go ahead," he replied, giving him a gentle shove.

He shook his head ruefully at Val. "He's never going to give up there."

Val's gaze followed Karl's progress across the room. "Oddly, I think he has every reason to keep at it."

"Really?" Was it possible that the stern and scary Kitty was softening toward the puppyish, yet determined, Karl?

Val shrugged. "Stranger things..." He kept going, clearing a path in the throng of partying men, his imposing figure parting the lesser humans without effort. He stopped at a small, two-seater table right at the edge of the dance floor. There was a 'reserved' sign literally embedded in the dark wooden top.

"Here you go, Duncan," the bouncer said with a flourish of his arm. "Front row seat. The show's about to start. I hope you enjoy it. Mackie and the boys have been working hard on the choreography."

"Thanks." Trey sat in the nearest chair. "I'm sure I will."

Val gave him a squeeze on his shoulder before leaving.

Alone with his thoughts, Trey started worrying about his meeting with Harry again. He took in the room as he did so. There wasn't a huge difference from the old décor. Everything was still mostly black and silver with red accents and more deep purple ones. He knew these were colors that resonated with the aliens. Black was standard for warriors, while the red represented blood, naturally. The purple echoed the hue of their irises.

And silver? Well, apparently that was the queen. At least, that was what Emil had told him. Trey hadn't dared ask any follow-up questions. The look of reverence in the alien's eyes at the mere mention of their ultimate leader was too intense for casual conversation.

The whole space was still the epitome of luxury, regardless. Everything was shiny and plush. He'd felt out of place when he'd first entered the club months ago while investigating a murder. Now, he felt comfortable. The velvet seat embraced his backside with the softness of a cloud. The muted lighting managed to make everything appear sexy. There were still platforms with stripper poles at the four corners of the dance floor. Boys already gyrated around to the delight of the patrons. There was some new talent, as well, and he couldn't help but appreciate the beauty on display.

An ice-cold glass of beer appeared in front of his eyes. "Here you go, honey. Kitty thought you'd want to start with this." A gorgeous boy with mocha skin, chocolate eyes and wearing only shiny silver boy-shorts batted his eyelashes as he put the beer down. "If you want anything else, I'll be close by." He turned and sauntered away with a swish of his narrow hips.

Trey didn't have more than a second to appreciate the sight before Kitty's voice boomed over the sound system. She asked for everyone to clear the dance floor because the show was about to begin. This was new — actual routines by the go-go boys. He'd caught bits and pieces of their practice sessions during their mission. He knew it was going to be good and a way to take his mind off his impending 'talk' with Harry. He settled back with his beer at his lips as the overhead lights dimmed and the men's conversations dropped off.

The raucous alternative rock music cut out and the opening strains of something more classic started. It took him a second to realize it was U2's *Mysterious Ways*. Spotlights flared on and four boys strutted out onto the dance floor from the back. They were modestly attired compared to the ones still at the poles, wearing white, ribbed, sleeveless T-shirts and ripped jeggings. Their feet were bare, but their hips were draped with scraps of plaid. Mackie and Demi pulled a few paces ahead of Quinn and Jase as they all began their coordinated routine. The boys on the poles began to gyrate around, also in sync with each other.

None if it mattered, of course. Trey's focus was on one boy only — Demi. The others were only so much fluttering around the main attraction as far as he was concerned. And that hybrid boy's gaze homed in on him in a millisecond, too. As he pranced his way forward, Demi kept Trey a captive by his attention. No matter what way the boy twisted and turned, he always landed his stare back on him. Trey couldn't have looked away if the club caught on fire again.

The boys' efforts brought the house down with cheers and clapping. His beer forgotten, Trey leaned forward as if he could get an even better view. Alex and the others had been generous with the position of the table. There was no way that he could be closer to the action or see the dance routine any better. Still, he tried, scooting his chair so close to the brass railing that his knees banged into it. He then gripped it with sweaty palms and white knuckles.

All the boys were good, but Demi outshone them with an inhuman grace that not even Mackie could mimic. He practically floated across the floor, his feet carrying him so smoothly that it was almost as if he didn't touch the ground. Trey's gaze landed on the mesmerizing swing of the boy's hips. He wasn't so far possessed that he didn't notice the pattern of the plaid draped there. He'd assumed Mackie wore his own family's tartan. The other boys, who knew? But, the pattern and colors hugging Demi jolted a deep memory in Trey.

It's the Duncan plaid.

Demi was honoring Trey's family in a way that caused a welling of possessiveness deep within him. It left him breathless. This was *his* boy, whether he willed it or not. Demi believed it to be so, and God help him, Trey did as well. His cock hardened and he didn't even bother to try to convince it to stand down. Right when Bono admonished the boy in the song to get down on his knees, the dancers dropped in unison. With thighs spread, they threw back their heads and made an O face. That brought the house down, and Trey nearly came right in his pants like a teenager. Then they ripped their tops in two from collar to hem and tossed the shredded remains to the audience. Of course, Demi sent his sailing directly toward Trey. He caught the scrap of fabric and clenched his fingers around it.

The newly-bared chests were painted in colorful symbols. All the men around him undoubtedly thought they were looking at nonsense markings to accentuate the boys' toned chests. But Trey knew differently. That was the alien script, although what it said or meant, he had no idea. It only served to highlight Demi's alien nature, and while it should have scared him, it didn't. Nothing could put him off his desire for Demi at this point.

As the show came to an end, the club members tossed money onto the floor. The boys blew kisses to their audience while scooping up their earnings. They all managed to dodge grabbing hands at the same time. In comparison, the boys on the poles jumped off their stages and worked the crowd for tips and cuddles. Naturally, the main four were not going to expose themselves to the kind of attention that could lead their alien lovers and husband to having murderous fits — or in the case of Demi, an avenging father.

Not if I get there first. That possessive thought reared up and he disturbingly didn't even try to tamp it down again. He even bared his teeth at a guy who leaned over the rail in an effort to make contact with Demi.

Trey needn't have bothered. Demi easily side-stepped the grabby hand and sidled up to the rail by Trey. He grinned coyly. "Did you enjoy the show, Sergeant Hottie?"

By way of answer, Trey took out his wallet and liberated the Benjamin he'd put there earlier in the day. He'd known about the dancing in advance, and while Demi had access to money Trey could only dream of, he wanted to show his appreciation. It was the only safe way he knew how to. He held it up.

With his smile firmly in place, Demi gripped the railing with one hand, while plucking the bill from Trey's grasp with the other. Their fingers touched for a brief moment, the feel of it electrifying. At least for Trey it was. His dick jerked and his face heated. He could tell from Demi's expression that he knew what effect he had. He morphed his pretty lips into a kissing purse as he leaned closer.

Trey froze with indecision. He wanted to press his mouth to the boy's, to take what was being offered. It would be like playing with fire. He knew it would, yet the impulse to take and taste and savor was overwhelming. His ass was half off his chair before he realized what he was doing.

It all changed in a second. Demi's expression fell and he pulled back. It took Trey a moment to realize that someone had come to stand behind him. That's where Demi's eyes were now fixed. And it didn't take a lot of thought or imagination to know who it was. Sweat broke out all over Trey's body as he sat back and looked up.

"Hi, Harry." He tried for a polite smile but feared he failed miserably.

Surprisingly, Demi's father didn't grab him by the throat and snap his neck. He didn't even shoot him a menacing look. Instead, he inclined his head with a mere tightening of his lips. "Good evening, Sergeant Duncan."

The man's attention shifted back to his son. "Demi, go back to the dressing room now before the patrons get the wrong idea about your—*availability*."

Surprisingly, Demi didn't so much as frown at the order. "Yes, Papa." He batted his eyelashes at Trey, however, before he twirled around and practically skipped away.

Trey took the opportunity to down a good amount of his beer before facing Harry again. "Um, you wanted to talk?"

Harry watched until his son had left the room before replying. "Yes, if you would please come up to our apartment. This is too public a place and Lucien insists on joining us."

Okay, that added an element of concern. As scary as Harry could be, his human husband put the capital F in the word fierce when it came to their son. Trey figured the goings-on at Dracul's castle must have been conveyed to the man and he had a few choice warnings he wanted to personally give Trey. Not that he could blame the guy. Demi was precious and in need of protection.

He took another slug of his beer before putting it down and standing. "Yeah, sure. Lead the way."

He walked through the club in Harry's wake like a man condemned. It took a few seconds for him to remember he still clutched the ruins of Demi's T-shirt. He stuffed it into his pocket, knowing it was still visible but unwilling to drop it. Fuck it. If Harry and Lucien didn't like this obvious show of devotion, they could kill him for all he cared. It would be worth it.

* * * *

Demi headed straight for the boys' dressing room, both delighted and suspicious that his fathers wanted him to be there. They'd been acting weird since returning from Wales. There had been lots of furtive, quiet discussions that always stopped the moment Demi came into the room. Something was up, and usually that meant he wasn't going to like the turn his life was about to take.

In the meantime, though, he was going to bask in the glory of the show being such a success. And in particular, the thrill of receiving the hundred-dollar bill that he clutched from Trey was making it nearly impossible to keep his feet at human speed. He wanted to race with glee. After a couple of months of nearly no communication, Trey had not only come tonight, he'd bathed Demi in the warmth of his undivided attention.

The man wanted him. There was no denying that now. It had been one thing for Trey to offer up his vein to keep Demi alive and get hard in the process. It was something else entirely for him to focus his attention on Demi as he had tonight. That had been unpremeditated and unscripted. The man's hard-on had been visible to Demi's excellent vision, and knowing Trey desired him was an emotional and physical high that sent him into a delirium of happiness.

"Oops, sorry." Jase almost ran into him racing out into the corridor.

The guy was buttoning up his white coat as he undoubtedly headed to the kitchen. Dancing was fun for Jase, but he loved cooking and he loved Emil. The usually mild-mannered chef had gone into full possessive-warrior mode when other men had pawed at the boy. Jase hadn't intended to linger on the dance floor once their routine was done so that Emil would have no cause to go medieval on some guy's ass. It was kind of sweet, actually, and the obvious devotion on both sides was enviable.

"No worries," Demi called out to Jase's retreating back before continuing on.

The dressing room was packed, Alex having given Mackie free rein to hire more go-go boys. Club Lux was back, better than ever. There was a relaxed, almost carefree, feeling about the place that Demi had never experienced before with his family. Dracul's demise had lifted the pall that had blanketed everyone for centuries before Demi had been born. It was easy for him to slip in and go through to the shower room without the others noticing. He wanted a few more minutes to himself.

He had his own cubby here now, where he kept some clothing. He headed directly there to take off what little he had on. The jeans were no big deal, something he tossed into the communal hamper once he'd shimmied out of them. The plaid was different. He managed to leave it in place, even as he pulled off his pants. The feel of the wool along his skin was delicious. Had Trey noticed how this was the Duncan tartan? He expected so because Trey was sharp like that, missing nothing. It had been an honor to represent the Scottish clan that he dared to hope he'd someday join.

His cock took advantage of its freedom by springing up almost immediately. It caused him to whip off the plaid so as not to risk soiling it with pre-cum. Thank God no one else was around to see his lack of control. Having waited an eternity for his body to mature in this way, once it had, there was no stopping it. It had only been a few months, ever since he'd started to feel weird, since his dick had been making demands. After a lifetime of just lying there, it had suddenly become the one thing his day had to revolve around.

It was ridiculous, yet perfectly normal. So said Papa after Dad had mortifyingly entered Demi's room one morning while he was taking his morning wood in hand. Yeah, that had been a kill-me-now kind of moment followed by an equally cringe-worthy 'talk' with his non-human parent later in the day. Apparently, his alien side was mega horny. He had an indeterminant number of years ahead of him where jerking off multiple times a day would be necessary if he didn't want excruciatingly painful balls.

Grabbing a scrunchy for his hair, he raced to one of the showers. By the time he'd twisted his hair up into a messy bun, his cock was practically jerking itself. It was as if the thing was sentient. He could practically hear it calling to him to hurry up and give it relief. He curled his fingers around the shaft with one hand while turning the water on with the other. The spray hit his chest around the same time that he came.

Honestly, it was almost clinical, like peeing, simply a biological necessity with little pleasure to be had, although the intensity of the orgasm made his head spin. He pitched forward, slapping his free hand against the wall to remain upright. He bit back the low groan pushing past his lips, too. The last thing he wanted to do was call attention to himself. Likely he wasn't the first or last boy to masturbate in this shower, but he still didn't want to become an object of teasing. His emotions were volatile these days, and he didn't trust himself to take it with good humor.

When he felt steady enough to let go of the wall, he clutched at his balls and squeezed. He continued to milk the shaft at the same time, determined to drain every drop of cum. Later in bed, he could do this again with less urgency. At least, he hoped he could. He wanted to enjoy it while picturing the look on Trey's face as he'd watched him dance.

Once his dick hung spent, he lathered up his chest to wash off the symbols painted there. He hated to remove them because they proclaimed his love for the human cop. The writing had been Mackie's idea, and each of the boys had latched onto it with enthusiasm. It was a secret message for their husband and lovers. No one else in the club would know it to be anything other than pretty pictures. Of course, only Demi had known the language. He'd painted the others before Quinn had copied the writing onto Demi's chest. While he knew Trey hadn't understood what he'd seen, it had still been one of the best parts of the show for Demi.

He didn't care, either, that his family could read the message. He wasn't ashamed of how he felt about the human. After all that Trey had done for them, they should welcome him, too. Nevertheless, he was prepared to get an earful from his fathers later that night. Or, maybe not. They weren't acting their usual selves, so he had no idea what they were thinking these days.

The sounds of raucous laughter cut through the pounding water. He quickly finished up, dried and threw on a fresh T-shirt and jeans. Having spent the vast majority of his life living with adults, he was happy to be able to hang out with boys of his own age. Sort of. He didn't like dwelling on how different he was from the others. It was enough that they saw him as a contemporary. Years of loneliness had made him awkward around others. He hadn't known how to act with people of his own level of maturity, so he'd lashed out, been bratty as a kind of defense. He felt differently now. Although his emotions were running riot along with his physical discomforts, he was also more comfortable in his interactions. He liked being with other boys.

"Demi, sweetie," Mackie called out from across the room. "Come join us. We're celebrating our smashing success."

The redhead sat on one of the new sofas in the expanded dressing room along with Quinn. They were sipping what looked like flutes of champagne. Mackie held a full one out to him as he approached.

Demi eyed the glass. "If you think I'm going upstairs with alcohol on my breath..." Part of him was thrilled at the idea, but the more practical side knew his fathers would kill him if he did.

Quinn giggled. "It's only sparkling cider. We're not trying to get you into trouble."

"Oh." Pleased that his friends were concerned about him, he took the offering and plopped down between them. The cold drink was marvelous and the bubbles tickled his nose, just like how the real stuff was supposed to.

Neither of the other two had bothered to shower. They sat with their painted chests still on display. All around them, go-go boys bustled about, getting ready to go on, or coming back to clean up from their previous rotation out on the poles and giving lap dances. Demi liked the company but didn't envy any of them. His dancing was purely for fun, and his ambitions went beyond being an entertainer, even if his fathers would allow him to be a go-go boy. Which of course, they never would.

It didn't matter. He intended to follow in Papa's footsteps and become a doctor. His experience caring for Dafydd had cemented that interest. He knew he could be good at it. His other ambition was more prosaic, yet within reach and more thrilling. He wanted to be like Mackie, a husband—Trey's husband, to be exact. Silly as it was, since returning from Wales, he'd started imagining what his wedding would be like. He'd also secretly tried out various versions of his new name—Demetrius Duncan, Demi Duncan, Demi Stelalux-Duncan. That last one was a mouthful, so he was leaning against it. The family name was entirely made up anyway. It had no real meaning other than as an effort to fit into human culture. Whereas, the

Duncan name was a continuation of Trey's family line. He wanted to be part of that tradition.

Mackie nudged him with his elbow. "So, Duncan came. All that worrying was for nothing. I told you he would."

Yes, Mackie, the eternal optimist, had been reassuring on that point. Demi grinned. "Yeah, you did." He sipped more cider and visualized how Trey had watched him during the show.

"He was super into you, too," Quinn added. "I mean, the rest of us were invisible as far as he was concerned."

Demi frowned despite his good mood. "How would you know?" He inwardly winced at the jealousy dripping from his question.

Quinn merely grinned. "Down, boy. I'm Alex's, remember? I just notice how the club members act, that's all. I have to be attuned to them, especially to make sure none of them are getting too close or handsy with me." He sighed. "Alex is possessive enough as it is. If I'm going to keep dancing, I have to make sure he doesn't have anything to worry about."

"I'm amazed he's as chill about it as he is," Mackie remarked.

Quinn snorted. "You think so?" He shook his head.

Leaning over Demi, Mackie said, "Oh, sweetie, are you having trouble?"

Demi was content to just sit and listen, but he was genuinely concerned about Quinn, and if he was having problems with Alex, Demi wanted to help. He waited intently for his friend to answer.

Quinn wrinkled his nose and squirmed. "Ever since we got back from Wales, he's been pestering me to go to school. He thinks I should get a college degree or something. Thinks dancing is a dead-end," he added quietly so the other boys in the room couldn't hear.

"I can see his point," Mackie said, equally quietly. "I mean, I'm taking online courses in accounting and management so that I can do my job here better. And," he added, looking at Demi, "you're thinking of being a doctor, right?"

Pleased to be included in the conversation directly, he nodded. "Yeah, I'm definitely going to do that."

"Well, that's great for you two. I just want to dance and be with Alex. I'm thinking of, you know…" Sliding down farther into the couch, he whispered, "Having him change me."

"Oh!" Mackie scrunched closer so that the three of them were in a tight, little scrum. "It's amazing. You should definitely do it."

Quinn grimaced. "But Alex says we have to wait. I'm too young to commit yet."

Demi gasped and so did Mackie, which just made Demi feel even more included. They huddled even closer, so much so that he could feel the warmth of the human bodies. He closed his eyes briefly and imagined it was Trey pressed up against him. Other than with his father, who wasn't wholly human anymore, he hadn't had much experience with the sensations he now felt.

"My fathers are endlessly saying the same thing to me," he dared to offer, afraid the others would scoff and remind him that he *was* really young.

They didn't.

Mackie patted his arm. "Sweetie, they have learned differently now, haven't they? You were like the hero of the day back in Wales."

Demi beamed at the praise. He couldn't help it. "They have been giving me more space lately."

"Ugh," Quinn scoffed. "I wish Alex would give me less. I mean, I want to be with him. I don't understand why he's pushing me away."

Before Demi or Mackie could reply, Quinn stood and downed the rest of his drink. "I'm due on stage. I need to put on a thong, but I'm not going to scrub off the paint so that maybe Alex will get the message that I'm his, no matter what I do."

Mackie sat back. "Good luck, sweetie."

"Yeah," Demi added, although he was sorry that the confab was ending.

"So," Mackie said after Quinn had left, "what's up with your hanging around here?"

Demi shrugged. "I don't know. Dad told me to stay down here until Papa comes to collect me." He finished his drink. "I was shocked that they let me dance, but I'm frankly more surprised they didn't force me back upstairs right after. Funny, Papa came over when I was talking to Trey, so I thought they'd changed their mind."

"Um." Mackie grabbed the bottle of cider and refilled both their glasses.

"What?"

"Nothing." The other boy busied himself with drinking.

Demi grew more alert. "You know something."

"Not really." Mackie averted his gaze. "I just overheard Harry asking Val the other day if he knew whether Duncan was coming tonight. He, ah, wanted to speak with him, I guess."

Demi shifted to face Mackie. "Why? About what?"

Mackie turned wide eyes on him. "Sweetie, I don't know. Val didn't ask because he's, you know, *Val*. So uncurious about other people's private things. It's really annoying sometimes. *I* would have asked."

"Huh." Demi slumped back, not sure whether he should be worried or excited. What could his fathers want with Trey?

Chapter Two

Trey had never been in Harry's private quarters before. While plenty of gatherings had occurred in Alex's suite, this part of the family's living space had always been off limits. He wasn't surprised to find that it was tastefully appointed with what appeared to be very expensive furnishings and trappings. A few accent pieces from Asian cultures caught his eye as he followed Harry into the living room. He wasn't sure what Lucien's background was, but he imagined the pair had traveled quite a lot in their years together. From what he could tell, the Stelalux clan had frequently moved around.

Unsurprisingly, Lucien was waiting for them. He sat demurely at the far end of a sofa with a chubby baby in his arms. The kid was sucking noisily on a bottle. This was Dracul's son, Idris, and he was way bigger than he'd been when Trey had cradled him in his own arms right after birth.

"Jesus, the kid's growing like a weed." The observation was out of his mouth before he could think better of it.

Lucien gave him an indulgent smile. "Yes, he'll grow significantly in the first two years, then slow down for many decades afterward. At least, he will if Demi is any indication of hybrid physiology."

The reminder of Trey's romantic and sexual obsession brought his worry back. This wasn't a social call. Of that, he could be sure. Still, he kept up the pretense of chit-chat as he took a seat in a nearby chair.

"Is Dafydd taking any interest in him yet?"

Dracul's former sex slave was living here in Boston, instead of back with Malcolm. It had been decided that the Highlander and his lover, Brenin, had enough on their hands rehabilitating the other Dracul captives. They didn't need the added burden of dealing with the clearly traumatized and potentially suicidal Welshman.

Lucien shook his head. "No. He stays in his own room and refuses to see his son."

Harry sat next to his husband and ran a hand down the baby's head. "At least Dafydd has fully recovered from the surgery and eats properly. I no longer worry about him wasting away." The doctor eyed Trey. "He owes his life to you."

Trey furrowed his brows. "Not really. You did all the work and Demi kept him alive with his blood." The reminder of that night still caused his guts to tighten. It had been a risky procedure all around.

"True, but I don't believe Demi could have spared so much blood without feeding off you. I would have stopped the transfusion and let Dafydd bleed out before allowing Demi to die. So, by logical deduction, you saved the man. He might even one day thank you for it."

"I doubt it, and it's not necessary in any event. I'm a cop. I did what had to be done." While talking about the Wales adventure—especially as some heroic effort on his part—made him uncomfortable, it was putting off whatever tongue lashing he was in for. He was fine with that delay.

"For Demi, yes?" Lucien asked. He kept his gaze on Trey while pulling the empty bottle out of the baby's mouth and hoisting him against his shoulder. "You care for our son."

Trey had to work at not squirming. He was a grown-ass man, not a middle school kid sitting in front of the vice principal, for God's sake. He didn't give in to the urge to brush off the assumption about his feelings, either.

"Yes, I do." He kept his answer simple. There was no point in elaborating anyway, given that he was hard put to understand the complexity of his feelings toward Demi himself.

Harry shared a veiled look with his husband before saying, "We knew it already, naturally, after what has transpired. But, decorum required that we confirm it with you before we proceed with asking for a favor."

Now, Trey was more intrigued than worried. Gripping the chair's arms, he leaned forward a little. "What kind?"

The men didn't answer right away. As he patted the baby's back, Lucien stared at his husband for a few seconds before nodding. "I must put Idris down for the night. Harry will explain."

With that, Lucien stood and walked out of the room. Harry's gaze followed his husband's journey until he was out of sight. Even from an angle, Trey could see the utter love and devotion the alien had for his human partner.

Harry slowly shifted his attention toward Trey. "He is and always will be the most exquisite man I have ever seen. My dear, sweet Lucien," he added with a rueful smile. "He brings out the most protective instincts in me, and yet has the power to fell me with a single, disapproving look."

Trey said nothing. He didn't know what to say in response, although he kind of understood what the guy meant. Although he'd fought his feelings from the beginning, Demi had a similar effect on him.

"Would you like a drink?"

The question surprised Trey. "Ah, sure, whatever you've got is fine."

Harry stood. "I have some of Malcolm's most excellent Scotch."

"Perfect. I'll take mine neat. Thanks."

There was a small bar set up on a sideboard across the room. Harry went there, poured a couple of stiff drinks and brought them back. "Lucien is trusting me to discuss this delicate matter about our son with you man-to-man."

Trey took the glass being offered. "*Okay.*"

Harry smiled as he sat. "Please don't be alarmed. I'm not going to threaten your life or anything."

"Glad to hear it." Trey took a healthy swig of his Scotch. Damn, it was smooth.

"Lucien was painfully young when I found him. He was perhaps fifteen by human years, although he wasn't sure himself of his exact age." The man sipped his drink. "He'd been sold as a very young boy by his father to a warlord to whom he owed money. Lucien's life became a blur of sexual servitude to men with no conscience. The last thing I wanted to do was exploit him further.

"But he surprised me. He was naturally submissive, yet had a will of steel. He wore me down with his devotion and determination. Eventually, I succumbed to his charms and my own weakness. I made him my lover, then my source of blood and eventually the carrier of my son. I've never fully let go of my guilt over it."

"Given that it produced Demi, I can't blame you for your choices. And," Trey added with a sigh, "I'm hardly one to cast stones."

"Because you believe Demi is too young."

Trey snorted. "I know it."

"How old do you think he is?"

Trey waved with his arms. "I don't know, sixteen, seventeen?"

"He's one hundred and five."

In the midst of taking a slug of his Scotch, Trey choked on the information. "Jesus," he wheezed, "I guess I shouldn't be surprised by that. I'm not sure it matters, regardless. It's more than the number of years that have passed. It's about mental and emotional maturity."

"True, except that you judge him by human standards." He clammed up for a few long seconds, as if gauging what to say next. "Lucien remarked that Idris will grow quickly at first. And that's true. By the time he's technically two, he'll appear more like six or seven. Then he'll seem to stay in that young state for many years to come. Another growth spurt will give him the appearance of a young teenager. Again, he'll plateau at that level for decades. At least, that is how it was with Demi and with the other hybrids I've had a chance to monitor."

The man got up to fetch the bottle of Scotch. He brought it back with him this time and topped off Trey's glass along with his own before putting it down on the coffee table.

"As strange as this is for humans, it's more so for our species." He sat heavily, obviously struggling to deal with whatever was going on. "Our growth is very long and mostly even. By our standards, the hybrids mature very quickly in all respects."

Trey drank half his glass before responding. This was an even weirder conversation than he'd expected, and where it was heading wasn't clear in the least. "Right... I get that. He's old and young at the same time. But, that's all physical, right? Demi acts like a kid, no matter how long he's been alive."

Even as he said that, however, he realized that wasn't entirely true. Demi's behavior had changed since they'd first met. He *was* maturing.

"By your estimation, perhaps, although his mental growth has also occurred in fits and starts. All of which is beside the point, unfortunately."

"How so?" The question came out more sharply than he'd intended. Something in Harry's tone was worrisome.

"Demi has entered puberty, for lack of any better word to use."

"Well, yeah, he's obviously a teenager, not a little boy."

Harry shook his head. "No, that's why the word is inadequate. For you humans, there is a many-year process of transforming from childhood into adulthood. Sexual maturity is part of that, where biology readies their bodies for reproduction before they are truly capable of such responsibility. For our species, it's a far quicker process, a matter of Earth months rather than years."

No longer interested in his drink, Trey leaned over to put his glass down and concentrate on what Harry was saying. "I'm not following."

"I'm sorry. I know this is difficult. You see, up until a few months ago, Demi was physically, by my species' standard, a child. Then he started puberty, which meant that he could get erect and achieve orgasm for the first time, just like with humans."

Trey couldn't help wincing. *Wow.* This was so not the conversation he wanted to have with Demi's father. It was more painful than when his own had given him 'the talk' after he'd turned thirteen and was soiling his sheets with wet dreams.

Mercifully, Harry plunged on without requiring any response. "He also had the classic symptoms of overheating, clumsiness and tremendous blood lust. I'd started him on daily bags a few weeks before we left for Wales, whereas he'd only needed the occasional drink before. Yours was the first direct feeding he'd ever had," he added with a pointed look in Trey's direction.

He'd known that, but hearing it again gave him a weird sense of pride—and possessiveness. As he instinctively rubbed at the spot inside his wrist, he had the instant thought that he didn't want Demi to feed off anyone else, which was dumb. He had no claim on the boy.

You're fooling yourself.

He closed his eyes on that painful truth. "Can you please cut to the chase here, Harry?"

"Certainly. I'm sorry, but the bottom line is that Demi needs his manhood initiation."

Trey popped his eyes open. "Huh?"

"I wish there were a better way to put it in English — or any Earth language. There isn't. It's such a beautiful word in my own tongue, although your ears wouldn't think it so. It simply means that he needs to lose his virginity — and soon."

Now all the spit dried in Trey's mouth. He emptied his glass in a futile effort to wet it again. "Needs?" That was the only word he could croak out before grabbing the Scotch and pouring another stiff drink.

"Yes. I mean that in the real sense of the word. It's not hyperbole. On my world, when a boy matures into a drone, he's given to whichever queen directly governs his family to be initiated into mating. For some, such as Alex, that meant the High Queen, a singular honor. But regardless, the queen shows him what it means to be intimate with another, and from that point forward, the drone can be sexually active with either gender."

Hot jealousy stabbed at his heart. "You mean he has to sleep with a woman?"

Harry gave him a wan smile. "Ideally. That would be the obvious way to handle matters, but who would that be? Someone willing, that goes without saying. We would never force our ways, including blood-drinking, on a human. That was Dracul's habit, never ours. Kitty is the only one we could even ask. Given Logan's struggle with her own demons, we would never impose on her."

Trey flashed on the image of the bartender with his precious Demi. The fury he felt scared him. It was a stupid reaction. Kitty could be trusted in all things, except... "What does Demi say?"

"Nothing. We haven't spoken to him yet."

Trey turned a sharp eye on the man. "Why not? This is *his* life, *his* body. He gets to decide."

Harry sighed. "I agree, of course. I do, as does Lucien. We must protect him, though, and we don't want to raise his hopes only to have them dashed."

"Meaning?"

"Regardless of whether Kitty would be willing to help, Demi wouldn't want her — or any woman, for that matter. He has only ever showed an affinity for his own sex — and for you in particular. Simply put, he has a massive crush on you."

Trey felt his cheeks warm. "Yeah, well, I kind of feel the same way about him."

"Exactly. That's why Lucien and I are asking you if you will do us the honor of initiating our son into manhood."

On an expulsion of breath, Trey flopped back in his chair. He crossed his legs to hide how quickly and violently he'd reacted to the idea of bedding Demi. "Jesus," was all he managed to say.

"We understand we are asking a great deal of you. By your view, Demi is young and humans largely take this issue of sexual initiation almost as seriously as my species does. We wouldn't ask if it weren't so critical that Demi be deflowered as soon as possible."

Trey rubbed his forehead at a growing headache. "Why? What's the hurry, exactly?"

Harry didn't answer right away. He stared for long seconds at his drink. "This is not a thing that is delayed. There is no reason to on my world. I've never known a hybrid to go through an extended period of puberty, so I don't know the effect. I only know that its symptoms will continue to plague Demi and prolonging them may lead to a permanent damage I can only guess at."

Trey's physical pain vanished. He sat forward again. "What kind? Is he at risk of real harm?"

"Yes, he is." This came from Lucien, who had quietly re-entered the room.

Harry stood in courtly fashion to escort his husband back to the sofa. They sat with their bodies touching from shoulder to ankle, a unified front in all respects.

"How so?" Trey didn't even care that he was barking out questions as if he had a right to know everything.

"I can't say, precisely," Harry admitted. "I only know that he's suffering and we won't take any chances with him. As much as we would like to keep him our little boy longer, this is out of our control. He must take this step, and we are asking you to gift him with your body. It's a tremendous request. We understand that."

Trey waved that concern away. "No, it's not. I was prepared to sacrifice my life for him. This, whatever it ends up being, is nothing." He took a deep breath and let it out slowly. "What do you need me to do?"

"Allow Demi to…" Harry didn't get a chance to come up with the right words.

Lucien jumped in. "Penetrate you."

Trey's hole clenched at the stark words. He hadn't bottomed since his late teens when he'd been experimenting with what it meant to him to be gay. Given his natural dominant inclination, he'd learned early that he was a top all the way. But this was Demi's health and possibly life at stake.

"Okay, fine. Where and when?" He wasn't one to dither over things. Besides, in all honesty, being 'forced' into making love to Demi was what he wanted anyway.

Harry and Lucien traded looks. Apparently, they hadn't expected him to be sold on the idea so easily. That only meant they hadn't been paying attention as much as they thought they had. Once Demi had literally sunk his teeth into him, he'd claimed Trey in a way that was undeniable and irresistible.

"Well," Harry finally said, "there is a ceremony of sorts. I'll need to speak with Alex about how we might recreate it with a human twist." He licked his lower lip. "It might not matter to Demi, but it will to me. In this, I want to be selfish."

Trey frowned, a frisson of concern creeping in despite his determination. "You don't mean like a wedding, do you? Demi is definitely too young to be making that kind of decision right now, especially if his hormones are clouding his judgment."

"No." Lucien was quick to reassure him. "It's purely about sex, and we agree with you on the marriage part." He lowered his gaze demurely. "Although having once been Demi's age and in love, I disagree with you and my husband as to whether Demi knows his own mind on this."

He raised his eyes again to stare directly at Trey. "Demi loves you, has since the first moment he saw you, just like I fell instantly in love with Harry. I knew that despite how men had exploited and abused me my whole life, that he was different. I wanted to be with him forever, and I haven't had a moment of regret."

"My love," Harry said softly before lifting one of Lucien's hands and kissing the inside of the wrist.

It was an act of aching tenderness that made Trey long for a connection just like it — with Demi. *No, he's too young.* And Demi was a twenty-first-century young man with a vast array of choices in life waiting for him.

He didn't need to be tied down to a cop careening into middle age. Sex was one thing. A permanent commitment was something out of the question.

He fisted his hands. "I'll do whatever you want to make this experience special for Demi, so long as it's understood that he's free to make whatever decisions he wants before, during and after."

"Agreed," the boy's fathers said in unison.

"Okay then, let's roll." Even as he gave the green light, he wondered what exactly he was getting himself into.

Probably something that would break his heart in the end.

* * * *

"Thanks for helping me, guys. I appreciate it." Damien, Emil's sous chef, steered Emil's SUV through the narrow streets of Boston, avoiding the few joggers who seemed to think that because it was early Sunday morning, it meant crossing streets without watching for traffic.

"Sure," Jase replied. "I've been meaning to get more involved with the food bank. I want to give back to the community, and all this uneaten food would go to waste if we didn't donate it."

From where he sat in the back seat, Demi chimed in. "And, I'm just glad to get out, no matter where I'm going."

He almost added more about how happy he was about his lockdown period being over. But then he remembered that Damien wasn't privy to his family's true nature or knew anything about the war with Dracul. Jase, who sat directly in front of him, stiffened a moment before relaxing again when Demi said nothing more.

Damien flashed his gaze at him through the rearview mirror. "You're 'rents are super protective of you, huh?"

It took Demi a second to understand the question. He smiled. "Yeah, my two dads think I'm made out of glass and totally stupid into the bargain. I'm lucky they figure you and Jase make for good chaperones."

Damien chuckled and said nothing more about it. Demi was glad and also not surprised. While he barely knew the sous chef, he found the guy to be pretty likeable and totally devoted to Emil. The fact that he was also dedicated to helping a soup kitchen targeting mostly homeless teens was also a point in his favor. Demi knew that the boy had been living on the streets for a while himself before Emil had given him a job. Emil was like that — always taking in strays and helping out humans. Demi liked that about him and figured tagging along this morning would be the next step in his own education for becoming a doctor.

"This should only take about an hour." Damien turned a corner and pulled into an alley between a small stone church and another building. "Father Ted usually has a couple of boys with him to help unload. I like to get the warming trays set up for him, too. After that, more volunteers come in to serve. I promise you'll be home and in bed soon. I know how tired you both must be after staying up all night."

Jase let out a loud yawn. "I can't deny sleeping is high on my list of things to do right now."

"I'm fine," Demi countered.

It was the truth. He didn't need the amount of sleep most humans did, and he preferred doing it during the day. Besides, he was so excited about what his fathers had told him a few hours before, he still was too wired to sleep.

Trey is going to make me his.

The news had been shocking. He could almost believe it was merely some fever dream he'd had. But he wasn't prone to flights of fancy — only dramatic, desperate hope. He'd wanted Trey Duncan since the first time he'd seen the man. What had started as a childish infatuation had matured into a relentless need, one that seemed impossible to obtain. And yet, his fathers had sat him down after Papa had come to fetch him from the dressing room and they'd told him the plan.

Trey was going to fuck him. That was the bottom line, no pun intended, although he giggled inwardly every time he thought it. The sexy cop was going to pop Demi's cherry, and hearing it had caused his dick to harden right in front of his parents. He had been so overwhelmed with joy that he hadn't even cared if they could see his arousal. His desire for the man was officially sanctioned by the powers-that-be. He didn't have to hide a thing now.

Of course, Papa had stressed how this was not some prurient event. There was going to be a formal ceremony and everything, where they gave him into Trey's care with all the solemnity their alien culture demanded. It wasn't about pleasure. It was a matter of *health*. Demi needed to be initiated into sexual activity the way he would have been on Papa's home world. It would alleviate the physical discomfort he'd been experiencing for months. He wasn't about to treat this whole thing like some wild sex ride. They were making do with what they had, taking into account Demi's wants, too, naturally. And wasn't it kind of Sergeant

Duncan to willingly help the same as he'd done by giving Demi his vein back in Wales?

Blah, blah, blah.

Demi had nodded in agreement with every lecturing word, all the while bouncing with glee on the inside. When they'd finally let him go, he'd raced to his shower and jerked off for about the millionth time. On this occasion, unlike all the others, his fantasy was a vision of what was to actually come. More than anything else, Trey's agreement to do this was proof that despite his insistence to the contrary, the man wanted Demi, maybe as much as Demi wanted him. It didn't matter. Demi's love would be enough to carry them both. He had a lifetime to make Trey happy.

Oddly, knowing what was to happen soon had already made him feel better. As he waited for Damien to park the SUV at the end of the alley, he felt calmer and more at ease with his body than he had in a long time. He looked forward to unpacking the food and helping to set up. The mundane activity, coupled with the good feeling of helping others, wouldn't have been something he would have been up for less than a year ago. Things had changed.

He had changed.

He hopped out of the vehicle feeling more lighthearted than he could ever remember and followed Damien and Jase around to the back. It was packed with all the uneaten food from the celebratory reopening of the club, plus a few staples to stock the soup kitchen. Emil was a soft touch, always had been since Demi had known him. Helping humans, especially by feeding them, had been the man's greatest passion before Jase had come into his life. Besides, the family had more money than God—or so said Papa. They could all afford to be charitable.

Damien hefted out a large open crate and handed it over to Demi's waiting arms. Although the sous chef didn't know about his hybrid nature, he had learned that he was stronger than he looked. Damien pulled out another of the same size and carried it over to the door in front of the SUV. Jase followed with a couple of lighter-weight bags, and Demi brought up the rear. He glanced around, not having been there before. It was a typical Boston alley, except it was fairly clean. Damien had said the boys whom the priest ministered to were always lending a hand to keep the church and its surrounding areas in good shape.

Given the early hour, there was no one around and the city sounds were muted. Demi supposed that most of the people the charity catered to had spent most of the night out, partying or panhandling. This wasn't somewhere for families or a shelter for overnight stays. Those that would come looking for breakfast were still somewhere else, sleeping the night off.

Bracing the crate against the wall and on top of his knee, Damien fiddled with the doorknob. He pushed the door open and gestured for Jase and Demi to go ahead. The inside was dark and cool, musty smelling the way old buildings often were. He stepped to one side to let Damien pass and show the way. Jase did the same thing. As they followed the chef down the corridor, Demi became vaguely aware of another scent. By the time he realized what it was, they'd already entered a stark basement room.

His feet tripped along with his heartbeat. "Wait," he called out, but it was too late.

Damien uttered a short cry and dropped his crate. Demi emptied his own arms just as quickly and pushed past Jase to grab Damien's arm. He didn't even consider how fast he'd moved. Damien was too busy gaping at the horror in the far corner and making a beeline for it. Damien wrapped his fingers around the boy's biceps and tugged him to a halt.

"Don't. He's dead and we can't contaminate the crime scene." He felt stupid saying the words, like some kind of terrible TV-show character.

There was no denying not only that the priest was dead, but that he'd been murdered. There was no sound of a beating heart or blood rushing through veins. He could tell from across the room that was the case, his hearing being almost as keen as his papa's. The humans wouldn't be able to tell, however. That, plus shock and overwhelming emotion, explained why Damien fought his hold.

"Father Ted!" Damien screamed and struggled to get free. "Let me go to him."

Jase came to join them, taking Damien's other arm and flashing a wide-eyed look at Demi. "Damien, stop. Please. Demi's right. There's nothing to do except call the police."

"Trey." Demi said the name with a breathless voice. Letting go the second Damien's movements slowed and pulling out his phone, he pressed the one number still on his favorites app and listened to it ring with growing concern.

"Demi?" Trey's tone was both sleepy and sharp. "Is something wrong?"

The sound of the man's voice was instantly calming. "Yes," he replied in a weaker voice than he'd intended.

"What?" Now Trey spoke with that sure and commanding tone that Demi loved.

It calmed him even more. "I'm at the soup kitchen that Damien brings food to and, um, the priest who runs it? He's dead. Killed."

"How do you know that?" There was rustling, and Demi could picture Trey getting out of bed and wrestling with his clothing.

Demi shifted his gaze over toward the body. "There's blood everywhere."

The priest was sprawled on his back, arms spread wide. His throat was slashed from ear-to-ear. A chair was turned over nearby and a pot of some kind of stew had spilled by the man's feet.

"Okay. Don't go near the body."

"I won't. We won't. I stopped Damien and he's sitting on the floor with Jase a few feet away from the door." He had to look away from the priest and focused on the other two boys. While blood was a central part of Demi's life now, seeing it spilled through a violent act made him queasy. He couldn't stand looking at it anymore.

"Good, that's good. Give me the address."

The minor praise made him feel better. He gave Trey the information and focused on the sound of the man getting ready. The simple rhythm of his breathing was somehow soothing. Trey kept him on the line, too, as he left his house and got into his car. He asked Demi for details about when they'd arrived and what exactly there were doing. Was anyone else there? Those mundane questions aided in Demi regaining his sense of peace.

"Okay, put me on hold and call nine one one. Let them know that a homicide detective is on his way. I'm going to do the same with you and call Karl in. You with me on that, babe?"

Demi was so thrilled at the casual endearment, he almost didn't respond. "Yes, got it. Back in a sec." He did as Trey said, glad to have a task, and stilled, feeling centered now that Trey was literally on the case.

He walked back down the hall and out to the alley to meet everyone and lead them to the right place. Trey came back on the line and kept up a steady, casual banter while Demi waited for him. Even though there was no one about, he didn't feel alone with Trey on the phone. By the time the emergency vehicles arrived, Trey was also pulling up. The sight of him getting out of his car gave Demi a shiver of pleasure. When Trey fixed his gaze on him, Demi couldn't resist running to his side. They hung up a moment before Demi launched himself at him.

Trey absorbed the blow with the same rock-solid control that he'd done in Wales. And as he'd done then, he briefly hugged Demi to him before setting him aside.

"Are you all right?" The man pierced Demi with concerned eyes.

Demi nodded. "I'm fine. Really. Whatever happened, it was over before we got here."

Trey nodded once. "Good. Now, I'm sorry, but I have to be professional here. I can't treat you like I..." His lips formed a thin line.

"Have affection for me?" Demi offered with a coy and hopeful smile. He didn't know what kind of label Trey wanted to put on their relationship before the deflowering ceremony.

"Right. That."

"I understand." He was determined to show how much he'd matured. He no longer wanted to act the brat. And his future was heading exactly where he wanted it—right into Trey's arms and life. Demi needed to adjust to the idea of being with a cop and supporting his man's career.

"What do you want me and the others to do?"

Trey hitched up his pants as he eyed the EMTs entering the building. "Go into the church proper, if you can. We'll need a clear area to handle the crime scene, and we'll come interview each of you when we have time."

Demi nodded. "Okay, we'll do that. I'm sure Damien knows the layout of the building and will find a spot for us to wait."

"He knew the victim, right?"

Demi nodded again. "Father Ted, yes. He does outreach work with LBGTQ homeless kids, including this soup kitchen. I think he was a big influence on Damien before Emil gave him a break."

"Got it." He offered a quick smile that sent a little zing racing through him. He could picture getting that smile every day. "Off then, you."

"Right." Demi had a strong urge to hug the man again or blow him a kiss. He didn't. Maturity was the watchword of the day and he was determined to abide by it. He also tried not to feel happy about how some poor human's death had given him this unexpected chance to see his man.

It was impossible not to feel that way, so he didn't try. Instead, he did as he'd been told, returning to the back door of the church with the sensation of Trey's gaze on him.

Chapter Three

Trey watched Demi walk away, transfixed more then he should have been on the way the boy's hips swayed and the pretty shine of his black hair against the early sunlight. Jesus, how sick was he that seeing the boy made him happy, even as he was on his way to view a murdered priest? He blamed it on the residual of his dreams. When Demi had called him, he'd been hard and aching. Since leaving Lux, his discussions with Harry and Lucien had caused his mind to reel more and more with the implications of what he'd agreed to.

"Damn, Trey, it's too early for murder after a night like I had."

Trey turned to a bleary-eyed Karl. "Really? I lost track of you once I came down from my meet-up with Demi's folks. Are you saying that you and Kitty..." He didn't know how to end the question.

Karl gave him a smug look. "I'm not one to tell tales out of school. Let's just say I made progress on that front." He glanced around. "How did we catch this one? It's a little out of our district?"

"We haven't yet, officially. I got the call from Demi. He, Jase and Emil's sous chef, Damien, found the body. I've put a message in to the lieutenant to square it with him."

"Is that wise? I mean, if the kid's involved…" Now it was Karl's turn to run out of words. "You don't mean it's"—his voice dropped—"our old space friends making trouble?"

"Nah." Trey made sure no one was about. "Demi would have said. It's just an ordinary murder." He frowned. "At least, I think it is. Come on. No sense standing around with our thumbs up our asses."

The back of the church led them directly into an open room. It held long tables on one end and a variety of scarred and rickety-looking ones scattered along with mismatched chairs around the rest of the room. It was easy to see how it functioned as a place to serve the needy a quick meal.

None of that held his attention for long, though. The priest lay sprawled across the room in a pool of blood. He didn't need Demi's otherworldly sense of smell to detect the metallic scent of the stuff. He zeroed his gaze on the victim's throat and let out a breath he hadn't realized he was holding when he saw that it had been slashed, not ripped.

"That answers that, I guess," Karl observed. "Just plain old murder."

"Yeah."

Trey trod lightly toward the body, peering at it as best he could without disturbing the coroner, a new guy named Vincente, and the rest of the crime scene crew that was already in the process of collecting evidence. He squatted down on his haunches and focused on the neck wound.

"Looks like a single slash," he observed to no one in particular.

"Yes," Vincente agreed. "No hesitation cut, just a quick one, deep enough to nearly take the head off."

Trey winced. "Christ, who'd do this to a priest?"

"I doubt the motive was money, given the poverty of this area," Karl chimed in.

"I see no signs of a struggle." The coroner stood and quickly made the sign of the cross. "It's a terrible thing, a priest of all people. I can't fathom it, not that any murder makes sense to me."

Vincente sighed. "I'll know more once I've had him on my slab, but I'd say he was grabbed from behind and killed within seconds—no time to fight back, not likely to have been able to utter a sound. Not that there would have been anyone lurking around to hear."

Karl grunted. "One of his flock, maybe. I bet a lot of these kids are on drugs. Maybe it was a simple matter of robbery after all."

Trey stood. "How much could a parish priest have on him?"

"A few bucks, but then that's all it takes for a few tabs of Molly."

On the surface, it sounded plausible. He'd seen strung out people kill for less. Still, it didn't quite sit well with him. "Let's go talk to the boys, see what this Damien in particular knows."

Leaving Vincente and his team to carry on, they left the scene and headed in the direction the boys had gone. They found them huddled together in the vestry between the back room and the small chapel. The sous chef, Damien, was sandwiched between Demi and Jase. They were giving the grieving boy as much comfort as he supposed they could, patting his back and murmuring soft words too low for Trey to make out.

Damien's head was bowed and he was obviously crying.

Trey hated to intrude on the kid's misery, but such was the nature of his job. "Hey, guys."

Three heads popped up. Demi's face lit up for a second, making Trey feel ten feet tall, before his expression turned somber again. Jase's gaze didn't quite meet Trey's, but then again, Emil's boy was always skittish around him. After the life he'd led as a trafficked teen, that wasn't surprising. It was Damien who kept Trey's attention, though. Of any of them, he was the one most likely to know something of value.

The sous chef wiped the tears from his eyes and took a notably deep breath. "You want to speak with me, yeah?"

Trey approached. "That's right. I need to know exactly what happened here this morning and what you can tell me about who might want this Father Ted dead."

The boy shook his head. "No one. No one would want to kill him. He was an awesome man, really caring. He made a difference for lots of kids like me, making sure we didn't go hungry, at the very least."

He paused, shuddered then continued. "He helped many of us get off the streets, stop, you know, turning tricks for food and a bed."

"Huh." Trey eyed Karl and could see the wheels turning inside his partner's head. "He took a personal interest, did he?"

Damien's eyes narrowed. "Not like you're implying." He huffed. "I mean, I know what's happened with lots of priest, but Father Ted wasn't like that. He was a genuinely good man, no funny business. No weird vibes. Just real concern and a dedication for helping homeless kids survive in ways that didn't involve selling themselves. He made me see that I had more to offer, motivated me to apply for a decent job. That's what led me to Emil."

"Okay." He rubbed his chin while considering how best to proceed. It really wouldn't be appropriate for him to interview Demi, and he wanted to speak with Damien alone besides. "Hey, Demi and Jase, will you please take Sergeant Anderson somewhere else so he can run through what happened with you?"

A quick flash in Demi's eyes indicated he wasn't happy about that plan. To his credit, he quickly banked it, though. No bratty comeback, which delighted Trey.

"Sure." Demi stood.

So did Jase. "I've been here before and that door leads to a small office."

Trey waited until the three of them were out of sight before sitting in the spot vacated by Demi. "I know this is hard, Damien."

The boy eyed him. "It fucking sucks." He heaved a sigh. "But, while cops aren't my favorite people given my past experience, I do know that you're a friend of Emil and his family, so I trust *you*. And, I do want to help catch whoever did this. Ask me whatever you like. I'll answer as honestly as I can."

"Good. I appreciate it." Taking out his notebook and pen, he started running through the usual questions. "When you arrived, did you notice anyone or anything out of the ordinary?"

Damien shook his head while he stared at the back of his hands. "Nothing. The alley was empty, which it always is this time of day. Father Ted rides—rode—a bike. He always brings it inside because he wasn't naïve. This is not the kind of neighborhood where you leave stuff outside."

The boy sat up suddenly. "Wait. I don't remember seeing it where he usually keeps it over by the serving tables." His shoulders slumped. "Then again, maybe I just missed it, because all I could focus on was him lying there."

Trey said nothing. His cop's eyes had taken in the entire scene and there had been no bike. It was possible the priest had stored it somewhere else. He'd have a good look around, but it was also likely the killer had taken it. If so, that probably indicated that one of the priest's flock was the culprit. A street kid could use a bike. Or, someone wanted him to think that was who to look for. Trey couldn't rule out anything.

It was gratifying, as well, that this was something utterly human. He wasn't seeking an alien vampire for this crime. God, how his life had changed.

"Tell me about the way Father Ted ran his outreach program. Did he go into the streets himself, approach the kids directly?"

Damien nodded. "Yeah, he did. He used to hang out in what he called his priest-lite mode. He wore the collar so that we knew where he was coming from, but also dressed down in jeans and kicks that looked as old as he did."

Trey tapped his pen as he pictured the man. Hard to tell someone's age when their face was a grimace of deadly pain and fear. "He was, what, late thirties, early forties?"

"I guess. Sorry, but if you're older than twenty-five, you're like middle-aged in my book."

Trey winced. Not that he was surprised by Damien's viewpoint. He'd held the same one when he'd been in his early twenties. He didn't mind time marching on, felt just as young and liked the wisdom he was acquiring with each passing year. But for his unfathomable relationship with Demi, he wouldn't be giving his age any thought at all. When he pictured being with that boy, however, he felt every one of his years as if they were dog ones.

"No worries. So, what was his usual pitch when he approached kids? What did he say to you, for example?"

A ghost of a smile crossed Damien's lips. "He'd start with 'Are you hungry?', like any teenager isn't always. Then he'd take you to a nearby diner and buy you a burger or whatever." He pulled his gaze up toward Trey. "Of course, I thought he was just another trick. Some guys are skittish or think they have to butter you up by feeding you first."

"His collar didn't alleviate your concerns?"

"Nope. You know how it is on the streets. Trust no one and every guy is either a mark or a source of danger. I was really surprised when he ended our meal by giving me a card for a shelter catering to LGBTQ kids. Then he gave me another one for the soup kitchen. You have to leave the shelter during the day and it doesn't provide meals."

"I think I know the place." Such shelters were few and far between when it came to this part of the population.

"I almost threw them away, pissed because while the meal was nice, I'd hoped to make money by at least giving him a blowie. In the end, it was a good thing I shoved the cards in my back pocket, 'cause the next guy who approached me tried to beat the crap out of me *and* not pay. I could take the one, but not the other. I went to the shelter out of a desperate need for a safe place to lick my wounds."

This wasn't a new story. Trey had heard variations of it throughout his career as a cop. He imagined most of the boys working at Lux had similar ones. Mackie certainly did, as did Jase. The fact that the latter boy's abuse had occurred in nice bedrooms and not the streets hardly mattered. In many ways, the Stelalux family had done more to help humans than their own kind.

Damien continued his story without prompting. "Anyway, I came here the next morning and got to talking more with Father Ted. I eventually ended up helping out and realized I liked working with food. I've been trying to help whenever I can now that I have my life on track. Emil's been really generous, too."

Sniffing back tears, he ended with, "I just can't believe he's dead. Who would do such a thing?"

"That's what I'm going to find out. Did you ever know of him having a run-in with any of the boys? Pimps? Drug dealers?"

"Not that I can think of," the boy replied with a shake of his head. "I mean, maybe he ruffled some feathers, you know? But to kill him like that?"

He shook his head again and swiped at new tears making tracks down his face. "It was such a good night at the club. I love the new kitchen and it was awesome to be there, cooking with Emil. Coming here this morning with all the amazing leftovers felt so good. I was riding the high after being up all night, but it was all good because I know how much the kids count on this. Oh, shit! They'll all be coming around expecting to fill their stomachs and on top of everything else, they're going to go away hungry."

Crap. Trey hadn't thought about that. Maybe he shouldn't even care, given the gravity of the murder. Still, he could only imagine how dependent some of those kids had become on this handout.

He stood. "Let's go get the others and see what we can do about that. If you think of anything else, call me, yeah?" He held out his card.

With one last wipe of his face, Damien took the card. "Absolutely."

Karl and the others were easy to find. Seeing Demi again goosed his spirits in a way that made him feel guilty. He tried to ignore both reactions as he ushered the boys outside. As Damien had predicted, there were a couple of dozen teens milling about at the mouth of the alley. Some were openly crying, testament to how news of the murder had spread already. Hard to hide the coroner's wagon and the rest of the official vehicles and investigators.

His arrival was met with some openly hostile looks. A couple of kids took off, as if worried he was there to hassle them. He couldn't blame them for their distrust, given how often beat cops did stop and frisk these street teens, and for good reason. Drug use was rampant, as was prostitution. People like the late Father Ted were often the only thing standing between these tossed-away waifs and exploitation or even death. He tried to adopt an air of friendliness and non-aggression, but no one was buying the act. Gazes were averted, at the very least.

Although it earned him a few skeptical looks from his own people, he let his actions do his talking for him. He wanted to interview more than just Damien about the priest's recent movements and possible enemies. He knew that if he took one step closer to the huddled group, they'd all scatter like birds. So, biding his time, he instead allowed the boys to take the food they'd brought and carry it down to the street. He stationed a uniform nearby to keep an eye out and left Damien in charge of dispersing what he had in an orderly fashion.

It was a Band-Aid on the problem, but something told him Emil would be starting a new venture at the club involving homeless kids getting free meals. Fortunately, that wasn't going to be his headache, but this goodwill gesture would hopefully be remembered if he started chasing down leads among the homeless youth of Boston.

Before he could get back to work, however, Demi broke free and approached. He shot Trey a shy smile. "Thanks for this." He gestured to the pile of food. "It will help make Damien feel better and some of these kids really look like they could use it."

"Yeah. It's hard for people like us to remember that not everyone has a family that takes care of them."

Demi nodded solemnly. "I know. I never used to, but ever since...you know, Wales, I've really come to appreciate how great my fathers are. And you are too," he added with a fetching flutter of his lashes.

That coy look gave Trey's dick all kinds of bad ideas. He cleared his throat and said, "I don't know about that."

Demi stepped closer and lowered his voice. "Please don't be nervous about...you know..." He licked his lips, a provocative move that could have been staged. Trey's cock didn't care whether it was or not.

"My fathers told me about the talk they had with you, and it explained a lot about how I've been feeling lately. It's hard to believe that the one thing I want more than anything is actually going to happen in a few days." He put his palm against his flat stomach, drawing Trey's gaze. "I have to confess I'm nervous, though."

Trey chuckled briefly. "Me too."

"Really?"

"Yeah."

Demi's eyes got misty. "That's so sweet but you shouldn't. I trust you, Trey."

The simple statement of confidence made him feel ten feet tall. He made an aborted movement to touch Demi's face before remembering where he was and who was watching. "You leave all the worrying to me. I won't let you down. Now, go on. We've both got work to do."

"Yes, sir." A few more battings of his eyelashes and Demi practically skipped away.

"Dare I ask what's going on?"

The sound of Karl's voice so close startled him. "Nothing. Not yet, anyway," he added as he turned to go back to the crime scene. "I may need your help in a few days." The big event was being planned for the following Friday. He both wanted more time and less to pull his shit together.

Karl shrugged and swatted Trey's arm. "Sure. You know I'm good for whatever. I've helped you fight aliens, haven't I?" he said in a voice too low for anyone else to hear. "It can't be any harder than that, can it?"

Trey rolled his eyes as much at himself as his partner's question. "No comment."

"Oh, now my curiosity is piqued. What's up?"

"I really can't get into it now." He blew out a breath. "I promised Harry and Lucien I'd do this thing, and it's making me a little crazy already."

The details were sketchy in his mind. The idea was for him to have close family members with him when he accepted Demi from his fathers. And, there was no way he could ask his actual brother to do it. There would be too many awkward questions for which there would be no acceptable answers. At least Karl was in the know, even if he might not fully approve of what Trey was about to do.

"I'll explain later. Let's go do our best for Father Ted. If he's the good guy that Damien believes he was—and, God, I really hope so—I want to find the fucker who did this and put them in a cage for the rest of their life."

* * * *

Dafydd slipped into the kitchen with quiet steps. In the few months since he'd been living at the club, he'd learned how to maneuver around the building unheard and unobserved. He preferred his solitude, and even though he'd been assured that he was not a prisoner and free to come and go as he pleased, old habits died hard. He'd spent centuries as Dracul's slave and now really only knew one way to live. Alex and the others treated him with the utmost respect, and still their presence caused an animalistic fear to rise in him. He was tired of being afraid and not yet ready to decide what he would do with his life. He'd only ever contemplated escape or death. Nothing beyond that.

He hadn't run into anyone since leaving his room. The fact that he had a private space like that—beautiful, quiet and in which no one entered without knocking and invitation—was a blessing. He appreciated that fact. And it had been easy to go on these morning forages unremarked while the club had been closed for business. With the opening the previous night, he'd worried that his privacy had come to an end. Even within the private areas, he'd assumed members would wander about, leer at him, make his skin crawl—but no.

Relief was a fleeting experience. He'd learned long ago that he must always be on guard. His first instinct was to sweep his gaze around the kitchen to make sure it was empty. The chef, Emil, was likely up in his room with his boy, Jase. The other cook he'd caught sight of, Damien, was nowhere to be seen. Dafydd had made it his business to know everyone who lived or worked in the club, so he knew that Damien wasn't likely to return until later when the club's business picked up again. He had plenty of time to dish up a few meals so that he could stay in his room for the rest of the day and night. Emil was a scary-looking fucker, as were they all, but he'd kindly given Dafydd permission to take anything at all from the kitchen.

A quick scan of the refrigerator had him pulling out part of a ham and a salad made of potatoes. Roasted vegetables rounded out his choices. He didn't need hot food. Living with Dracul had made him grateful for anything that filled his belly. Tastiness was a bonus, as were sweets. He pulled out a platter of pastries that made his mouth water. Even before he'd been abducted by the monster, treats had been a rare thing in his poor life. He was a little embarrassed at how much he craved them.

He grabbed all he needed to start constructing thick sandwiches. Bits of ham made their way into his mouth as he did so. His appetite had never been so strong and he felt wonderful. Fully healed from his latest delivery, he was experiencing a kind of good health that he'd never known before. To be free of hunger and pain was almost miraculous. Every day, his body became more robust. All of that was without a diet that included alien blood. Harry had offered, warning Dafydd that he didn't know what foregoing it after some many centuries would do. If there was any ill effect, he'd yet to experience it. He hoped that all it would do was set him on a course to live and age in a natural fashion. It hardly mattered. Near immortality had never done anything positive for him anyway.

"Oh, I beg your pardon."

Startled by the voice, Dafydd went into survival mode, clutching at the knife he held and whirling around to face the danger. He knew even before he saw the man that there was no threat. It was only Lucien. But such were the lessons of his miserable life. He couldn't turn off his instinct to brace for a fight.

It wasn't only Harry's husband, though. In the man's arms sat a gurgling baby. *Idris.* The name had stuck, and Dafydd had tried to work up some resentment about that. He couldn't. Despite everything that he'd experienced at Dracul's hands, he still couldn't hate the child that had been cut out of him. He couldn't bear to look at him, either.

He loosened his grip on the knife and turned back to the table of food. "No apologies necessary. This is your kitchen more than mine."

There was a gentile snort and soft steps approached. "This is Emil's domain, make no mistake."

"He's given me leave to come and take what I will, like." He didn't enjoy how defensive he sounded, but at least he was free to speak in his own fashion. Since living with these new creatures, he'd rediscovered his Welsh identity. No one seemed to mind his accent or idioms. It was surprisingly liberating. He hadn't fully appreciated how much of himself he'd lost during the endless years with Dracul.

"Of course. I didn't mean to imply otherwise." Lucien stopped on the other side of the table. Idris gave Dafydd a drooling grin.

The carefree and wholly human look caught him by surprise. He froze and stared at the baby for a few seconds, his heart beating rapidly. He hadn't wanted anything to do with this creature of Dracul. His otherworldliness was on display, his size too big for the infant he was. Tufts of black hair stuck up all over his head and his eyes. *God...* That violet shade made Dafydd shiver. The knife slipped out of his hand, clattering on the table.

The baby made a squawking sound and screwed up his face as if getting ready to squall. Dafydd had to look away and put his hand against his chest. It was hard to breathe. He turned to leave.

Lucien stopped him. "I'm sorry. I don't want our presence to chase you out. Please stay. I'll only be a moment. Idris needs his breakfast and Emil said he left a bowl of porridge for him on the warming tray by the stove."

Saying nothing, Dafydd returned to his task because he was hungry, and it was stupid being afraid of a baby. The child couldn't hurt him, not physically anyway. Not yet. By the time he could, Dafydd would be long gone, although how and where was something he'd have to figure out eventually.

"Would you like to hold him while I fix his breakfast?"

Damn the man. The alien doctor's husband was surprisingly tough-minded for all his gentle demeanor. He'd been trying to get Dafydd interested in the baby since they'd arrived here in America. Seeing the earnestness in the man, not any kind of cruel baiting, Dafydd had worked hard at keeping his temper in check.

"What for?" Now the bitterness came out without his even caring. "He's none of my concern and yours for all that."

"I'm sorry again. I'm not trying to make you uncomfortable."

"Aren't you, then?" he shot back and immediately regretted his fit of temper. It never got him anywhere being stroppy, and again, he understood Lucien wasn't trying to be mean.

Dafydd slammed the top piece of bread on his sandwich. "My apologies. I'm being ill-mannered given that I am your guest."

"Not mine, Alex's," came the mild correction.

"And he dictates how you behave, no doubt, like Dracul did in his domain."

Lucien's mild expression turned flinty. "Not like that at all. I expect that's hard for you to accept, yet it is the truth nevertheless."

Dafydd shrugged and continued making his meal. "I expect it is, given that I'm standing here unfettered. Not sure it matters, like. I have nowhere to go and no way to take care of myself at the moment." He flicked his gaze up. "If he thinks I'll take the boy off his hands eventually, he's fooling himself and so are you. I don't want him."

He nearly bit his tongue saying those words out loud in front of the baby, then chastised himself for his own silliness. Not even Dracul's spawn could understand what was being said at such a young age. Soon, though, he would, and he'd grow strong enough to hurt his father with little effort. His fingers tightened their grip on the bread he held as he remembered how Dracul laughed delightedly the first time one of the twins had left marks on Dafydd's body. *No, I won't think of that. It's over.*

"I understand your emotions are still running high, given your ordeal for hundreds of years. No one expects you to recover from that within weeks. We don't want to pressure you to take Idris, either."

The human smiled down at the baby and let him grab hold of his finger. "For my own selfish purposes, I'm delighted to care for him. My own son is essentially grown now." He got a faraway look in his eyes. "I'm not ready to let go of him, but in less than a week's time, he will have passed into adulthood according to my husband's culture. There's nothing I can do to change that."

Dafydd could see how sad the man was. He had gone through this process with the twins, although he'd been and still was happy to have them out of his sight. Being treated with contempt from afar at least left him without bruises and pain. He could see Lucien's feelings on the matter were entirely different.

Maybe it is about of how they are raised.

No, he wasn't going to go down that path. Paternity was at the root of it all, anyway. Dracul had been viciously evil, so his sons had that blood coursing through their veins. Alex and his loyal crew had always been different, apparently. He'd never known for sure because from what he'd seen, it had been some kind of internecine war. Perhaps they'd simply resented Dracul's competition. Everything he'd experienced since fleeing Wales told him differently, but he didn't trust anyone—not now, perhaps not ever. Regardless, Lucien had raised Harry's son and now he was raising Dracul's. If he thought the child would turn out as kind as Demi, Dafydd feared he was in for a rude awakening.

He hurried to fill his plate. "Well then, you're welcome to him. Raise him if you want. Toss him in the river. I don't care."

Again, he wanted to take back his harsh words. Lucien stared at him with a look of more pity than rebuke. Shoving everything back in its place, Dafydd grabbed his meal and fled the kitchen. He craved the quiet solitude of the sanctuary he'd been given. He vowed in the future to pick his time for foraging more carefully. He still lacked the fortitude to deal with anyone. Or even his own life.

* * * *

"Hey, Sergeant Duncan!" Dr. Ric Paz hurried to catch the cop and his partner.

The two men stopped and turned, then waited for him. They both looked bleary-eyed, and given what he knew about the latest morgue delivery, he could bet he knew why. "Paz, what are you doing down here?" Duncan asked.

He shrugged as he stopped. "I've started a pathology residency. I like emergency medicine, but I want to see it from this end, too. I'm a bit of a lab rat, actually."

Duncan scratched the back of his head. "Yeah, I think I've heard that about you."

Of course, he had. Keeping the aliens' secret had meant being given access to information about how they ticked. While he hadn't had much time to do so, Harry had issued an open invitation to visit his awesome set-up in the basement of the club.

Speaking of which…

"I take it you two went to the grand reopening at Lux," Ric said. He pitched his voice low so that no one who might enter the hallway would hear. "I had to decline because of my early shift starting this morning. I guess you cops are better at burning the candle at both ends."

He tried not to envy them. It had been hard not to attend the opening. Not that he cared much for the club scene, but part of him had hoped he could at least ask about Dafydd. He had no illusions that the poor abused guy would be whooping it up. Recovery from his C-section notwithstanding, Dafydd had a long road ahead of him, given his years of horrific abuse. It wouldn't be surprising if he never overcame it.

And Ric had no business thinking about the not-quite-human anyway. He didn't have to take a psychiatric residency to know that his interest in Dafydd was inappropriate. The man had been his patient for one thing, and for another, he wasn't even necessarily interested in forming any kind of relationship with a man. Being Dracul's sex-slave didn't mean Dafydd was gay. And if he were and managed to overcome the psychological trauma of constant rape and battering, the last man he'd be interested in would be someone who would remind him of that time.

"Actually," Duncan's partner chimed in, "we got called into a case unexpectedly."

Duncan grimaced. "Yeah, Demi, Jase and Damien, Emil's sous chef, discovered a body. The case should have gone to someone else, but I snagged it because we were first on scene."

He nodded. "You mean Father Ted."

"Yeah, that's right. Did you work on his autopsy?"

Ric shook his head. "No, but I saw the name and double-checked that it was the same man as I remember from the ED a few weeks back."

That caught the men's attention. Duncan furrowed his brow. "You mean he was admitted to the emergency department recently?"

"Not him. No, he brought in a boy that I treated." Even now, the memory of it infuriated him. "An older teen, badly beaten and raped. He didn't want to be at the hospital, but the priest insisted. He practically sat on the kid until I was able to examine and treat him."

"Who hurt him?"

Ric rolled his eyes. "He wouldn't say."

"Of course not," Anderson muttered.

"But, Father Ted told me on the side at one point that some new pimp was corralling the street boys and putting them to work for him."

"Just the boys?"

"Apparently, although I don't know why he'd stop there."

Anderson scoffed. "Easy… They don't get pregnant."

"I guess."

The whole topic made Ric's stomach roil. The way that poor boy had been bloodied had nearly brought Ric to tears, and he'd drunk himself stupid that night when he'd gotten home. It wouldn't have taken much in his life to have been different for his path to have turned in that direction. He was grateful for the chances he'd been given.

"Anyway," Duncan continued, too hardened to the way of the world to bat an eye at what Ric had told him, "what did the priest tell you about this pimp?"

"Nothing really. I gather he's been preying on quite a bit of what Father Ted thought of as his flock. The priest was trying to track him down, or so he said. I did warn him that it was a police matter. He assured me he wasn't intending to confront him, just learn enough to take something to a cop he knew in vice."

Anderson nudged Duncan with his elbow. "Hey, maybe he meant Craig."

Duncan's eyes flashed. "Really, Karl? There's how many detectives in vice and you immediately think of him?"

Anderson held up his hands. "I was only suggesting…"

"Well don't." Duncan's tone brooked no argument. Obviously there was a story there, although Ric didn't have time to suss it out.

"Look... If I think of anything else that might help, I'll let you know."

"Got a name for the kid?"

"He said Mateo *Smith*. No insurance of course. Came in and was treated as indigent. Sorry."

Duncan nodded. "It's okay. Thanks for letting us know."

"Sure." When they turned to leave, his discipline cracked. "Hey, um, if you went to the club last night, did you see Dafydd by any chance?" He looked away. "Or, you know, heard anything about him and the baby?" The memory of that infant with the strange violet eyes still haunted his dreams.

"I didn't see him. Sorry." Duncan looked at Anderson, who also shook his head. "I've heard that both of them are doing well, though. They're in good hands, if you're worried about them."

"Oh, no," he was quick to reply. "I'm sure they are. I was only asking as a doctor. You know, following up on a patient's recovery." He flashed a quick grin and could tell by the looks on the other men's faces that they weren't buying that explanation.

"I'm sure it would be fine for you to go and see for yourself," Duncan offered. "Didn't Alex give you a membership card? And I know Harry is happy to have you visit."

Ric backed up a step, already uncomfortable with how he'd steered a professional conversation into a personal one. "Right... Yes, of course, Alex did and Harry is. But, you know...*work.*

"I'll see you around," he added before turning on his heel and taking off. He was halfway down the hall before he remembered that he'd been heading in the opposite direction when he'd run into the cops. Still, he kept going, because apparently the mere thought of

Dafydd and his baby boy was enough to turn Ric into a blithering idiot.

Chapter Four

"I don't know, Demi. I still think the Canali or the Boss classic black shawl jacket is the way to go."

Demi eyed Quinn's reflection in the mirror. "Boring. Epically so." He twisted and turned to assess his current choice. "I love this Hickey Freeman. It's a classic look but with a bit of pizazz."

Mackie leaned into his view. "Yeah, but it's blue and paisley. A little outside the lines for this kind of affair."

Demi tossed that concern away with a flick of his head. "As if there's a standard for what I'm doing." He dropped his voice so that the hovering attendant couldn't hear. "Papa says I would traditionally be presented *naked*."

A shiver ran up his spine. The idea of being handed off to Trey with nothing on but his skin was titillating — like a virgin sacrifice to the vengeful god, not that Trey was anything like that. Still, how sexy would it be to saunter up to him, proudly sporting his desire for the man? He could even picture tying a bright red bow around his dick then had to stifle a giggle.

"Dad said 'no' with that rare tone of his, which meant he wasn't going to submit to Papa's will on it." He sighed. "Wearing something pretty, but not stuffy, is the next best thing. I want to make Trey's eyes pop when he sees me."

Mackie grunted. "Jeez, Demi, he's already like a cartoon wolf every time he does. I don't think what you're wearing will register much."

"So, if it doesn't matter to him, I should pick what makes me feel sexy and desirable." With another turn to check the way the jacket fell from his shoulders, he gestured to the clerk. "I'll take this."

He peeled off the jacket and handed it over to the man before hopping off the fitting platform. Fortunately, given the time crunch, he'd managed to find clothing that didn't need altering. He really did have a great physique for clothing. And, thanks to the Amex black card Papa had given him in his own name, he could afford to shop independently — or with his friends. It was fun trying on clothes with the boys instead of a bored parent. He only wished Jase had been free to come with them.

He hurried into the changing room and removed the rest. Mackie and Quinn ambled over to take each piece to bring to the clerk. "You guys should really buy something to wear yourselves. My treat," he added, pleased to be able to pay for stuff.

"Thanks, but Alex has force-fed me a ton of clothing lately. My problem is going to be choosing which outfit I want to wear. There are so many choices now in my wardrobe that it's freaking me out, actually."

"I'm all set, too," Mackie added. "Although, unlike our frugal midwestern boy here, I can never have enough stuff. Good thing I married a generous man."

Demi flashed him a smile, disappointed that he couldn't shop some more. He also knew that, unlike Mackie, he wasn't going to have a rich husband. He'd have to learn to live on a budget, whatever that meant. Money had always been something that was magically there for him. But he didn't want Trey to feel like he couldn't provide for his family, so frugality was going to have to be something Demi mastered.

Except, not yet.

"How about lunch?" he asked while he slipped into his street clothing.

"I could eat," Quinn said.

Mackie nodded. "Always. There's a new sushi place around the corner. How about we try that?"

"Sounds perfect. Still my treat." He wanted to use his new credit card again before going home. It was silly perhaps. And it hardly mattered who paid, given that the family finances were basically one big pile of money.

The other two shrugged and let him lead the way out of the dressing room. The clerk merrily rang up the purchases, not batting an eye over how a teenage boy produced such a high-limit credit card. He also didn't mind charging for the delivery of the clothing. Demi wanted an unfettered walk to lunch. He practically floated out of the store. In only a few more days, he was going to be in Trey's arms, naked and in bed. It was hard to believe that it all wasn't some kind of dream.

The restaurant was quaint and fairly empty when they arrived. As they sat perusing the menu, Demi couldn't help venting. "It's too bad this isn't going to be an eating event. I'd love for Emil to set out the kind of spread you had at your reception, Mackie."

"Hmm, yeah I hear you on that. The guys want to replicate this whole thing as close as possible to the way it would happen back on...the home world," he ended in a near whisper.

Demi sighed. "I know." The server returned and they ordered a massive amount of food. "I don't know why it has to be so boring."

"Solemn," Quinn corrected. "Alex says this is a really big deal. He was telling me about his experience, and he talks like it was life changing."

"So does Val. He, like, almost choked up describing being led to his queen. You know how unemotional he is most of the time. It was super weird, given how I can't begin to picture him with a woman."

"He is bisexual, you know," Demi pointed out. "They all are."

Quinn frowned over his cup of tea. "Are you? I mean, I seem to remember your saying you were poly, but you never really said what your orientation is."

Demi opened his mouth to answer, then closed it with his own frown, as he considered the question. "No," he finally said. "I thought I was both bi and poly back when sex was purely an abstract idea. When I think about it, now, I can't imagine being involved with more than one person, plus girls just don't do it for me. Maybe it was a matter of meeting the right man to pique my sexuality." He shrugged. "I guess I'm totally gay."

"You must get that from your father. Lucien," Quinn clarified.

"I guess." Was Dad gay? He'd never thought about it. He knew how his parents had met, and at the time, there was no way his human father had had a choice about having sex with men. Up until Papa, Dad had been a victim of sexual assault, not a willing participant. Had he wanted a man in his bed or had he merely acquiesced out of gratitude? The thought made him a little sick. While he'd rarely considered it, he always assumed his parents truly loved each other.

"It doesn't matter," he said with a wave of his hand and determined to fully enjoy his outing. "I'm all about the penis, for sure." *At least, one in particular.*

Mackie giggled. "I hear you. I feel the same way. Hey," he added, leaning in closer, "have you figured out how this whole night of deflowering is going to play out?"

"What do you mean?"

Quinn rolled his eyes. "He means who's going to be sticking what into whom. Honestly, Mackie, as if it's any of our business."

Mackie tossed his head. "Like you haven't thought about it."

Demi intervened before his friends got into a tiff. "Wait! Why is that even a question? It's obvious."

"Is it, sweetie?" Mackie challenged.

"Um, yeah. Trey is the one with the experience, and besides, I'm so not into the idea of topping him." He gave an exaggerated shudder. "Can you imagine my commanding an alpha male like Trey?"

Quinn and Mackie exchanged looks, but before either of them could answer, the food arrived. Picking up chopsticks, they dove into eating like the starving boys they were. Demi's appetite was still off the charts, and shopping always gave him an appetite anyway.

Once he'd stuffed enough in to satisfy the worst of his hunger, he picked up the topic again. Chewing had given him time to consider the question and was curious as to why either of his friends thought he'd ever top a man. The mere thought of being impaled by Trey's dick sent his own cock into painful hardness. It was his daily fantasy to imagine how it was going to feel to be filled with that man's hard shaft. His hole clenched painfully, and he realized too late he'd be aching for release by the time they got back to the club.

"Seriously, guys, why do you think I might be the one to do the fucking? Oh, do you do that with Alex and Val?" He couldn't for the life of him picture such virile men being on the bottom. Quinn nearly choked on his sushi and Mackie giggled. "I take that as a no."

Mackie clasped the tag swinging down from his collar. "Have you forgotten what this means? I'm Val's *slave*. Slaves get fucked, sweetie." His eyelids drooped. "And how!"

Demi grinned at the purely erotic face his friend presented. "So I see." He looked at Quinn.

The boy shrugged. "I haven't. I know, though, if I asked, Alex would do that for me. He denies me nothing." He sighed. "Except he won't take my answer about going back to school seriously. Damn, he's like a dog with a bone about that one."

"Okay, so I ask again, why would you think I'd do that with Trey?"

"It's the nature of the beast, sweetie. Back *you know where*, every male sticks his dick into a queen. After that is like whatever… But they all do it that one time. You're part of that, um…culture, and I just assumed you'd do this thing the traditional way, more or less."

"Oh." Demi sat back. "I hadn't thought of it. My parents have certainly said nothing about it. They could barely look me in the eye when they told me about the ceremony. Papa, in particular, is being uncharacteristically delicate."

Quinn tapped his chopsticks against his plate. "This is new territory for all of them. They're trying to stick with a tradition that doesn't mesh with their lives now. As usual, you're causing your parents fits, Demi." He grinned broadly to show he was only kidding.

Demi took it more seriously. "You're sort of right about that. I am a bit of a bother in this case. They want me to stay a child, as well. I can tell they aren't quite ready to let go."

He was, though. He felt more than primed to assume an adult role in life. The fact that he would be going from his parents' domain to Trey's didn't faze him, either. However this all played out from the initial deflowering ceremony to life with Trey, he was prepared to make it work. He wasn't worried about anything because he trusted Trey to take care of him.

Of course, Demi would have responsibilities, and he would be earnest about them. After the sex would come the hard parts — meeting Trey's family, planning their lives together. *Shit.* He knew next to nothing about the man. Were his parents living? Did he have siblings? Would any of them like Demi? He would have to make sure they did. No more playing the brat. Whatever Trey expected of him, he'd do it with a smile and love. Sappy, yes, but still true. There was nothing he wouldn't do for the man who had stolen his heart without trying, long before he'd saved Demi's life.

Besides, Demi had faced down Dracul and his hateful men. He could weather meeting and wooing a few humans. And maybe Trey's family would insist on a church wedding. Ooh, he liked that idea. They were such pretty buildings and there'd be flowers and the trappings that Mackie had had, plus more maybe. Papa would deny him nothing. He almost bounced in excitement just thinking about it.

"You know what?" he said, spearing another piece of sushi. "It doesn't matter. I'll let Trey lead the way. Whatever he wants is fine by me." He popped the bite into his mouth and chewed with a grin.

* * * *

"You know I can do this alone," Karl offered.

Trey grunted. "No. Thanks, but no. I'm not so pathetic that I can't handle seeing my ex for an investigation without having a fit of the vapors. It's not as if he were the love of my life or anything — or even a great lay."

That last bit was a lie. Craig Jefferson had been an excellent lay. The sex between them had been off the charts volcanic, which was why it had taken so long for them to realize how incompatible they truly were. Trey had always been into football, while Craig was a hockey man. Craig liked quiet nights at home, whereas Craig was a clubber. And oh yeah, big deal-breaker — Trey had been faithful and Craig had been a cheating piece of shit.

A real potato-potahto kind of kind of problem. Trey had always considered monogamy to mean not having sex with other guys. For Craig, it meant only having sex with randos. *"No emotions in it, babe. I love you, so what's the problem with me getting my dick sucked by a twink in leather shorts?"*

"There are other vice squad detectives, you know." *God.* Karl was persistent in his own protective way.

"Yeah, but Jefferson is the best, and if anyone knows about a new pimp in town, it will be him. I have a feeling that this is a good lead on the priest's murder."

"Me too. I just don't want to have to keep you from committing the same crime."

"Ha ha. Don't worry, I'm going to keep this strictly professional." Trey hoped he sounded more confident than he felt.

Those proverbial butterflies plagued his stomach as they wound their way through Craig's shop to his desk. The guy fancied himself a modern-day Wild Bill Hickok in that he liked to keep his back to the wall. He'd snagged a spot in the far corner of the room. Trey spotted the man's nearly bald head halfway across, and despite his resolve, his heart stuttered.

Damn. Craig hadn't changed in the two years since they'd last spoken. Okay, yelled. His smooth, clean-shaven face, a few shades darker than Trey's, still made him look younger than he was. He hadn't lost any of his raw masculine beauty with his square jaw and sharp cheekbones. At six feet tall and sleekly muscled, he could have been a model. Trey's dick stirred with reflexive memory, making Trey mad at his own lack of discipline. By the time, he reached his destination, his eyes had gone flinty and his lips were tightly closed.

Craig looked up from some file he was staring at. His face registered annoyance, then morphed into a smug smile a second later. "Trey."

"Jefferson," he replied in a stony tone.

The vice cop sat back in his chair. "Oh, is it last names now? Okay then, what's up, Duncan? Anderson?" he added with a nod toward Karl.

Part of Trey was irked that his former boyfriend could switch to professional mode so quickly and seemingly effortlessly. Wasn't the guy's stomach churning the way his was? What difference did it make anyway? He should be happy that all Craig was interested in was whatever business Trey was bringing to his doorstep. Trey was being ridiculous.

Sucking up his emotions, he got to the point. "We're investigating the murder of a priest."

Craig tossed his head back and huffed out a breath. "Father Ted."

"That's the one."

Craig grimaced. "I heard first thing this morning. It sucks. I met him a few times, and he was a good guy." He lowered his gaze to Trey. "You know at first I had my suspicions. All those young boys in particular that he ministered to? Seemed fishy to me. I guess I'm jaded that way."

Asshole that he was in his personal life, Craig was a damn fine cop and genuinely worked tirelessly to bring justice to sex crime victims in particular. "We had the same ugly thoughts, but the boy I know that found the body assures us the priest was on the level."

"That was my ultimate conclusion. Which kid?"

"Damien Winter."

Craig nodded. "I know him. He's one of the few success stories out there, isn't he? Found steady work as a cook or something."

"That's right." Before Trey could decide whether he wanted to admit more details, Karl chimed in.

"At Club Lux."

"Oh yeah?" Craig's eyes narrowed. "I've heard of it, a hotspot for the rich and kinky. Seems like it's been a magnet for all kinds of weird shit too, huh?"

Trey looked down at his feet and cleared his throat. "I don't know about that. We, ah, got to know the family that runs it because of that serial killer last year. Anyway," he added before Craig could ask any follow-up questions, "the club's chef had been donating food to Father Ted's soup kitchen for street kids. Damien and a couple of other boys from the club were making a delivery when they found the body."

"And they called *you*." Craig's dark brown eyes had always been expressive. His thoughts practically popped out.

Damn, no one could ever accuse the man of not knowing how to add two plus two. Trey kept his gaze steady as he said, "That's right. They know and trust us."

Craig rocked back. "Uh, huh. So how can I help you?"

Karl stepped into the conversation again, which was all to the good. "We learned that there is a new pimp throwing his weight around. A doctor we also know said that he had a rape and abuse victim brought into the ED by Father Ted. We were hoping you could shed some light on the guy. Maybe he figured the priest was interfering with his stable."

Now Craig's expression took on a hard edge. Trey knew that look. His ex was pissed. "I know who you're referring to. I call him the Dark Knight."

"Why, is he a brother?" Trey asked.

"No, actually, I hear he's a white dude. Like, super white. The guys I pull in are scared shitless of him — the boys and the other pimps. No one seems to know exactly who he is, or they're too afraid to say, but he blew into town a couple of months ago and is making his mark quickly and with extreme prejudice."

"Why the cutesy moniker, then?" Karl asked, although as he did, Trey's gut started tightening again.

Craig shrugged. "It just seemed to fit. According to my sources, this guy is huge and is really into black leather." He winked at Trey. "Sounds like my kind of guy."

Trey ignored the baiting because now his nerves were heading into full-on red alert territory. "And he comes out at night." It was a statement, not a question, because *fuck*...

Craig didn't appear fazed by the question. "Well, yeah, but that's true for most of these scumballs. The boys do their best trade after dark. From what I hear, though, this guy holds court underground somewhere. A basement, I assume, but no one's talking with any kind of useful detail. He has his lieutenants pound the pavement and keep the boys in line. He never goes to anyone. They're always brought to him."

"Christ, Jesus," Karl muttered.

Craig sat forward. "Look, I'd give you more info if I had it. From what I can tell, this guy wouldn't blink at killing a priest. I'm surprised the streets aren't more littered from his muscling out his competition. He's crafty, staying below our radar for the most part by either co-opting anyone who crosses his path or somehow disposing bodies in ways we don't discover. If he's behind the Father Ted murder, my guess is he's sending a message."

"To whom, I have no clue." He leaned back again. "So, what can you tell me?"

"Nothing," Trey shot back. "No one saw or heard anything and forensics is coming up with zilch, too."

"Pity. You'll keep me apprised of your progress, though, right? As a return on professional courtesy." He gave Trey a lazy smile that used to make his dick hard in an instant. It almost did again, except the information bomb that Craig had provided — and Trey was working hard to appear sanguine about — was acting as a good boner-killer.

"Of course." Trey had mastered hiding his feelings from his ex. It was easy to fall back into the habit. "Thanks for your help."

"Any time. And, Trey?" he added as Trey and Karl turned to leave. "It was good to see you again."

Because the guy appeared to genuinely mean it, Trey forced himself to nod and smile before leaving. He waited until they were in the hall before cursing loud enough for his partner to hear.

"You're thinking what I'm thinking?" Karl asked.

"Yeah, but that's crazy, right? The fucker is dead."

"Is he? You said no one saw it with their own eyes."

Trey led the way out of the building. "Alex and the others are sure, and that's got to count for something."

"Maybe they're so desperate for their war to be over that they're willing to ignore the obvious doubts."

"Maybe," Trey conceded as they jogged down the stairs to the parking lot. If that were true, then he was in the same category. Carrying Demi out of that castle of horrors, he'd hoped and prayed with all his will that the fight was truly over. Maybe he'd been fooling himself.

"Plus, it doesn't have to be *you know who*. Thing One and Thing Two escaped, as well as a few others, right?"

"God, I hate it when you're smart."

"Gee, thanks."

They strode over to their car. "I guess we need to take this to Alex. He and Val will be better judges of whether we have overactive imaginations or if a real threat exists. Plus, I want to talk again to that Damien kid." He unlocked the doors.

"Maybe Logan can do some sniffing around for us," Karl offered as he rounded the car to the passenger side.

"Good idea." Trey slipped in behind the wheel. "Oh, damn, I still need to ask you for that favor." He'd meant to finish the discussion he'd started back at the crime scene over a beer, but this case wasn't going to give them a lot of down time.

"Sure, like I said, anything."

Trey eyed his partner. "You need to hear me out first. This is going to be weird."

In the process of buckling up, Karl shot him a grin. "Seriously? What about our lives hasn't fallen into that category lately? I'm amazingly good with weird, as it turns out. Go figure."

"Yeah, well…I kind of need a best man."

"Fuck me, you're getting married? To Demi? This is the promise you made to his parents? I can't believe they'd be down with that instead of measuring you for a coffin."

"Not exactly." *Jesus.* That was on him for using the wrong terminology. The ceremony was already outside his comfort zone. No way was he ready for a permanent commitment. Besides, Demi was too young for that. Wasn't he?

"I need to do this thing on Friday with Demi. A sex thing." He winced at his awkward explanation.

"A sex. Thing?"

"Sex. Just sex, Karl. I have to have sex with Demi." *Jee-sus.* Could this conversation get any stranger?

"Have to?"

Trust Karl to focus on the inanest of his word choices. "It's basically a medical necessity."

"Uh-huh."

"Really. The way Harry described it, Demi is going through some kind of physical change that requires, ah, deflowering."

"Shit, that's almost poetic."

"Fuck you," Trey said without heat. He started the car and pulled out of the space. "I have to pop his cherry. Is that better for your perpetual thirteen-year-old self?"

"You're going to fuck him. I get it. Me and Young Karl are fully engaged with this plan."

"I'm glad someone is," Trey muttered. "Actually, technically he's going to fuck me."

"Hmm, interesting."

"That's one word for it."

Karl coughed once. "I guess if I thought about, which I definitely have not, I would've expected you to be a top kind of guy."

Trey couldn't resist playing out a brief fantasy of what it would be like to sink his cock into Demi's cherry-tight ass. He felt guilty a split second later, but for a glorious moment, he was in heaven. Unfortunately, it only served to make his pants tighter.

"You wouldn't be wrong, but this isn't me picking a random up at a club. I'm simply trying to provide a service based on their species' customs and physiological needs." *Like a science project. Homework. Duty.* If he kept telling himself that, he might convince his cock and all the rest of him. Probably not. *Shit.*

Karl was silent for a few seconds in which Trey imagined the guy was trying hard to scrub certain unwanted images from his brain. "*Right.* Am I supposed to witness this event? I mean, is it like medieval times when people stood around the bed and watched the consummation?"

Trey almost ran off the road. "Christ, no!" Except, come to think of it, he hadn't nailed down that kind of detail with Harry. *No, no way.* That couldn't be the case.

"I'm supposed to have some kind of entourage, for lack of a better word, when Harry and Lucien hand Demi over. I was hoping you could, you know, stand with me."

"Well, sure, no problem. I'm, like…honored or whatever. But shouldn't it be family or something?"

Trey flicked his gaze at his partner. "Seriously? How would I ever explain this to my brother? Hey, Dante, I'm going to do something that makes me look like a pedophile, but it's all good 'cause he has alien blood in him and he doesn't mature lineally. How about you act as my wingman as I carry him up to bed?"

Karl snorted. "You're right. That was a stupid thing for me to suggest. He *is* kind of young," he added. "How are you handling that?"

"Badly," he confessed. "No matter how long he's been alive or how much Harry explains the physiology of a hybrid, I still see Demi as a kid—and one that I want more than my next breath," he confessed before he could think better of it. "Christ, I *am* a pedophile."

Karl chuckled. "You so are not. Look… I get your reservations, but you have to trust Harry on this. No way he'd be setting this up if it weren't beneficial for his son."

"I suppose." It still felt wrong, and yet too right at the same time.

His dick had no conscience. It was straining in his pants in a way that hadn't happened with Craig. That had been another problem with his relationship with the man. They'd both been alpha males vying for control, even though he'd always been attracted to men that looked much like himself. Or that's what he'd thought until he'd stopped fighting his impulses and allowed his attraction to twinks come to the fore. Demi was his dream lover. No question about that.

"I know you, Trey," Karl persisted. "You're the best guy I've *ever* known. Truly. I'll be proud to stand with you on Friday."

"Yeah? Thanks, man. I appreciate it. Thanks, too, for accepting this whole alien thing. Keeping that secret from you was killing me, and I'm not sure how I'd have handled all of this without you by my side."

"Ah, Jesus, listen to us," Karl scoffed. "Turn on sports radio, for God's sake, before we each grow ovaries."

Trey shook his head. "So un-PC, man." He did as his partner asked anyway, happy to end the conversation. If for no other reason, he needed his dick to settle down before he arrived at the club.

* * * *

"Alex, I'm not going to have this conversation again."

Quinn's angry voice caught Trey's and Karl's attention before they reached Alex's office. The door was open, so they became privy to the heated discussion whether they wanted to or not. They exchanged glances before slowing their steps by unspoken agreement. Whatever was going on with the two lovers, they didn't want to get involved.

Val was pulling up the rear of their little convoy. He had no qualms, apparently, as he passed them the moment their steps faltered. "Jesus, this again," the guy muttered.

"Darling boy, I'm sorry to inform you that we are." Alex's smooth words held a hint of an edge to them.

Quinn came rushing out of the room, nearly crashing into Val. The bouncer moved in a blur to get out of the boy's way, not that Quinn got far. With equally fast movement, Alex came to grab his arm and pull him up short.

"I said that we're *not* done with this discussion." Trey had never seen Alex this forceful outside of an actual fight. "This is too important for you to act the brat."

"Oh!" Quinn jutted his chin up and shot fiery eyes at his lover. "You mean that what you want matters and what I want doesn't."

"That is not even remotely close to anything I've said." The alien leader's tone was icy and commanding.

"Yes, it is." Quinn jerked his arm, but of course, there was no way for him to free himself unless Alex let go.

Trey eyed Karl and could see that his friend was thinking the same thing. Neither of them was going to stand by and let Alex hurt Quinn, not that they stood any chance of overpowering the guy. And, from everything he'd seen of this alien, Trey didn't believe that Alex would ever do anything like that anyway. Val hung back with his arms folded, his usual stance, with an expression that conveyed annoyance but not alarm. Trey supposed the bouncer knew Alex better than anyone, and if he wasn't worried, there was probably no reason to be. Then again, would Val ever challenge his superior?

Quinn and Alex seemed uninterested in their audience, regardless. More importantly, Quinn didn't appear afraid, only seriously pissed off.

"You consistently dismiss everything I say about how I want my life to be."

"Because you aren't acting rationally."

Quinn's mouth popped open on a gasp right before he pounded his fist once against Alex's massive chest. "You think I'm being overly emotional because I'm too young to think things through."

"I didn't say that, either. I'm simply pointing out that you have the opportunity to enhance your education and make more of your life."

"I don't want more!" Quinn nearly shouted it out. "I want to dance and warm your bed and…and, I want to be changed," he finished with a hitch to his voice that sounded suspiciously like he was going to cry.

God. Trey really felt like a voyeur. He wanted to slowly back away but also didn't want to call attention to himself or Karl.

"You're so young." Alex's voice dipped down low and soft. "There's plenty of time for you to make the decision to change. Once it's done, there's no undoing it. I don't want you to end up like Dafydd, stuck with no longer being human and perhaps forever dependent on something you don't want."

Quinn scoffed. "How could I ever be like him when you are nothing like Dracul?"

Alex's expression hardened. "I will be if I allow this to happen without deliberation."

Quinn shook his head. "See? There it is. You say we're a couple, but we're not equals. You're the boss of me, and I would be fine with that if you would only acknowledge that I have ultimate control and that when you insist on something, I have the right to refuse."

By the hold on his arm, Alex shook the boy, once and not hard, merely for emphasis. "We *are* a couple and you *do*. Changing you is something *I* have to do, though, and I will not do it unless and until I think you are truly prepared to make that irrevocable decision."

"Right, sure." Quinn huffed. "You decide, not me, when and if I'm ready. Admit it, Alex. You can't commit. That's the real problem. You don't want marriage and children. You don't want me."

"Darling boy, that's not true. I want you more than the breath I take or the blood I drink. There's simply no rush for you to make decisions that are irreversible."

"The only pressure I'm feeling right now is from you, and I don't like it. I won't tolerate it, Alex. I know my mind, and what I want is to spend the rest of not just my life with you, but the rest of your life. I refuse to grow old and die centuries before you do. If you can't understand or accept that, then we have nothing left to discuss."

"Quinn."

"Now let me go. I need to practice."

"You don't have to dance." Alex's tone sounded weary, and that was new in Trey's experience.

"That's where we disagree. Let. Me. Go."

For a second, Trey really worried that Alex wouldn't. Then suddenly, he released his hold on Quinn and stepped back. The two men stood staring at each other for another second before Quinn turned and strode away. Not fast enough, though, for Trey to miss the sheen of tears in his eyes.

Christ. He had to agree with Alex, however. Quinn was maybe nineteen at this point. What was the hurry in making a life-altering change? And for that matter, where was the harm in furthering his education? From what Trey knew, Quinn had taken the job dancing at the club out of desperation. He had choices now, ones that lots of kids, like the ones Father Ted had ministered to, would give anything to have.

Alex's gaze stayed on Quinn's retreating back for a few more seconds, before he trained it on his visitors. "Gentlemen, sorry for the wait. How may I be of assistance?"

The guy acted as if they'd disturbed nothing more than paperwork instead of a knock-down, drag-out fight between him and his lover. *Okay.* If he wanted to play it cool, that was fine by Trey. Apparently, alien men were just as good as human ones in pretended their hearts weren't being ripped out and stomped on.

Trey started forward. "We may be jumping the gun on this, but Karl and I have a problem. And," he added with grunt, "we're afraid it might be a Dracul-adjacent one."

Alex's eyes narrowed. "Indeed? You'd better come inside, then. It appears our brief period of peace and quiet may be at an end."

Chapter Five

"That bastard!" Mackie uttered his harsh assessment of Alex once Quinn had finished stammering out his tale of the big fight.

"Mackie, that's not helping," Jase admonished before patting Quinn on the back.

Demi held his tongue, silently agreeing with Mackie, yet not wanting to stir up trouble for himself. Not now. They were all sitting huddled at the big table in the kitchen, keeping their voices low so that Damien wouldn't hear their precise words. The human was super chill in Demi's experience and easily becoming part of their group. He still didn't know their big secrets, though, and probably never would. So, they couldn't afford for him to hear about Alex refusing to change Quinn. It was enough that there were clearly relationship issues and that Jase needed to take a break from kitchen chores to lend comfort.

Mackie made a face. "I call them like I see them." He blew out a breath. "Honestly, these men treat us like infants sometimes."

"Isn't that kind of your thing?" Demi asked. He knew very little about the BDSM lifestyle because his fathers had kept him far away from what went on in those second-floor rooms. He was intrigued, though. Not that pain sounded like fun but being restrained held some titillation. He'd imagined during more than one jerk-off session what it would be like to have his wrists tied to the bedposts while Trey tortured him with pleasure.

He shuddered and his dick stiffened — again. God, it had been a little more than an hour since the last time he'd drained his demanding balls. He kind of wanted to save himself for his night with Trey. His body had other ideas. Of course, Trey was at the club, and while Demi wanted to be supportive of Quinn, he was also really hoping to catch a moment with his man.

Mackie looked down his nose at him. "If you knew anything about what it means to be a slave, you'd know that I ultimately wield the control in our relationship. Val does nothing without my consent."

Demi shrugged. "You're right. I don't get it."

It made no sense to him. Maybe it was the difference between how humans saw things and his own alien nature. While he'd chafed at his fathers' control for his entire life, the idea of giving himself to Trey, totally and completely, left him feeling calm and steady. Some primordial part of his brain was maybe connecting to the hive nature of his people. There was a hierarchy and the certainty of it was oddly liberating. Then again, perhaps it was a fantasy and the reality of it would be quite different. Quinn was certainly miserable, when Demi would have bet anything that the boy loved being commanded by someone as, well, *commanding* as Alex.

"He'll come around eventually," Jase comforted. "In the meantime, would it be the worst thing in the world to look into classes? I'm going to enroll in a local culinary school because Emil thinks it's the best way for me to learn."

Quinn made a face. "Except you like cooking, so it makes sense for you to follow his advice. I want to dance. I love it, actually. And, I love getting fucked by Alex, too. I want him and only him forever more. Plus, I've been spending a bit of time with Idris. I started doing it to help Lucien then found I really like it. I want to give Alex sons," he added in a near whisper.

Demi did, as well, truth be told. Too bad Papa said that hybrids were wholly male. Unlike Mackie and the others, he wasn't going to be able to actually carry Trey's babies. Still, they could adopt. Lots of humans needed parents. Not that he was in any hurry. Trey wouldn't need to pressure Demi to take time to finish his education. Demi was determined to go to medical school, just like Papa.

Although, he realized with a sudden jolt that, as a human, Trey wasn't going to live as long. They didn't have much time together. He hadn't considered that. And the idea of Trey dying within a few decades gave him a pain right where his heart was. Maybe there was a way to alter that. What if he fed Trey his blood? Would it extend his life? He'd have to ask Papa.

Mackie patted Quinn's hand. "Like Jase said, he'll come around to your way of thinking. You just have to stay firm and wait him out." His face took on a sly look. "Where are you sleeping tonight?"

"Oh." Quinn sat back. "I hadn't thought that far ahead." He shrugged. "I'm not sure I can face Alex, but it's not like I have a bedroom of my own anymore."

That was true. Dafydd was ensconced in the guest room.

"You could maybe hang out with me," Demi offered. "My bed's queen-sized." He'd just have to do his nightly jerking off in the bathroom. "A sleepover could be fun."

Mackie clapped his hands. "Perfect."

"I don't know, guys," Jase said. "Isn't there some kind of rule about not going to bed angry?"

Mackie batted that concern away. "Nonsense. This will give Alex a taste of what it's like not having Quinn around. An object lesson," he added with a firm nod.

Jase didn't look convinced, but Quinn seemed happy with the idea. And while he really didn't want to piss Alex off and worried that his parents might put a stop to the plan, Demi decided that if he was going to enter adulthood, he was capable of asserting himself. He would have to put his foot down.

Except his thoughts on the whole thing fled in the next instant at the sight of Trey entering the kitchen. His faithful partner was hot on his heels, but Demi didn't care. Trey took all his attention. He was up and heading toward him before his brain registered the idea. He frowned as he saw that Trey hadn't noticed him. He was approaching Damien, who stood by the stove stirring a huge pot of something.

"Hey!" he called out and picked up his pace, careful to keep it at human speed, even though the effort was almost painful.

Trey glanced at him, flashed a smile and kept his focus on the sous chef. "Damien, got a minute?"

The boy tapped the big spoon in his hand against the edge of the pot and set it on the counter. "Um, sure. What's up?"

"Let's sit down. I have a few follow-up questions about Father Ted."

"Of course. Whatever I can do." Turning, he headed to the other end of the table from where the boys still sat.

The cops followed. "Guys, if you don't mind, I'd like to question Damien without a big audience."

The others got up before Damien said, "I'm cool with their being here—you know, if you are."

"No, that's fine," Mackie said for all of them. "We need to practice anyway."

"I don't," Demi countered with a grimace. He didn't want to lose a chance to spend time with Trey, no matter what was going on. It was bratty of him, maybe. Then again, he didn't feel much like being grown-up right at the moment. His dick ached and a flash of heat crept up his skin.

Trey shot him an admonishing look, yet ultimately said nothing when Demi joined them. "So, Damien, I got some information from other sources about a new pimp controlling the boys out on the street." He went on to describe someone that sounded way too familiar.

Demi's stomach dropped at the growing suspicion that one of Dracul's men or sons had infiltrated Boston. For a brief second, he managed to convince himself that he was being overwrought. Then he caught Trey's grim look and understood that no, he was right on point. The cop was worried about the same thing.

Damien listened and nodded. "Yeah, maybe. I've heard some whispering about a mean motherfucker edging out the competition. The boys are more skittish than usual, that's for sure."

"Do you know a boy named Mateo?"

"Um, yup. I do. He's been out there a while, a little older than me, I think."

"Could you help us track him down? We'd like to ask him a few questions."

Damien snorted. "Nah, you're playing me now, Sergeant. I show up anywhere with you two in tow and I'm going to get a rep as a snitch. No one will trust me afterward, and they won't give you shit anyway. You know that."

Trey pressed the bridge of his nose with thumb and forefinger. Demi wanted to jump up and massage the tension out of him. He sat on his hands instead, determined to be a good boy and not a distraction.

"Right, I do know that. I still need to get more info on this pimp."

"You think he had something to do with Father Ted's murder?"

"You tell me. Father Ted tried to get the boys off the street, right? Not exactly a popular move with the men preying on these kids and making money off them."

Damien nodded. "I hear that. So, how about I do the asking without you?"

Trey shared a look with Anderson. Neither of them liked that idea. It was clear from their expressions. "That could be dangerous. I don't want any attention on you when you're isolated."

"There already is. I worked with Father Ted for months. And, Emil and I are scoping out a spot to rent near the church to establish a new soup kitchen. Talking to boys I used to hang with is a thing I do. Nothing out of the ordinary, and hey, I can take care of myself."

Not against my people, you can't. "How about I go with him?" The offer was out of Demi's mouth before he could think better of it.

Trey turned hard eyes on him. "No fucking way."

A little frisson ran through him. He liked it when Trey went all alpha male on him. "Why not?" He tried batting his eyes.

Trey's expression turned even stonier. "Because if I allowed that, your fathers would kill me and dine on my entrails."

That was sort of true in the very literal sense of the expression. "I'll be fine. Like Damien, I can take care of myself."

"He's surprisingly strong for a skinny dude," Damien agreed.

"No." When Demi opened his mouth again, Trey simply repeated himself. "No."

Now Demi stamped his foot. He couldn't help himself. "You're being ridiculous, Sergeant Duncan." He worked to keep his tone calm and firm. "You've seen how capable I am. And, it's not as if I'm heading into a fight or anything. Damien and I are just going to hang out on the streets and chat with other guys. Right?" he added, giving Damien a pointed look.

"Um." The kid's gaze ping-ponged between Demi and Trey. "I guess. That's what you're asking me to do, right?" he asked Trey. "It's not like we're going undercover or anything freaky like that. Truth be told, most of the boys I'd approach are more Demi's age than mine. He might do better if they think he's one of them."

"See?" Demi flashed Trey a sweet smile. "I'll be fine, and Damien will be safer with me." He shrugged. "Honestly, it's not as if I need your permission to go out in public and hang with some —"

He squeaked as Trey grabbed him by the arm and dragged him out of his chair and across the kitchen. Although he could have put up a fight, and probably would have won, instead he let his man pull him into the pantry and slam the door behind them. The overhead light popped on and Trey stared at him with furious eyes.

"Are you out of your fucking mind — or are you just trying to drive me either crazy or into an early grave?"

Demi didn't answer immediately, not sure if it was a rhetorical question or not. He didn't get a chance to say anything anyway.

Trey kept going, his fingers pressing into Demi's flesh. "Seriously? Being snatched off the streets for your little adventure in Wales wasn't exciting enough for you? Are you that unfazed by having been mauled by Dracul's asshole guard that you'd risk something like that again, because you do know that odds are whoever this new pimp is he's one of them? Maybe one of the twins, God help us all."

Trey's chest was heaving as if he'd run a long time. His pupils were blown wide with either anger or arousal. *Both?* Demi didn't dare look down to check.

His mind digested the mini-rant and latched onto something. "Wait! You know about what Kronid did? How? I was careful to keep it from Papa."

Trey's lip curled. "I'm a cop, remember? And my former boyfriend works vice. I know all about how kidnappers and hostage-takers brutalize their captives. I didn't need anyone to tell me what you'd been suffering all that time. I was scared, still am, that it was worse than what it appeared to be."

"No," Demi was quick to reassure him. He put his palm on Trey's chest. He could feel the rapid beat of the man's heart. Hear it. "He only groped me like some stupid villain in a John Hughes movie. It was nothing."

He tried to be cool about it, but his voice hitched in the end.

Trey pulled him in closer. "No, it wasn't. Shooting that fucker was the most satisfying thing I've ever done. If your kind didn't turn to dust, I would have gladly emptied my clip in him."

"Really?"

Trey nodded, and their gazes stayed locked. Tension mounted between them like a tangible thing. Demi's dick went into overdrive. *God.* He wanted this man inside him. His hole clenched painfully, launching him forward on a whine. Before he could stop himself, his mouth slammed into Trey's.

The moment their lips touched, there was no holding either of them back. It wasn't only Demi that wanted this. Whatever discipline that had been keeping Trey in check up to that point snapped. He yanked Demi flush against his body. They clawed at each other, trying to close the gaps that remained. Teeth and tongue entered the fray, a rough kiss that was nevertheless better than anything Demi had ever imagined.

With his erection pressed painfully against his fly, he couldn't help humping Trey's pelvis. There were close in height, so no surprise when his hard cock brushed up against an equally firm one. He moaned at the delightful friction then whimpered when Trey surprised him by cupping his ass and pressing the dicks together.

He wants me as much as I do him.

The discovery was thrilling. Every dream was coming true and forget about any dumb ceremony. His man was dry fucking him right here in the pantry. Demi's breath sped up and his cock swelled and jerked. His fangs punched down before he could hold them in check. He nicked Trey's lip by accident and the taste of the man flooded his mouth.

Delicious.

This was better than it had been before when necessity had driven them to it. The small amounts of blood he sucked in tasted better than what he'd consumed in Wales. As it trickled down his throat, he convulsed in an orgasm that left him mindless. He thrashed his way through, moaning and huffing into Trey's mouth. His man held him tightly as he rode the wave and shuddered into the end.

Breathless and limp, Demi let his head loll back. Trey's handsome face wavered through Demi's blurry gaze. A bead of blood welled up on the man's lower lip. Demi flicked out his tongue to lap it up and close the small wound.

Trey's grip tightened. "Oh my fucking God."

Demi gave him a lazy smile, feeling more content that he had for weeks. Except, he wiggled his hips. Trey was still hard. He hadn't come.

"Oh." He reached down between them to palm the length through the fabric of Trey's pants. "Let me help with this."

Trey grabbed his hand by the wrist. "No. Don't. This has gotten way out of line. This isn't the ceremony."

Demi's eyelids drooped. "I know. Isn't it awesome?"

"No. I mean, yes, this was great, but no, we have to stop now. It's not...sanctioned."

"Who cares about that?"

Demi didn't wait for a reply. His imagination had already been cut loose. Using his superior strength, he freed himself and dropped to his knees. His otherworldly speed had Trey's pants open and his dick out before the man could utter another word of protest.

Then Demi dove right in, putting his mouth around Trey's cock, robbing the man of the power of speech.

At least that was his interpretation of the animalistic sound that passed the man's lips before he dropped his hands and leaned against the pantry door. Demi had no real idea of what he was doing, yet he didn't care. The feel of Trey's heavy shaft on his tongue was mind-blowing. It was the best treat he'd ever had, almost. The salty pre-cum slid down his throat the same way the blood had, reminding him of the one thing that he loved to consume the most. So long as it was Trey's.

He could have spent hours feasting on the hard flesh, except the moment he took it all the way down and swallowed, Trey spasmed. The dick swelled and cum spurted out with surprising force. He pulled back to work the dick with his tongue in order to get more of a taste.

Curse words flooded over his head as he milked Trey completely dry. Only when Trey uttered a weak plea to stop did Demi let the cock slide completely out of his mouth. He licked his lips to get every drop and sat back on his heels. He smiled shyly at Trey.

The man still had his eyes closed. He banged his head against the door a couple of time. "Your fathers are going to kill me. That's assuming I don't slit my wrists with guilt."

With a frown, Demi stood. "You're being melodramatic. You're not going to kill yourself and my fathers aren't going to find out."

Trey's eyes opened to slits. "You think Karl and Damien have any doubt about what's going on in here?"

"And why would they tell anyone?" he countered. He waved at his front. "There is no visible evidence, either.

My T-shirt is covering up the cum stain and I didn't spill a bit of yours."

Trey grunted and stood straight. He put himself to rights in quick order, disappointing Demi, who would have liked to do it for him. "We're not doing this again, and you're not going out with Damien."

"I can wait until the ceremony to get my hands on you, but I am going to help Damien ask around." Before Trey could argue further, Demi rushed on. "Think about it. Damien doesn't know the score about what could truly be going on. He can't protect himself if he's in the dark, and even if we tell him, he's still at risk. Someone who isn't a cop or big and scary like Val has to watch out for the guy and keep his ears open to information that wouldn't mean anything to Damien but would prove useful. I'm the logical one. You know I am," he added, folding his arms.

"Even if I agree, your fathers never will."

"They won't have a choice if Alex orders them to let me."

"Which he won't if it upsets your parents."

"He will if you convince him of its wisdom. You know it makes sense."

Trey closed his eyes again for a second and ran his hand over his head. "Fuck me."

Demi hid a smile. "I intend to on Friday. Before then, let me go out and see what's going on. None of us are safe if one of Dracul's minions is out there. Whoever he is, he wouldn't have bothered to come to Boston just to be a pimp. He could do that anywhere. He's here to cause us trouble. We'll be back to playing defense if we don't get ahead of whatever trouble is brewing now."

"Fuck me," Trey said again, although this time his tone sounded more resigned. "Come on. Let's go talk to Alex."

Demi tried not to show how gleeful he was at winning their first argument as a couple. Friday couldn't come fast enough.

* * * *

"Thanks for letting me ride along, guys." Ric leaned onto his elbows as he peered through the space between the front seats. He felt a like a dog on a family trip, but that was fine. Having spent the day in the morgue, a place without windows and where one could easily lose track of time, Ric was happy to be outdoors. The night was warm enough and the idea of playing cop appealed to whatever little boy was left in him.

"I've always wanted to do a stake-out," he confessed.

Duncan glanced at him through the rearview mirror. "Technically this is a tail. Although, it looks like Damien and Demi are going to hang around this spot for a while."

The tight lines along the man's mouth conveyed how stressed he was about their night's activities. No surprise there. Ric had seen for himself in Wales the closeness of the cop and the hybrid son of the alien doctor and his human husband. He couldn't imagine that Duncan would have gone along with Demi being out and about with the street kids if there had been a better choice.

"That's good." He wanted to be reassuring. "We've got a great view of what's happening. I can't see how they can come to harm here. It's too public."

Duncan's expression managed to turn extra grim. "You'd think, but shit happens in the blink of an eye and you're royally fucked."

Ric knew when to back off. He'd learned that lesson working in the ED, where he had to balance accurate assessments of a patient's condition with hope. Some people were more willing than others to grasp any thread of it, while others were too savvy to let go of any amount of worry. Duncan fell squarely in the latter category. Of course, he did. He was a cop. He'd seen the worst and would see even more of it before his career ended.

So, Ric focused on the positive aspects of the night's doings. He'd been itching from the beginning to insert himself more into the aliens' lives. Although he'd expressed it as scientific curiosity, he really had to face the fact that it was more personal than that. As a child, he'd loved sci-fi in all its forms. What could be better than to learn that there was at least one other world out there with intelligent life, and like every sci-fi movie made, those creatures had come to Earth. The vampire intersection only made the whole thing more awesome.

What had happened in Wales had been an off-the-charts stupendous journey. He'd dreamed about it, especially the wan young man who was actually centuries old. Ric relived the moment when he'd helped pull a squalling hybrid from a male body. Surreal didn't begin to cover it. Nor did he have any words to describe what it was like to hold Dafydd in his arms, tend to him, heal him from his most recent trauma. That face, that ethereal, beautiful face, haunted him. Parting from him once they'd reached Boston had been harder than he could have imagined. As inappropriate and pointless as it was, he was looking for any excuse to see Dafydd again.

The opportunity had come in form of sitting in an unmarked car with two casually-dressed cops, watching a bunch of homeless teens pass around obvious bottles of booze in paper bags and fatties. Ric's ass had already started to go numb and he was bored as fuck but also intrigued and a little frightened. If what Duncan had said was true, they'd brought the danger from Wales that they hadn't stamped out back with them. And that was his ticket to this slow-moving drama. If things went south and Demi or anyone else ended up injured, Ric was there with more medical supplies at his fingertips than the AMA would have normally sanctioned for a doctor to carry around. It was, according to Duncan, the terms set by Demi's fathers.

It was good to be useful. He wasn't going to be any help in a direct confrontation, but unlike Harry, he was probably entirely unknown to whoever had been in the castle. He hadn't been part of a fight, so he'd hopefully remained unseen as well. Anderson hadn't been there at all, meaning he was also possibly not on anyone's radar. If Duncan was a known quantity, even an alien with their extraordinary eyesight would be hard put to notice him under the ball cap set low on his face. The deceptively piece-of-shit car they sat in blended into the general environment, even though it was illegally parked.

Anderson passed him small binoculars. "Do any of those boys look like Mateo?"

This was another possible good use for him. They were looking for the kid he'd treated, and while the sous chef, Damien, professed to know him, Duncan figured it couldn't hurt to have Ric scanning around, too.

Ric peered through the lens at the loose group gathered on the Esplanade. The sight of all those lost children tugged at his heart. Tossed or chased away from their families or having slipped through the cracks in a system intended to help them, they had few choices. Drugs and alcohol numbed their pain, while selling their bodies earned enough to buy more. It was a vicious cycle that evil people preyed upon. For that alone, Ric wanted to help catch this alien fucker exploiting vulnerable humans.

The magnification allowed him to see Demi more clearly. The boy had already been leaving with Damien by the time Duncan had picked Ric up. He'd only seen the hybrid from a distance since returning from Wales. He was surprised by how much the kid had changed. He looked different in ways that were hard to pin down. It wasn't only the streak of red hair dangling alongside his face or the grubby clothes he wore. There was something about his features that appeared more mature, as if he'd aged a year in mere weeks. He still looked painfully young, just not as much, which undoubtedly was part of the stress eating away at Duncan. Ric could relate, given that Dafydd had the face of a teenager despite his ancient age.

Shutting down his own musings, he swept the view of the binoculars down the messy line to the far end then held it there as he fussed with the magnification. "I think I see him."

Duncan straitened. "Where?"

"At the far-left end."

The cop swung his binoculars in that direction. "The one with the spiky green hair?"

"Yes, that looks like him, although he was a redhead when I treated him."

Duncan tapped an ear bud with his finger. "Demi, head all the way down. Paz says the boy at the very end who looks like The Joker stuck his finger in a light socket is our guy."

Of course, the Stelalux family hadn't sent their precious boy into possible danger without as many safeguards as possible. Demi also had an ear bud that allowed Duncan to speak to him. Although no one had explained it to Ric, he assumed Demi could also communicate back.

Demi nodded his head as if to some musical beat, then slung an arm around Damien and leaned in to speak with him. They sauntered away, passing other kids and heading toward Mateo. Duncan followed their progress through his lens. Ric did the same. His heartbeat ticked up to a more rapid pace. Likely nothing of consequence was going to happen, yet he felt more primed to react to trouble than he had in the ED.

Damien and Demi took their time, not making it obvious that they had a destination in mind. He had to admire how cool they played it, when Ric figured he'd be a bundle of noticeable nerves if he were in their position. He supposed Damien had learned to hide his feelings and intentions on the street. While Demi's sangfroid was innate to his species, from what Ric had seen.

It felt like forever, but eventually, the pair ambled up to Mateo. Damien greeted the boy with the usual multi-stepped handshake that was popular with those far younger and hipper than Ric. Demi hung on Damien, as if they were lovers, and waved in a flirty way at

Mateo. The boy had a joint, which he offered to both of them. Damien took a quick hit. Demi demurred. *Smart kid.* Duncan uttered something like 'good call' at Demi's refusal. The brief interaction made Ric wonder if aliens got high. He knew they drank, although he'd never seen any of them drunk or even tipsy. Maybe that was something they did to blend in with humans, yet remained unaffected. He'd have to ask Harry. After tonight, he figured they owed him something. It would give him a chance to casually ask about Dafydd, and maybe if he were lucky, run into him.

Another few minutes ticked by while the three boys chatted, seemingly amicably. Ric was about to lower his binoculars when another boy came into the frame. At least, he thought it was a boy. Hard to tell when the kid was dressed all in black with a watch cap pulled down to his eyebrows. He was riding a bike slowly along the path where the rest of them sat. Although Ric couldn't be sure, he thought there was a subtle shift in everyone's demeanor. It was as if a ripple of unease ran through them, where each person in turn went on guard as the bike rider rolled by.

As he approached Damien and Demi, Mateo's gaze shifted. Like the others, his body language indicated he'd gone into high alert. Damien turned to see what Mateo was looking at. It was something out of a movie where the frames are slowed then sped up for dramatic effect. Damien's reaction to the newcomer was at first nothing more than he'd done for everyone else since he'd arrived. In an instant it changed. The boy's expression morphed from friendly to furious in a blink of an eye. He shouted, pointed then sprinted toward the bicycler, shaking Demi's arm off in the process.

"Fuck!" Duncan and Anderson both swore in unison before Anderson grabbed the binoculars out of Ric's hands to get a better view.

Ric leaned in farther, as if that would help him see better. "What's going on?"

Even as he asked the question, the kid on the bike sped past Damien, who swiped and missed stopping him. There was a moment of almost pandemonium as the others tried to distance themselves from what was unfolding. It gave the newcomer a chance to avoid Demi, too, by swerving onto the street before returning to the walkway.

There was another one of those weird slow-down, speed-up moments as Demi's head swiveled from one direction to the opposite way. Then he took off after the bike boy.

"Goddamn son-of-a-bitch." Duncan's swearing rocketed out of his mouth. Banging his binoculars onto the hump between the seats, he said, "Demi, stop!" The cop's head shook. "No, don't go after him. Do you hear me?"

Duncan pushed something on the consul and suddenly Demi's voice was coming through the speakers. "He's riding Father Ted's bike. We can't let him get away." *Christ!* The kid didn't even sound winded, even though he was sprinting down the path alongside the Charles River.

"You fucking well can!" Duncan's fury was impressive. He started the car and had it leaping forward like a gazelle. "I'm going after him. Stand down."

"Can't drive on the Esplanade," came Demi's retort.

"Watch me. I mean it, Demi. Stop chasing him right this goddamn minute." Now there was fear in the man's tone.

There was no reply, only the sound of breathing. *Smart kid.* He knew he wasn't going to win the argument, so he had elected not to have one at all. Meanwhile, Duncan was doing the reputation of Boston having rude, aggressive drivers proud. Ric slumped against the back seat as the car swerved into traffic on Storrow Drive. He fumbled with difficulty to get his seatbelt back on as horns blared and Duncan swore ripely over and over again.

"That cocky brat. Friday can't come a moment too soon. Once that ceremony is over, I'm going to lock his sweet ass in chastity and board him in his room for the next fifty years."

Anderson clung to the handle above his door. "You might be dead by then," he noted mildly.

"I can only hope so," Duncan sneered.

"What ceremony?" It was stupid to be asking such a mundane question under the circumstances, yet his curiosity had been piqued and it was better than pissing his pants in fear.

Duncan barked out a laugh. "Demi's manhood initiation, if you can believe that. As if this kid has any business being treated like an adult. When this night is done, I'm going to turn him over my knee and..."

While Ric understood the man's feelings and saw it for the hyperbole that it was, he couldn't help thinking that Duncan was underestimating Demi. From what Ric could see, the boy was more man now than kid. And as he caught sight of Demi chasing the bike rider closer to the river, he figured right now, he was their best hope of winning.

Chapter Six

Catching the kid on Father Ted's bike would have been dead easy if not for the irritating need to hold himself back. As he closed the gap between them, Demi fought a constant battle with his muscles' natural abilities and his cerebral understanding that with so many humans in sight, he couldn't give them a show that was unexplainable.

He had to block out, as well, Trey's haranguing through his earpiece. He'd known the second he'd taken off after this guy that Trey would have fits. It was no surprise that he kept ordering Demi to stop, to let him handle it, to stay away from danger. Except that way was doomed for failure. If Trey risked driving onto the Esplanade, the chances of an innocent person getting hurt were unacceptably high. The man was too good a cop to do that, yet the boy on the bike had the advantage of being able to evade capture by going where the car couldn't.

Whoever it was, he was skilled, commanding the bike as if it were an extension of his own body. The small compactness of the rider allowed him to crouch low over the handlebars to cut down on wind resistance. He seemed utterly unconcerned with falling over, which made him harder to catch because he treated the trees and other people like pesky obstacles to maneuver around with ease.

Demi, of course, was equally facile. His agility was inhuman and his ability to keep himself falling, cat-like. He always landed on his feet. The speed with which he ran didn't even strain his lungs. The only thing bothering him was Trey's stream of furious orders to stop. While he could have turned the earbuds off, he didn't. In a strange way, the sound of the man's voice buoyed him. He felt connected to him and it was almost as if they ran side-by-side. Any fear he might have felt chasing someone tied possibly to Dracul's men eased with the knowledge that he wasn't alone. It might be crazy, but he had an unwavering belief that Trey would always keep him safe.

The least he could do was help by catching this asshole. His chances increased as they sped past the bulk of people around and headed into a more secluded part of the Esplanade, given that it was night. There were so many paths along the grassy route, the bicycler had no trouble forging ahead. Except he didn't stick to the parts designed for his ride. Instead, he cut closer to the river, bouncing along the uneven grass. The obstacles didn't seem to bother him, and they for sure were no issue for Demi.

He took the risk of picking up the pace and closing the gap between them. The boy he chased rose up off his seat and dared to turn his head to look at Demi. It was a stupid move because no one retained complete control by doing something like that, and it served to slow him down, as well. When the bike wobbled, the kid overcompensated and headed straight for the river bank. Then he hit a big bump and went head over heels past the handle bars and straight into the water.

Demi didn't hesitate to follow. Kicking off the ratty sneakers Damien had made him wear, he catapulted himself off the ground and dove into the river. He deliberately overshot the spot where the other boy had made his splash. The half-formed plan was to loop back underwater and grab him by the legs. He took a deep breath as he went in, unbothered by the coldness that enveloped him. Like all of his species, it was heat that bothered him, and in the last few months, particularly so. And swimming came easily to him. He had no trouble opening his eyes and peering through the murkiness to catch sight of his quarry.

The human flailed in a clumsy effort to get back to the surface. The moment he broke through, however, Demi was already on him. He wrapped one arm around the boy's thighs and propelled them forward by kicking and take long strokes with his free arm. His captive wasn't going down without a fight, though. Demi grunted out precious air when a knee rammed his chest. He had to contain the thrashing boy with a bear hug, leaving only his legs to finish the journey. It wasn't hard. This kid was small and skinny. A stray thought crossed Demi's mind that there was no way this was Father Ted's killer. The priest had looked like a pretty big man. But, if the boy had the man's bike, he'd been a witness to the murder or arrived shortly afterward. Either way, Trey would want to question him.

Thinking of the cop goosed his efforts. He definitely didn't want Trey jumping into the river. Getting soaking wet wasn't going to help what was likely an already bad mood. Better if Demi could present the kid in a nice package on the bank. With that driving intent, he hauled the still-squirming boy up onto the grassy slope. He flipped him onto his stomach and kneed him in the back.

"Knock it off!" Demi issued the command in as stern a voice as he could manage.

"Fuck you!" The pinned boy threw his head back to hit Demi's face. Demi was too quick for him, though. "I'm going to scream for the cops if you don't let me go."

Demi pushed him down by his shoulders. "No need. They're here."

That was no lie. Trey had jumped the curb in the car and come to a screeching halt. He was out of it and running toward them before the wheels stopped spinning. The look on the man's face was glorious — a thrilling combination of pissed off and relieved. What it wasn't was indifferent. Knowing that Trey cared enough about him to feel such strong emotions was worth sitting on top of a wiggling body with water dripping everywhere.

Trey slid beside them like a rookie making his debut at Fenway Park. He yanked Demi off the prone body and rolled him away. Anderson replaced him before the kid could mount an escape, but none of that mattered because Demi ended up lying under Trey. The man he loved held him down by the shoulders, much as he'd done with the boy, except in this case, they were face-to-face. Demi's breath caught as he looked up.

"Are you all right?" The way Trey snarled out the question, it sounded more like an accusation.

"I-I'm fine." He tried for a pretty smile.

Trey bared his teeth, obviously not charmed in the least. "Are you sure?" When Demi nodded, Trey shook him once. "What the fuck were you thinking? I told you not to chase that punk."

"He was getting away and on Father Ted's bike. He's obviously a witness or something. You need to question him."

"You think?" He roared out the response loud enough to send a shiver through Demi.

"He was getting away." His tone sounded petulant to his own ears. He slapped his palm against Trey's chest. "Let me up."

Trey leaned in closer. "Not until I'm sure Karl has that fucker secured. Christ Jesus, Demi, are you trying to give me a heart attack? You were supposed to watch Damien's back, not go all *Die Hard* and tackle a suspect. In the fucking Charles, no less."

"Um…"

Trey deflated in the next instant, his shoulders sagging and he sat back on his heels. "You scared the crap out of me." He stuttered out a breath. "I couldn't stay with you while driving the car, and I sure as shit couldn't run as fast. Then I saw you go into the water and…goddamn, I thought you wouldn't come out again."

"Oh." Seeing how almost defeated Trey looked made him feel bad. He reached up and ran his fingertips along the man's jaw. "I'm sorry. I didn't intend to frighten you."

Trey sighed. "Demi, you scare me witless. Always have." Slinging his leg over, he stumbled to his feet and held out his hand. "Come on. Let's get you home."

Demi allowed himself to be pulled upright. "What about the kid? Aren't you going to question him?"

"Of course I am. Later."

Karl had the suspect standing and handcuffed. The hat had come off, giving Demi a clear view of who he'd been dealing with. A jolt hit him when he saw that it was a smaller version of himself, part-Asian with long, dark hair plastered around his pretty face. Various piercings winked in the moonlight and he stared at Demi with utter hatred.

"You're going to regret this," he spat. "My man will tear you apart."

Karl shook him by the hand holding his shoulder. "Shut up. You can do your talking after we've booked you."

"For what? I didn't do anything. This crazy cunt chased me right into the water. I'm the victim here."

Pointing to where the bike lay on the ground, Trey said, "That right there says otherwise. At the very least, it's stolen property."

A couple of patrol cars came racing up and soon a uniformed officer was hauling the kid away. Trey left Demi to speak to the others while Paz came ambling up with a blanket.

"Here," he said, shaking it out and wrapping it around Demi. "Are you okay? Did you hit anything, like your head, when you dove in?"

"I'm fine," Demi reassured him, his gaze still on Trey. "Nothing hurts." That was mostly true. The kid had managed to get a few licks in. Demi's stomach ached a bit where the guy had kneed it a few times.

"Come back to the car. I need to check you out anyway."

Demi wanted to argue the point, wanted to stay within sight of Trey. Knowing that Paz had been brought into the whole thing to reassure his fathers, he gave in instead. He followed Paz to the unmarked car and sat in the back with him. He sat patiently through the doctor's exam, allowing his wet shirt to be pulled off, hissing only a bit when sore spots got poked.

Paz hummed. "Not bad. Nothing that requires treatment anyway." He pulled away with a sigh. "Not that my assessment is going to placate your fathers."

"They worry too much," Demi said absently. His focus remained on Trey, who was supervising the removal of the bike, as well as the perp.

"That's what parents do—at least, good ones. From what I've seen, your two fathers are the best. You may not appreciate that now, but you will in a few years. You'll see it for what it is."

Karl peeled away from Trey and followed the uniforms back to their vehicles. Damien appeared out from the gloom, having followed apparently at a slow, human pace. Trey met him, clapped a hand on the boy's back and headed over, his face not quite so grim as he said something to the sous chef. Demi tried not to feel jealous, failed then stewed for a half-second before reminding himself that Trey saved his harder side for Demi because he cared about him. He loved him. Maybe. Hopefully.

He had to look away. "Actually," Demi said turning to Paz, "after the way they acted when Papa and I were snatched by Dracul, I appreciate how badass they are."

The doctor grinned. "They are definitely that."

Trey opened the driver's seat door and slid in. "I'm taking you all back to the club."

Damien took Karl's old seat. He twisted his head around and grinned at Demi. "Dude, that was awesome. Thanks for catching him."

Demi shot him a smile. "You're welcome. Glad someone appreciates my actions." He tapped Trey on the shoulder. "What about..." Demi shut his mouth when Trey glared at him through the rearview mirror.

"Do you want me to drive so that you can go with Karl?" Paz offered.

"No. Thanks. I promised I would see Demi safely home, so that's what I'm going to do. I'll go question the kid afterward. Buckle up."

That was all he said before starting the car and driving away. Demi did as he'd been told, snuggling into the blanket and waiting for his body to calm down. He was thirsty, though. Not for water. His dry throat yearned for blood, the need almost overpowering. His gaze homed in on Trey's neck. Although he couldn't see the pulse, he could imagine it. Opening his hearing, he focused on the beat of Trey's heart. Paz's and Damien's intruded, though, confusing him and making it less enjoyable. He wanted a connection with his lover, because after what happened in the pantry, that's what they were to each other.

Soon, they'd be engaged, then married... His cock stiffened at the idea. He had to be patient. It was only a few days away now. He would have to settle for the bags of blood his fathers gave him and finding pleasure in his own hand. Except shit, with Quinn sharing his bed, he was going to have to do both in the bathroom. Not the sexiest place. He'd have to deal with it unless and until Alex came to his senses. He snorted inwardly, as if that were even possible. The captain had risen to his high rank by being determined and he was not one prone to second-guessing himself. Demi rather expected that poor Quinn was going to have to be the one to give in.

Not his problem. Demi had other, more urgent concerns. Trey had been right about Papa and Dad pitching a fit when they heard what happened. Demi harbored a slim hope of running up to his room to change before the story of his dip in the river reached his fathers' ears. It might not sound so bad if they couldn't see the aftermath. No such luck. When Trey pulled up to the club's side entrance, they came hurrying out along with Alex and Val. Damien must have texted them that they were on their way back. Dad had Demi engulfed in a tight hug by the time he'd put both feet on the pavement.

"Why are you shirtless and wet?" he demanded. His keen gaze swept Demi up and down. "You've lost that expensive dyed hair extension that Mackie loaned you," he added, swiping his hand over Demi's head.

Even though he'd had the entire ride back to come up with a way of telling the tale so that it didn't sound too bad, he found he had no words. Instead, he leaned into his father's embrace. Two sets of arms wrapped him up, held him securely as Papa joined them. He knew he was loved and that he was safe, unlike that kid he'd chased down, who likely had learned to do terrible things to survive. He hadn't felt sorry for him as he'd wrangled him. Now he did.

"I'm okay."

"Is he?" This from Papa.

"Yes," Paz replied. "I've checked him out and he's fine."

"I'll explain everything before I head back to the station." Trey's voice sounded weary.

Everyone trooped inside, slipping into the private elevator in a group. It stopped on the floor where Demi shared rooms with his fathers, and Dad hustled him off while the others stayed.

Demi dragged his feet. "Wait. I want to go to the debriefing."

"No." Dad's tone brooked no dissent. "You've done enough, apparently, and Papa will tell me all about it later. You need to take a shower."

Paz stepped out to join them. "I'll come, too, if you don't mind. I've had it for the night."

"Of course," Dad replied before propelling Demi forward.

Demi had a second to look over his shoulder. Trey's expression as the elevator doors closed was unreadable. He tried not to let it worry him. After all, Friday was coming up, and once they'd rid him of his pesky virginity, things would be different. They had to be.

* * * *

The knock on his door was so soft that Dafydd thought for a second that he'd imagined it. Then another came, and he had to decide whether he even wanted to answer. This room he'd been given was his haven, a place where he could spend the days and nights alone, reading, as he was now, or watching TV. There was an endless array of channels to choose from, as well as the Internet. There was also a large supply of books in Alex's private library. He'd been told to peruse at will, and he had.

The one good part of being Dracul's slave for centuries had meant some time to learn a few different languages. He could switch between Welsh and English easily out of necessity, given that Dracul and his men had done so. Survival alone had forced him to be bilingual. It made slipping into life in America easy. Easier, that is, because nothing about his life was other than hard.

Another knock had him putting aside his book and sliding off his bed. He unlocked the door and opened it a sliver to see who it was. Dr. Paz peered back, the man's expression conveying his own unease. Although tempted to shut the man out, Dafydd couldn't bring himself to be quite so mean.

"Yes?" He allowed some annoyance to seep through.

Paz's lips quirked up briefly. "Sorry to bother you. I happened to be in the club, and I was hoping to see how you are doing."

Dafydd dropped his gaze. "I'm fully healed with no lingering effects from the…" He licked his lips and fell silent.

"That's good to hear, but I was more concerned about your, um, mental health, frankly."

Dafydd raised his eyes again. "I seem to be managing feeding, washing and dressing myself all right." He winced inwardly at his stroppy retort. He'd been raised to be polite. Years with the monster had dulled his childhood lessons, yet they weren't completely destroyed.

He opened the door more. "Forgive my rudeness. I appreciate your concern. As you can see, I'm truly fine."

The doctor flashed a smile. "I'm glad to hear it." He stuck his hands in the front pocket of his pants, drawing Dafydd's gaze there.

The man was dressed down in a simple shirt and worn jeans, much as Dafydd was. The luxury of being fully clothed whenever he wanted was something he was still getting used to. He hadn't yet mastered the idea of wearing smallclothes, something totally foreign to him, but soft baggy denim and sweatpants suited him very well. The doctor's pants were tighter, hugging his slim hips and cupping his crotch in a provocative way. Dafydd hated that he noticed such a thing. So, turning, he walked away.

"May I come in?"

"Do as you like." Dafydd was back to being difficult. He threw himself on the bed and sat up against his amazing mound of pillows. Not being used to staring at anyone in the eye, he focused his gaze on his own bare feet, mostly. It was hard not to keep glancing at his visitor.

Paz padded in, leaving the door open. "I don't mean to be intrusive. I happen to be up with Lucien and he said you stick to this room for the most part. I was worried," he added with a shrug.

"You needn't be." Dafydd waved his hand at the room. "I live in perfect comfort, as you can see. I haven't been this safe, well-fed and pain free in my entire life. I want and need nothing more."

"Hmm." The doctor made a circuit around the room. "I have no doubt you see it that way." He poked at the heavy curtain hanging closed against the window. "There is a whole world out there, you know. Eventually, you'll want to go out into it."

Now it was Dafydd's turn to shrug. "Perhaps. Not today, though."

Paz let go of the curtain. "It's night."

Dafydd blinked back at him. "Is it? I've lost track."

"I'm not surprised. People who live in isolation tend to form a twenty-five-hour cycle instead of keeping to the twenty-four-hour one."

Dafydd expected more, like a lecture about how he needed to leave his room. Instead, Paz stayed silent as he studied the stack of books Dafydd had amassed.

"I saw Idris." The remark caught Dafydd off guard. Paz returned to the bed, hands back into his pockets, rocking on his heels. "He's gotten so big and is very robust and happy."

Something sharp poked at his heart. He swallowed hard. "He's a monster. They grow fast. Wait until he's big enough to rip your throat out. I expect that will make him very happy indeed." How many times had he witnessed such barbarity by Dracul or their sons? The memories turned his stomach.

Paz inched closer. "I don't think that's going to happen, not in this environment where the Stelalux family works so hard to protect humans. This club will be a good place for him to be raised."

Dafydd said nothing. There was no point to this conversation. The doctor was naïve, never having lived the horror of being Dracul's slave. He'd heard stories, no doubt. To experience the true level of evil that had been Dracul was all it took to beat any hope or optimism out of a man.

A thought occurred to him. "Why are you here? In the club, I mean. Are you a member?"

Paz snorted. "This is a place where rich men come to play. That's not me. Not yet, probably not ever. Although Alex has been kind and extended a membership to me in gratitude for what little I've done, I'm not really comfortable hanging with this crowd, not on a routine basis. Maybe on a Friday or Saturday night, but this is the middle of the week."

"And yet, here you are." He wasn't sure why he was prodding the conversation along. He should be working to kick the guy out.

Paz screwed up his face. "I was helping out again on a small matter."

Of necessity, Dafydd had developed an excellent sense of trouble brewing. "What?" he asked sharply.

"Nothing of consequence." When Dafydd stared hard at him, the man elaborated. "There was a murder of a priest recently and there's a guy corralling some of the street boys as their pimp. I was asked to be part of a sort of undercover effort to learn more. That's all."

The fuck it is. "What are you not telling me?"

Paz's face went through all sorts of contortions, which might have been amusing if not for a tightening in Dafydd's gut telling him something bad was happening. Finally, the doctor explained. Dafydd's heartbeat sped up and his lungs labored as his breathing became harsh.

"It's probably nothing related to Dracul," the doctor tried to reassure him. He raced up to Dafydd's bedside and dropped to his knees. Clasping Dafydd's wrist, he pressed his finger on the pulse. "Take it easy. You're safe, no matter what."

Dafydd yanked his hand free and scuttled into the middle of the bed. "You don't know that."

Paz stood. "I'm sorry. I didn't intend to frighten you."

"I-I'm not. Fear was beaten out of me long ago." *Liar.* Mostly. It was more fury making him react this way. It was supposed to be over. Plus, Paz's touch had freaked him out, not because he hated it, but because he *hadn't.*

"It may be one of the twins." He forced the words out.

"Why do you think it's one of them in particular?" the doctor asked. "Assuming it has anything to do with Dracul at all. We don't know that it does."

"Don't we?" Dafydd spat back. "I'm not even convinced the monster, himself, is dead." No body, no ashes, no certainty... Not that he had anything to fear in that regard. He would die before being enslaved again, either by his own hand or by Dracul's.

Pushing down his emotions, he worked with the facts he had. "The twins were banished because they fucked up their mission here. I think they were still in the castle after that, but I can't be sure. They could have been long gone before the night you rescued me."

Memories swamped him for a few seconds—the agony of childbirth, the reassuring touch of the doctor and his insistence that Dafydd wasn't going to die. He wouldn't have thought it possible, and yet the man had been true to his word.

He worried the comforter he lay on. "I know my sons. They've spent their entire lives trying to live up to their father's standards of monstrous success. It would suit their perverted view to achieve power right under their enemies' nose. I should perhaps talk to Alex." The thought of facing the alien leader, as well as the one called Val, made his stomach knot. It was too reminiscent of Dracul and Petru, even though he knew they were nothing alike.

Paz held up his hand. "It's all right. They've already considered that. They are working with the local police and seem to have it well in hand. They aren't complacent by any means. I'm sure if they need anything from you, they'll ask."

Dafydd relaxed back against his pillow, more relieved than he wanted to be. "Very well. Thank you for telling me the truth."

"You have a right to know what's going on. You're part of this, more so than I am."

"You seem quite in the middle of it to me." He didn't mean it to be an accusation, yet it came out sounding like one.

Paz shrugged. "I was in the right place at the wrong time and know how to keep my mouth shut. I'm fascinated by all of this, to be honest."

"I'm a specimen in a jar, am I?" *God, now I really am being cruel and rude.*

Paz's expression hardened. "No, you're not." He took a step closer. "You matter, Dafydd. I, um, care about what happens to you. This isn't me looking for entertainment or a Nobel Prize if and when this whole alien thing becomes known." He paced away then continued. "It started out that way. I'd be lying if I said it hadn't. Sometime while I was helping birth Idris and keeping you alive, it became more personal." He stopped and stared into Dafydd's eyes. "I hope I'm not entirely out of line saying that."

Dafydd dropped his gaze again and ran his finger long the spine of his book. "I can't honestly say. My moral compass is, if not broken, hopelessly malfunctioning. And after accepting my imminent death and making peace with it, I find living mystifying. Being free should make me happy. Instead, I am confused."

He stared up at Paz from under his lashes. "You know I am hollow inside. I have nothing to give anyone."

"I don't believe that."

"It's true." His voice caught.

"Give it time. You'll see that it isn't."

* * * *

Trey dropped into the ass-killing interview chair, tossing his folder on the table. "So, mystery boy, now that you've had a couple of hours to consider your situation, do you want to give me your name?"

The skinny kid slumped across from him remained silent. He'd said nothing other than a string of vile curses since his arrest. That was according to Karl. Once they'd wrangled him out of his wet clothing and into dry prison issue, he'd gone silent. His fingerprints didn't match any in the system so far. They'd run them through IAFIS with no luck. The kid hadn't been arrested before, which seemed unlikely — or perhaps his offenses had been juvenile and therefore sealed.

Trey tapped his fingertips on the file. "I guess I'll just call you 'kid', then." He pulled out a picture of Father Ted lying in his own blood where he'd been killed. "You know this guy?"

He slid the picture closer. The boy's gaze flicked over it before skittering away again.

"That's Father Ted, but I bet you know that already. He used to do good work with street kids like you."

According to Damien, this boy might have hung around the soup kitchen before. He couldn't be sure. And if this was one of the members of the new pimp's stable, he probably wouldn't have needed the food hand-out.

He presented the picture of the bike next. "That's what you were riding tonight, and oddly enough, it belonged to Father Ted. It went missing the morning his throat was cut."

Something flickered in the kid's eyes, and he shifted in his seat. Sensing he was breaking through the façade of indifference, Trey took out another picture of the body, this one from the morgue. There was something about the sanitized view of the corpse that was worse than the murder-scene one. It was starker, more realistic, not something that every teenager saw in video games and in movies. No fake blood pooling around someone who looked merely asleep, only a hideously pale dead man with his throat gaping open.

"Nice guy. Everyone said so, a real man of the cloth. He wanted to help kids like you, get you off drugs and the streets. Give you a way of surviving that didn't involve selling yourself to sweaty men in their cars or a back alley. And yet, some asshole slit him open like a fucking carp."

The boy's gaze turned away again. He tightened his lips into a narrow line, and his thin chest rose and fell on a harsh breath.

Trey pounded his fist on top of the last picture. "Look at him!"

The kid jumped, his fuck-you demeanor cracking even more.

"You know," Trey said, lowering his voice to a more conversational tone. "We don't have the death penalty anymore in this state, but we still put punks like you away for life. I hear Sousa is handling the overflow of mean motherfuckers from Walpole. Those dogs will tear a little thing like you apart."

The perp scoffed. "You think I'm scared of prison? I can handle myself. I'll just find the biggest daddy there and he'll protect me. I know how to make a man happy," he added with a toss of his head.

Shit. For a second there, the gesture and the way the hair swung reminded Trey of Demi. In fact, this boy looked way too much like him. Trey'd been so pissed off back on the Esplanade that he hadn't noticed the similarities, not that it meant anything. It shouldn't throw him. He couldn't let it.

"Sure, sure, I bet you do, so long as you stay young and pretty." He snapped his fingers. "Oh, wait, that won't happen. A lifer like you will age out of cute in a few years and sink right into old and ugly."

Now, the boy was pissed. "I won't get life." He barked out a laugh. "As if anyone will believe that I could kill that tall priest from behind." He shut his mouth with an audible click of his teeth when he realized he'd said too much.

Trey leaned forward. "Interesting. You knew Father Ted and you know the way he was killed. And you're right. You're too short. So, who did it and why?"

The boy folded his arms. "I have no idea." He shrugged. "Yeah, I knew him. *Of* him. Fucking do-gooder. Not content with handing out food. He had to hand out shitty advice about things there were none of his business."

"He liked to help kids stop whoring. That pissed off pimps, I hear. Ones like yours?"

Now a look of smugness crossed his face. "You have no idea about who you're dealing with."

"Why don't you tell me?"

A snort and an eye roll were all he got.

Trey sat back and acted relaxed. "I'm thinking it's this guy who wears leather like he's perpetually in cosplay." That slight earned him a narrowing of eyes. "Big, fat maybe."

"Muscular," the boy spat out, then actually put his hand over his mouth.

"Yeah, 'cause a street rat like you has choices. Nothing but the best when it comes to men you bed for a few bucks, a warm place, maybe a shower."

"It's not like that. I am *not* a whore."

"Right. Of course. Not now. You used to be, though, huh? But this new pimp has taken you off the street because he's your *boyfriend*." He put as much of a sneer into the last word as he could manage.

It did the trick. Sitting up, the boy jabbed a finger at him. "I take care of him. And in return he shoves his huge dick so far up my ass that it chokes me." He dropped his eyelids in a creepy attempt at seduction. "You're nothing compared to him. He could snap you like a twig if he wanted."

"Like he slit Father Ted's throat, almost severing his head?"

"Exactly. That fucker won't meddle anymore in my man's business."

Trey said nothing more. He merely sat staring back at the boy while the enormity of what he'd just said sunk in. The piss and vinegar in the kid slowly leaked out. He deflated, slinking down into his chair. He blinked rapidly as if holding back tears.

"I'm not saying anything more," he added in a small voice.

Trey almost felt sorry for him. Except for the image of Father Ted lying in front of him, as well as the nearly worse one of Demi diving into the Charles River in pursuit of this little shit, he might have. Instead, he gathered up the pictures and shoved them back in his folder.

"Maybe after a night in a cell you'll change your mind." He stood. "He's not coming to save you, kid. You're already as good as dead to him, and some other boy is getting his ass reamed in your place.

"I'm not the enemy. He is. You have no fucking idea how much."

Chapter Seven

"I can't believe I'm doing this in the middle of a murder investigation." Trey eyed himself in Alex's full-length mirror.

Karl brushed at something on Trey's shoulder. "When are you *not* in the middle of one? There's never a good time on this job to do anything personal. We've hit a dead-end anyway."

That was true. The kid in the tank wasn't talking. Having been baited into confirming their suspicions about who killed the priest, he'd clammed up good. Interviewing him had become an exercise in futility, and that was before his court-appointed attorney had entered the picture. John Doe, as he'd been processed under, was officially off limits unless his lawyer was present.

"You're right. Nothing's happening tonight." Other than a ceremonial sex act that made him more nervous than he'd been his first time.

Running a hand over his own head, Trey checked out his barbershop trim and shave, as well as his choice in clothing. "I guess I look presentable enough. Not sure about the suit, though."

It was the best he had. He'd considered renting a tux, but that seemed overblown. This wasn't a wedding, after all, more like a junior prom kind of situation—formal, but not too much so. Still, the few hundred bucks he'd laid out for this suit was nothing like the multi-thousand-dollar ones he could expect the Stelalux men to be wearing. He just couldn't compete.

"You look sharp, Trey. You always do, not that the kid is going to care."

Trey closed his eyes briefly. "Please don't call him that. I'm freaked out enough as it is."

"Young man, then. Come on, Trey. If I thought you were doing something wrong, I'd pistol-whip you, tie you up with duct tape and toss you into the trunk of my car."

Trey forced a grin, appreciating how his friend was trying to ease his worries. "Yeah, I know that. Hell, I'd help you."

He flicked at some imaginary fleck on his collar while patting the pocket of his jacket to make sure he'd put the lube in. Harry had assured him that no disease could be transmitted between them, so no condoms were necessary, but a dry fuck was not on the agenda. The very thought of it made his hole clench—and not in a good way. And it was on him to prep himself. Demi didn't have the experience to know what to do. He'd spent the last few nights loosening himself up with his own fingers.

It had been more fun than he'd expected. Not a chore at all, especially when he jerked off at the same time with thoughts of Demi fueling his imagination. Of course, those fantasies involved him doing the fucking.

Well, tough. Tonight was all about what Demi needed and wanted. Trey was a mere vessel. It kind of helped thinking of it that way, actually, made it more medical and not prurient. Yeah, that was how he had to approach the whole thing.

Alex loomed up behind Karl. "Gentlemen, it is time, if you will."

Trey took one deep breath and let it out before turning. "Sure thing." He winced at his casual awkwardness. Although no one had given him a script or anything, he still felt that there had to be a solemn way for him to play his role.

"I am ready, sir," he added.

Alex smiled. "Relax, Sergeant. The ceremony itself is brief and fairly simple. The tough part will come once you return to this room."

Because the idea of doing this back in Trey's apartment made everyone uneasy, Alex had loaned out his own bedroom for the night. That was fine by Trey. He definitely didn't want to take Demi's virginity within hearing distance of the guy's parents. Plus, rumor had it that Quinn was occupying that bed for the moment. Alex didn't seem particularly tense, but he must be seething inside at how he was sleeping apart from his lover. Oh well, that's what came from entangling himself with someone so young. Quinn needed time to figure out who he was. Like Demi. This night was about sex, not the rest of his life.

Reminding himself of that helped. Not a lot, but he'd take anything at the moment.

He followed Alex into the living room, Karl at his heels, a solid presence that Trey really appreciated. The group gathered there was small — Val and Mackie, Emil and Jase, Kitty and Quinn. No Logan, though, and that didn't surprise him. The veteran was great in a fight, yet she still struggled with everyday life and interpersonal stuff. Demi and his fathers hadn't arrived, which he knew was by design. They would come up from their suite shortly now that he was there waiting.

As he'd expected, everyone looked like a million bucks. On the long coffee table sat beautiful cut-crystal glasses filled with red liquid, enough for everyone. Trey's stomach tightened even more than it already was. *God.* He hoped drinking blood wasn't part of the deal. Harry certainly hadn't said anything about it. Then again, perhaps he hadn't dared.

The elevator chimed and there was no more time for him to dwell on what made him nervous. A few seconds later Demi came walking into the room flanked by his fathers. From that moment on, he was all that Trey saw. Beautiful, as always, Demi slowly approached with an uncharacteristically shy expression. His features were clearly visible because his hair was drawn back in a loose tail, the strands softly framing his face. He was dressed formally, but with a cute flair that made Trey smile.

Trey took a step toward him. Karl stopped him with a quick grip of his arm. Of course, he was supposed to let Harry and Lucien escort Demi to him. What few rules there were had been passed along to Karl as his otherworldly wing man. In this proceeding, Trey was the queen, and those lofty females were pursued, *never* the pursuers. It was hard, but he stayed where he was and watched Demi make his slow progress forward. Trey's palms itched with the desire to reach out and touch. He held himself in check with difficulty, but there was no holding back his dick. It hardened, not caring about protocol and not the least bit conflicted about what he was about to do.

The trio stopped a few feet away from him and bowed. It felt weird being on the receiving end of that kind of courtesy. He almost returned the gesture, except this time, he remembered his lessons.

Then Harry stepped forward. "I am Horatiu Stelalux and I humbly offer you the precious gift of my son, Demetrius."

Trey blinked. He'd sort of known Demi's full name, yet hadn't ever thought of him as anything other than Demi—or 'that brat', except that moniker didn't fit anymore. Mostly. The adventure on the Esplanade remained a sore point.

Karl poked him in the ribs. Trey sucked in a breath. "I welcome you, Horatiu, and your family."

He kind of felt stupid, especially as he wasn't even in his own home and really didn't have the right to entertain here. He stuck to the script because this mattered to these aliens who had become his friends. This was their culture as much as they could honor it in this setting. He needed to help them feel comfortable in what they did. That was as important as treating Demi right. After all they'd done, sacrificed, on behalf of the human race, it was the least he could do.

The reminder had him straightening his spine.

"Do you find our gift acceptable?" Harry asked with nobility but not certainty.

Trey didn't hesitate. "I do." He wanted to say more, because Demi deserved more enthusiasm than two words could convey. That's not how a queen would see it, though, so, again, he kept to the convention.

Lucien guided Demi forward. He and Harry each took hold of Demi's left hand and slowly raised it. No further words were spoken as they silently waited for Trey to make his move. He knew what to do, but before he took what was offered, he glanced around the room. While everyone wore serious expressions, the humans also showed happiness underneath. The aliens, though, were different. There was a depth of emotion there that Trey had trouble reading. It was almost a sadness, as if what was playing out hurt — or perhaps mattered so much that they couldn't maintain the façade of confidence that they always presented.

It startled Trey, so much so that he took the time to gaze at each person. Emil, always more familiar than the others, had his arm around Jase and held him close. His hand made circles around the boy's shoulder, as if soothing them both. Val stood behind Mackie, clasping the tag that hung below the boy's collar. The possessive gesture was only outshined by the rapid movement of the bouncer's massive chest. And Alex, his gaze steady on Demi's outstretched hand, slid his own over to where Quinn stood beside him. He fumbled for the boy's fingers and latched onto them. For a brief moment, Trey thought Quinn would reject the touch given the troubles between them but no. He instead entwined their fingers in a solid hold that perfectly conveyed how strong their relationship really was.

His perusal of the room seemed to take a long time. It had only been a couple of seconds and had done surprising wonders for his nerves. He returned his gaze where it wanted to be, on Demi. Then he reached for his hand and took it from the boy's fathers. Without looking, he raised it to his lips, turned it over and pressed a kiss to the inside of the wrist. A shudder ran through Demi at the touch, something Trey had no trouble detecting. He grinned and was rewarded with a shy smile in return.

The tension, or whatever it was, in the room evaporated. *Seriously?* As if anyone was actually worried that he would reject Demi. In any event, the mood turned positively joyful. Harry and Lucien beamed before clasping their own hands and sharing a quick, sweet kiss. Not that any of that held Trey's attention. He tugged Demi to his side and wrapped his arm around his waist. While their heights were closely aligned, the half-alien boy was far more slender. He fit neatly against Trey's broader body.

Emil and Jase started passing the glasses around. Trey swallowed hard as Emil handed him one before doing the same to Demi. Except up close, Trey could tell that the drinks weren't the same. His was thinner and the scent of wine wafted up even though Demi's blood-filled glass produced a stronger smell.

Once everyone had been served, Trey waited for some sign that they should all drink. A toast maybe. None came. Instead, the others merely drank eagerly, talking in low tones and sharing quiet kisses and other forms of affection. Kitty strolled over, taking Karl's attention. Under other circumstances, Trey would have been tempted to ogle what was going on between the two of them. Now, however, wasn't the time. Demi was where his focus needed to be.

He clinked his glass against Demi's. "Here's looking at you, kid." Cheesy, but the best he could come up with. The wine's hearty bouquet hit his tongue with a burst of flavor. Of course, it was some likely hideously expensive vintage.

Demi's pretty lips pursed. "I'm not a kid. Well, not for much longer anyway." He batted his eyelashes in an irresistible way before taking a sip of his drink.

Trey first placed a quick kiss on that luscious mouth, then said, "Your movie education needs improvement."

"I get the reference. I'm just saying." He lay his head on Trey's shoulder. "I don't want you hesitating tonight because you think I'm young."

Now Trey kissed the top of his head. "Don't worry. I don't have that much control or sense of morality. I want you. All you have to do to be confident of that is glance down. I'm surprised my pants haven't ripped right open."

Demi giggled and rubbed his face along Trey's neck like a cat. "I'm the same. Why don't we go now?"

"Um, is that okay? Won't it be rude or something to leave before everyone's at least finished their drink?"

"No, silly. I'm yours for the night. You call the shots. Whatever you want, goes."

Wow. That was so not the thing to say in front of his dick. It pulsed while his balls tightened. He'd better get started before he hurt himself with the waiting. "Okay," he said after another quick head kiss, "go on ahead of me. I'll be there in a second."

Pulling away, Demi gave him a sly look. "Don't keep me waiting too long." Another quick flutter of his lashes then he was sashaying away, putting a provocative swing to his slender hips.

Trey downed the rest of his wine in one gulp.

Karl's hand came out of nowhere. "Let me take that for you, boss."

"Thanks." He grimaced. "I'm tempted to have more, like an entire bottle."

Karl shook his head. "Uh-uh. You need a clear head more than Dutch courage."

"You're right." He clapped a hand on his partner's shoulder. "Thanks again for being here."

Karl's eyes shifted to the side. "Like it's a hardship for me to have an excuse to hang with Miss Kitty."

"Yeah, right. Enjoy."

Next, Trey approached Harry and Lucien, feeling the need to say something before trotting off to deflower their son. Harry had his hand cupped around the back of his husband's head and they were hunched in toward one another. They turned to him when he got close. Tears swam in Lucien's eyes, causing Trey's stomach to drop.

"Oh, God, don't cry." The words were out of his mouth before he could stop them. "I'll take good care of him, I promise. Unless you've changed your mind?" The thought caused a lump to form in his throat. *Mary, mother of God, please don't do that.*

In the next instant, Harry allayed his fears. "We have not. We can't. Biology drives us all in this matter." He rubbed his thumb along his husband's cheek, catching a tear that had escaped. "It's hard. That's all."

Lucien blinked rapidly before setting his gaze on Trey. "We trust you, Sergeant Duncan. Please pay me no mind. Like any parent, I suppose, I find it difficult to accept that my son is grown up." His lips quivered in a parody of a smile. "That reminds me that Idris needs tending. Damien was kind enough to watch him, but the child is my responsibility."

Trey was tempted to say something stupid like 'hey, we should be on a first name basis' but he held his tongue. With a bow, Lucien turned and walked away with a straight back and no hesitation.

Harry's expression conveyed his love as he watched his husband leave. "It took nearly two years before he could look me in the eye, three more after that until he welcomed my touch as something more than duty—or at least convinced me that was the case. I waited for that signal, fought my own desires all the while, because hurting him was anathema to me. Even now, I sometimes worry that he's merely doing what he'd been brutally trained to do—submit to whatever powerful man possessed him with a convincing smile."

"He loves you." Trey was kind of crap at reading other people's emotions, but even he could tell that much.

Harry looked at him with wide eyes. "You think so? It is all I've ever wanted since the moment I first saw him. Certainly I've given him safety and comfort."

"And Demi."

"Yes, he loves our son. Of that, I have no doubt. He trusts me, as well, and I've always strived to never give him regret that he does. He believes that you must take Demi to bed tonight because it's medically necessary. I've assured him of it, and so he has fought his own instinct to keep our son away from the carnal pursuits of a man. It must bring up painful memories for him."

Trey cleared his throat. "I get that. I promise you, though, Harry, that I will treat Demi with the care and respect he's due."

Something frighteningly feral crossed the man's face. "I'm certain you will. If you don't, you know I will suck your blood dry, rend your flesh and grind your bones to dust."

Trey coughed as if he'd been hit in his solar plexus. "Got it. But if you don't mind, I'm not going to dwell on that right now. Otherwise, I'll be no good to Demi."

Harry inclined his head. "Naturally. I wish you a good night." With another quick bow, he walked away.

Trey stood frozen for a few seconds.

Once again, Karl proved his worth. He ambled up and said, "Shake it off, Trey, and get in there." He jerked his head in the direction of the bedroom.

Trey snorted. "Who are you, Yogi Berra?"

"Tonight I am, apparently. Didn't we say our goodbyes like five minutes ago?" He waggled his thumb.

"Right. I'm going, I'm going, coach."

Hitching up his pants, he headed for the bedroom. No one seemed to pay him any mind, which he sincerely appreciated. The bedroom door was tipped shut. He pushed it open with his fingertips and stepped inside. Once again, he froze, all executive functions having shut down in his brain.

Demi lay propped up against the pillows, having turned down the bedding. He was stark naked, his silky black hair cascading down his shoulders and his glass of blood dangling in one hand. And, his slender cock stood ridged against his flat stomach.

"What took you so long?" The question was asked in a low, breathy voice. Demi took a sip of his drink while he kept his gaze on Trey.

Trey didn't have any words, wouldn't have been able to get them out of his dry mouth anyway. Instead of answering, he kicked the door shut with his foot then stumbled his way to the bed, shucking clothing as he went. Maybe he was supposed to do this with some kind of finesse. A striptease perhaps? A slow seduction, drawing out the anticipation for them both.

Fuck that.

He didn't have the control. Buttons popped off, a hem ripped, shoes and socks went flying. Nothing mattered except getting naked and into bed with Demi as fast as he could manage it. The boy's eyes flashed at the show. A giggle bubbled up, too.

"Careful, Trey. Don't hurt yourself before you get the deed done."

Trey tripped as he pulled off his pants. He had to grab the edge of the bed to keep from falling. "I'd have to be dead for that to happen. Even so, my dick would remain hard."

The weeping head of his cock already peeped out from the top of his boxer-briefs. It was miles ahead of him, but it couldn't be allowed to run the show. *Slow down. Demi needs patience.* For all his provocative presentation — and that blow job in the pantry notwithstanding — Demi really didn't know what he was in for. No one did until they'd had intercourse for the first time. The fact that Demi was going to be the object and not the receptacle hardly mattered. Joining bodies was a profoundly intimate act. It required care and prep, for both of them.

That reminder had Trey scooping up his jacket and grabbing the lube from the pocket. He dropped it on the nightstand before taking the glass out of Demi's hand and doing the same with it. Then he knelt on the bed beside him and simply stared for long seconds. He wanted to soak in the beauty, study it, memorize the curves and angles before he dared to touch.

Demi's eyes showed bright. "You look at me with such..."

"Reverence," Trey supplied in a voice thick with sudden emotion. "You are precious."

Demi touched Trey's knee, the gentle brushing of his fingertips along his skin causing Trey's cock to jerk. "Not too much so, I hope. You can touch me, you know. I won't break."

Trey snatched up his hand and played his thumb along the knuckles. "You could, though, if I'm not careful."

"Don't be silly." Demi giggled. "I'm very strong, as you well know."

"I didn't mean physically." He lifted his gaze to stare back at his lover. "You are painfully young and this is your first time. I don't want to fuck it up. It will set the tone for the rest of your sex life."

"Oh, Trey. Think of all the boys in our orbit that you know and how many of them have proven that's not true. Even Brenin overcame his horrors to find love and happiness with Malcolm. You can't scar me for life or anything."

"Look at Dafydd." The former slave hadn't been at the ceremony. No surprise there. He was in self-induced seclusion in his room, might never truly come out.

"I'd rather not, if you please," came Demi's mild rebuke. "This isn't a night for sad thoughts."

"You're right."

Trey knee-walked up to cup Demi at the back of his head. Leaning in, he kissed him. Unlike the pantry experience, this time it was soft and gentle. He teased the boy's lips with his own, opening them up slowly before sliding his tongue in. There was the metallic taste of blood at first, but he didn't let that throw him. This was Demi, the essential nature of him, and that made it okay. After a few sweeps of his mouth, that tasted disappeared and was replaced by a sweeter one that was both foreign and familiar.

Demi didn't remain passive. He roamed his hand up Trey's hip before sliding it down over his butt cheek. Trey made himself relax, assuming the next stop was his hole. Demi would want to explore that part of him, and he was determined to let him do that without tensing. The boy fooled him, though. Instead of moving over to Trey's cleft, Demi skittered his palm down Trey's thigh then back again to clasp his cock.

Trey's breath hitched and he pulled away from Demi's delicious mouth. "Easy, baby. I'm not as young as I used to be." Covering Demi's hand with his own, he tugged it off his dick. "I don't want to come too soon. It will be better if I wait until you're inside me."

He traced his tongue along Demi's jaw.

Demi shimmied. "What?" He clutched at Trey's hand and scraped the nails of his other along Trey's back.

Trey nipped at the spots he'd licked, then worked up to the earlobe. "I'll come like a rocket when your dick pegs my prostate." Taking the dangling bit of flesh between his teeth, he bit gently.

"Oh!" Demi arched into him. "That shouldn't feel as good as it does."

"Yeah, I know. One of life's little mysteries." He swirled his tongue around the shell. "I'll show you some others."

Demi moaned. "Can't wait, except—" He pushed against Trey's chest, forcing him to pull back. "Why do you keep saying I'm going to fuck you?"

Trey raised his eyebrows. "That's like the deal, right? You need to stick your dick into me to satisfy your biological transition to adulthood."

"Who says?"

"Um, everyone?"

"No one told me that. What if I don't want to? What if I want you to stick your cock up *my* ass? It's what I've been dreaming about."

That confession was all Trey's dick needed to hear. It pulsed pre-cum out to dribble down his shaft. His balls tightened even more. His fingers convulsed around Demi's in a tight grip. Everything went into overdrive from its already accelerated pace. He vaguely worried his heart might give out.

He shook his head slowly. "I don't know, baby. As amazing as it sounds to slide my cock into your sweet ass, I don't want to screw this thing up."

Demi licked his lower lip, a move that had Trey chasing after it. He couldn't resist claiming Demi's mouth in another kiss. This time, he held nothing back. He went in with teeth and tongue, chasing Demi's back and forth. He pressed his whole body into it, sending the boy down fully onto his back. Their cocks crashed into one another, dragging low moans from both of them. They clutched at each other, fingers digging into skin. Demi's was a little cool, but Trey's only got hotter. He could feel sweat trickling between his shoulder blades and along his inner thighs.

Because he needed air, he broke the kiss, although not the contact. He licked stripes down Demi's throat, pausing to place a kiss on top of the pulse on one side. Then he continued to forge a path that led him to hard nipples. Demi groaned and shuddered underneath him as he sucked each one in turn. The half-alien boy's hairless chest was a smooth feast that led him past a flat stomach to an equally hairless groin.

Trey paused in surprise. How had he not known this before, and why was it such a compete turn-on? No matter. A plan was forming in his fevered mind. Twisting around, he clasped Demi's thighs and pulled them apart. He settled between them and fixed his lips around the head of the boy's cock. The spurt of salty pre-cum on his tongue was reassuring. It tasted so very human.

Demi shrieked and bucked his hips. Trey was waiting for it, having taken a deep breath and relaxing his throat. When the shaft filled his mouth and cut off his air, he was ready. And eager. The cock was long, yet slender enough to take all the way in. Trey's lips pressed against that bald skin at the base of the shaft. He worked his tongue and swallowed hard. It had been a long time since he'd deep-throated anyone. He hadn't forgotten how to use his muscles to milk the dick. And he squeezed the boy's balls at the same time, rolling them with this thumb.

Demi came in an instant, his body flailing, and a keening wail filled the room. Trey winced at the sound, hoping anyone who might be close enough to hear it would understand that it was a good one. Who knew how aliens reacted to orgasming. He appreciated, however, that Demi's response to the intense pleasure was one Trey could relate to.

He worked the dick as he pulled off it, not really surprised that it stayed more or less as hard as it had been before he'd sucked it off. He remained kneeling between Demi's legs, huffing breathlessly, painfully hard, yet unwilling to proceed until he knew Demi was ready. It was going to take a while to prep him for Trey's penetration. He was not a small man, which normally gave him a sense of pride. Now, he worried that he'd hurt his lover.

Demi's eyes opened to narrow slits. "That was awesome. I'm so glad I got to do that to you first. I never imagined you'd do it for me."

Trey frowned. "Why not?" He rubbed his hand along the inside of Demi's thigh, enjoying the way it made his cock jerk. "Sex is about being generous. It's not your job to please me, but our jobs to please each other."

A smile broke out across Demi's face. "That's so sweet."

"Well, yeah." Trey ducked his head, uncomfortable with the naked admiration. "Plus, maybe that satisfies any biological imperative you have to stick you cock into something."

Demi giggled, which reinforced Trey's belief that his decision had been the right one.

"Ready to keep going?" he asked, reaching for the lube.

"Yes, sir, if it means you fucking me."

Trey bared his teeth. "Oh, it does." He held up the lube. "We have to take it slow, baby. I don't want to hurt you."

Demi sat up in a move that was like a blur to Trey's eyes. He threw his arms around Trey's neck and whooped out a laugh. "Didn't Papa explain to you?" He shook his head. "No, of course he didn't. He thinks I'm sticking it in, so no need to explain how my ass works, huh?"

Placing his hands on either side of the boy's head, Trey pulled him back far enough to stare into his eyes. "What are you talking about?"

"I'm bisexual by nature, if not by interest. My hole self-lubricates like a vagina when I'm aroused. And," he added, widening his eyes, "I'm totally am right now. How about you do something to ease me?"

It took about a second for Trey's brain to process what his lover was saying. Once it had, he wasted no more time. He might not have alien speed, but he put Demi back on his back in a flash. Although he mostly trusted Demi to know his own body, he still carefully inserted a couple of fingers inside him. The tight ring of muscle opened to him with little prompting and warm slickness eased the way. The snug passage presented no resistance to the intrusion.

But it was the totally contented sigh that Demi uttered that convinced Trey more than anything that his lover was ready to receive him. With trembling arms, he propped himself above the boy. Demi spread his legs without urging, raising them sufficiently to give Trey a landing spot. He lined up his cock with Demi's hole and pressed.

Like sliding home. He sunk in balls-deep with a slow, steady thrust. His eyes slammed shut and he held himself motionless while his arms shook even more. But he wanted this for just a few seconds — to savor the mind-blowing pleasure of claiming Demi, of being welcomed by him with no uncertainty. It was so perfectly right that he couldn't imagine what he'd ever worried about.

Demi clenched Trey's shaft and, grabbing him by the shoulders, tugged him down. The reminder that there was more to this coupling than Trey's mere pleasure, broke his inaction. He let himself be pulled down, and he began thrusting, angling his head to one side, he exposed his neck and tried not to tense as he waited for the strike.

When it came, he yelled, only not from pain.

Chapter Eight

Demi's senses were on overload. His mind and attention skittered from his ass to his mouth. Trey's cock was drilling him with fast, hard strokes while the cop's blood coated his throat. The intensity of the dual pleasures caught him by surprise. No wonder his family had fussed over this, treated it as a life-changing event—because it was. Everything he'd done before this, every sip of blood, every jerk-off marathon, was nothing compared to the transcendent experience of being fucked and fed in tandem.

He pulled deeply from Trey's vein, clutching him close. He wrapped his legs around the man's muscular ass to help him pound into Demi's greedy one. Nothing was enough. He wanted closer, harder, faster. A wave of orgasm crashed over him. He bit deeper into Trey's neck in response. Warmth spread over his torso and up his stuffed channel, confusing him until he realized that Trey had come, too. The noises the man made were primitive, fierce. They sent shivers down Demi's spine and caused him to come once again.

He shook and clawed and thumped his heels against Trey, mindless with it all, until the sounds his lover made changed tone. His papa's warnings came to the fore. Retracting his fangs, Demi licked the wounds closed before he went limp. Now the only thing joining him to Trey were the man's hands and cock still embedded all the way inside Demi's ass.

He forced his eyes open and stared at him. "Are you all right?" He looked for signs that he'd drunk too much or otherwise hurt the man he loved.

Trey smiled before he blinked rapidly a few times. "I think I'm supposed to ask you that question."

Trey carefully pulled out and slid over to lie beside him. Demi missed the vacancy immediately and wondered how long the man would need before he could fuck him again. Demi rolled onto his side and placed his hand on Trey's chest.

"I'm fine. Deliriously so. But I'm afraid I forgot my own strength. Did I hurt you?"

Compared to Demi's paleness, Trey's skin was too dark for bruises to be easily seen, at least not according to Demi's vision. He loved the contrast, though, when he looked at them touching.

Trey picked up his hand and kissed the knuckles. "Nothing you need to worry about." He sighed and his body went lax. "I just need a minute to rest up. That was…intense."

"Oh, you should have juice to replace the blood I took."

Tugging his hand free, he jumped off the bed and went over to the small refrigerator Alex kept in his room. Emil had already stocked it with Trey in mind. There were cold snacks, pastries and lots of refreshing drinks to get them through the night.

Demi grabbed an apple juice for his man and a lemon tart for himself. He raced back to the bed as he stuffed the treat into his mouth. By the time he got back, Trey was already asleep. *Poor baby.* Demi had worn him out. With a smile of satisfaction, Demi carefully got back up next to him and waited patiently for the man to wake again—tried to, anyway. It was all so exciting and better than anything he'd dreamed of. He wanted to do it again and again. Not only on this night, but for the rest of their lives.

* * * *

When Demi opened his eyes the next morning, he immediately knew he was in bed alone. Even after only one night, he'd already become used to having Trey's big body to snuggle against. Each time that they'd turned to one another, it had been amazing, and when they were too tired to fuck, they'd cuddled and eaten Emil's fabulous food. Those simple domestic memories were almost as good as the sex. He couldn't wait for the day to end so that they could do it all again, although they hadn't had a chance to discuss the transition of Demi over to Trey's place.

He traced the rumpled sheet by his side, feeling the warmth left there. Trey hadn't gotten up too long ago. Then he heard the shower running. Of course, Trey had to get an early start because he worked. Maybe, though, there was time for a quick one in the shower? He'd gladly blow Trey if that was how he wanted to start his day.

Throwing off the covers, he rose. Trey walked in before he'd taken more than a few steps, toweling his head and looking sexy as hell. Although not aroused. *More's the pity.*

The man stopped as he spied Demi. "Hey, sorry. I didn't mean to wake you. I have to get to the station and keep at the Father Ted investigation."

Demi tried to hide his disappointment. "That's fine. I understand. Except," he added with a frown, "isn't it Saturday?"

Trey paused in the act of picking up his underwear from the floor. "I'm a cop. Weekends don't mean shit, especially when I've got a case like this one that's stalling out."

"Oh, of course. I understand." He bent to help his man gather up his clothing. "Are you wearing this suit?"

Trey took the pants out of his hands. "Yeah, I really don't feel like going home to change, and while this is a little more upscale than my daily wear, it'll do."

Demi stood twining his fingers. "I could go and get something else for you, if you like. Bring it to the station. I mean, I should start moving my stuff to your apartment anyway."

In the process of zippering his pants, Trey paused. "What?"

A ripple of unease crept up Demi's spine. "That's where we're going to live, right? There's no room here, and I figured you wouldn't like that anyway. You're not a hive species, so you want your own space. I'm totally fine with that. As much as I love my dads, I don't want them underfoot while we're getting to know one another better."

Trey shook his head slowly. "Demi, you aren't moving in with me and I'm not moving in here, either."

The unease intensified before he understood what Trey was saying. He rolled his eyes. "Oh, please, don't be so old-fashioned. Is it your family? Are they like really conservative and no living together before we're married? Seriously, Trey, that's so nineteenth century." He sighed and moved away restlessly. "But I get it if it's important to you. I can wait. Just not too long, please," he said, eyeing Trey.

The man continued to stand and stare. "Demi..."

He shrugged. "So, a quick period of engagement, followed by a spring wedding. I do love pastels. And maybe tomorrow we can go out and get me a ring? I know it's kind of silly, but I like the idea of wearing one before the wedding. Tiffany is open on Sundays."

No, dummy, not there. It's too expensive. "Or, wherever you like to buy jewelry," he amended.

Trey's expression remained stony, unreadable except that it didn't mean anything good.

"Say something, Trey." Demi felt truly naked as he stood there waiting for his man to respond. It wasn't his lack of clothing. It was how he'd laid all his love, his hopes and dreams out before this man, and he was very afraid Trey was going to do something horrible with them.

Trey closed his eyes briefly before coming over to him. "Demi, there's no moving in together, no engagement and no wedding. Not now, maybe not ever. Last night was amazing, but it was a necessity for you and a favor from me. I'm sorry if you didn't understand that."

Demi's blood iced over and he had trouble catching his breath. "What do you mean a 'favor'? Like you fucked me to be nice? It was a chore?"

Trey grimaced. "I stated that badly. It was something that I did because your fathers asked me to. I wouldn't have done it otherwise because you're too young by my estimation. If Harry hadn't approached me about doing this, I would have continued to keep my distance. I've never intended to lead you on."

"You don't love me." Demi hated how small his voice sounded. How young and pathetic.

Trey swallowed hard enough for his bobbing Adam's apple to catch Demi's attention. It led him to the spot over the man's jugular where he'd taken his first real feeding of blood.

"My feelings for you are complicated."

"I don't know what that's supposed to mean."

"It means that I have feelings for you and desire you in way that bothers me. It has from the beginning, when you looked at me with those worshipful eyes from behind a teenage face."

"I'm an old man compared to you!" He flung the fact out as if it could somehow pierce the wall Trey was erecting between them.

"You know it's more complicated than that." Trey paced away, snatched up his shirt and shoved his arms in. "When I look at you, I see someone not quite grown. I've been really struggling with my attraction to you. A big part of me believes it's wrong, hates me for what I did last night."

Demi flung his arms out. "That's ridiculous. Even by the contrived birth information on my ID, I'm of legal age to have sex with."

"I don't give a fuck what the Commonwealth of Massachusetts thinks. I have to live with myself, by my own code of honor. You've always been too young to my eyes, and a piddling eight months or so isn't enough time to change that. I slept with you for your health and because the idea of any other man doing it made my head explode."

Trey fumbled with his shirt buttons before realizing some had come off the previous night and gave up. That small evidence of how much he'd wanted Demi helped ease the pain of the rejection a little bit. Only a little, though.

"So you do love me?"

"I don't know. Jealousy isn't love. I've heard plenty of murderers conflate the two to justify their actions. It disgusts me, and I'm not going to go throw around that same illogic to justify my actions. All I can say is that I care for you, enough that I'm not going to set up house and take away what's left of your childhood."

"I'm not a kid anymore, Trey." Demi held his arms out wide. "This is me all grown up. If you don't believe me, ask Papa."

"How about you ask your dad?" Trey retorted. "Ask your human father what he thinks of your giving up the choices in front of you to tie yourself to one man."

Demi dismissed the idea with a toss of his head. "Dad grew up in a different time, had a different experience. It's not relevant. I know my own mind on this. I want you."

Grabbing his socks, shoes and jacket, Trey said, "Yeah? You think? Tell me that again in five years. No, ten. Then we'll see."

"That's ridiculous. In ten years you'll be..."

"Old." Trey's lips thinned. "That's another thing, isn't it, Demi? I'm human, just that, not a hybrid or changed. I've got maybe fifty years left in my life, and everything at this point is all downhill. You like how I fucked you silly? Then what? I popped right off because, at my age,

I can't recover as fast as someone younger—alien or human alike."

Trey plopped down on the edge of the bed and tugged on his socks. "Pretty soon, you'd be lucky if I want to do it once week. I won't be able to keep weight off like I do now, no matter the amount I exercise. How does a beer gut sound to you of the *perpetually flat stomach*?"

Trey slipped on his shoes and tied one with enough force that the lace broke. He cursed and stood again. "Bad teeth, bad hair, sagging skin, liver spots." He shrugged on his jacket. "Death is both quick and slow for us mere humans."

Demi sniffed back tears that threatened to leak out. "I don't care about any of that. I love you, Trey."

"Maybe." He tossed his tie around his neck. "If you do, the ten years won't matter, especially for someone like you. It's a blip in time." He headed for the door.

"Don't you walk out on me!" Panic was setting in. He lashed out. "I'm not waiting that long for sex. I'll...I'll fuck other men."

With his hand on the doorknob, Trey turned to look at him. "Good. You should see what it's like with someone who isn't me. You won't truly know if I pleased you until you've had more experience."

Demi felt as if he'd been punched. "You want other men to have me?"

"Christ on a stick, no! But this is about what's best for you. This is for *your* own good, Demi, and that's the end of it."

With that parting shot that was like both a stab wound and a fervent kiss, Trey left and quietly closed the door behind him. Demi crumpled to the ground, despair washing over him. How had his beautiful ceremony ended like this? He threw back his head and howled.

* * * *

"I've got some shitty news, boss."

Trey turned and snarled at his partner. "Really? 'Cause this morning didn't start out sufficiently miserable already?" Karl's eyes went wide, making Trey feel bad. It wasn't his fault that Trey had made such a hash of things with Demi.

Karl held up his palms. "Whoa, sorry. I take it things didn't go so well last night?"

"Actually, they went great. It was the best experience of my whole fucking life. It was this morning that stank." He huffed. "And this isn't the time or place for my hissy fit. What's going on?"

"We need to get down to the holding cells. I got a call from the desk sergeant on my way over. She figured she'd start with me because we're old friends, and I assured her I would be the one to give you the bad news."

Trey's heart sank as he changed directions from the squad room to the elevator. "It's the kid, isn't it? He's dead." He didn't even bother to frame it as a question because, of course, that was the story. Nothing else of importance could cause Karl to be so grim.

"Yeah." Karl stood with his hands shoved in his back pockets. "They found him a few hours ago and spent the time since running through the correct protocols while covering their asses."

The elevator doors opened. "How'd he do it?" Trey entered and pressed the button.

Karl's expression turned sourer, if that were possible. "He didn't. It wasn't suicide, but straight up homicide."

"What?" For the second time that morning, Trey felt off kilter, as if the world had changed into something unrecognizable since he'd gotten into bed with Demi. Nothing seemed to be making any sense. "How is that even remotely possible?"

"That's what we're about to find out. The details are sketchy so far."

Trey was shaking his head before Karl finished speaking. "Except we don't really need them, do we? We know how it happened. Unless one of our people was bribed into doing it, the answer to how someone could break into a locked cell and kill a prisoner is obvious."

"Yup."

They said nothing more as they rode to the right floor, got out and followed the sounds of a whole bunch of people losing their shit. The relevant cell was surrounded by cops of various ranks. A lot of whispered conversations were taking place. One earnest-looking newbie stood talking to a sergeant with a red face and maybe tears in his eyes. *Christ, what a mess. And so predictable.* Trey felt ashamed that he hadn't worried about this eventuality, not that there was any way in particular that he could have stopped it from happening. There was no human-based protocol to prevent the aliens from doing what they were intent on. Still, the guilt ate at him. It made for a nice chaser to the crap already residing in his gut over Demi.

He and Karl pushed forward, everyone parting for them with various degrees of relief and resentment. As the arresting officers, they'd brought this trouble to their door, but that also made them point men on the problem. With a nod at the presiding officer, Trey stepped up to the doorway of the cell and winced at the sight and smells that greeted him.

Death was never pretty. All kinds of hideous things happened to the human body when it expired. He was glad that the room was cordoned off as a crime scene and he wasn't kitted up to enter, not that he needed a closer look at the sad remains of the kid who'd sneered at him during the interviews. The poor boy was lying naked and face down on his narrow bed, his head at an angle that was unnatural. His long hair obscured most of his face, and yet it still caused a flash of memory that grabbed Trey by the nuts and had him inhaling a shocked breath.

He saw Demi sprawled on his stomach beside him, breathing deeply in sleep. An almost smile graced his beautiful lips that were puffy from the many kisses they had shared. The slender back tapered down to a narrow waist before flaring out over a high, tight ass...

"Fuck," he breathed out the word and would have staggered back if not for Karl's sturdy presence.

"Easy, boss," his partner murmured.

"Sorry. He looks so much like —"

"I know. It's not though, yeah? And look... It's Paz."

That helped. Trey focused on the doctor examining the body. It was a stroke of luck that it was someone they could trust with the truth. He swept his gaze over the cell, and, seeing nothing out of place, looked down at the door's handle. It had been crushed. No surprise there. Although how their quarry managed to gain entrance to a cop shop and leave undetected remained a mystery for the moment. It would have taken nothing to break into the cell.

Paz rose from where he'd been squatting beside the body and came over. "His neck has been broken," he said without preamble. "I'd say during sex."

"I guess that explains why he's nude," Trey remarked.

Paz's gaze dropped. "Yes. Whoever did it at least made it quick, and coming from behind probably means the boy died without even knowing what was happening."

"Hard to believe it was intended to be merciful," Karl observed.

Paz's eyes turned flinty. "No, I expect it was merely a way to ensure it was quiet. I'll know more once we've done the post-mortem."

Trey raised his eyebrows. "They have you doing those on your own?"

"No, but I'm sure the coroner will be happy to have me do the scut work of informing the lead officer of the case." He quirked his lips. "I'll call you."

"Thanks." Trey backed away and turning, found himself face-to-face with the custody officer. "How the hell did this happen?" He kept his tone light because making enemies never helped, and he knew that no one had done anything wrong. All the cops were trained to deal with humans, not aliens with super strengths and a millennium of advanced tech.

The woman's expression gave nothing away, although she had to be pissed. "That's something we are still trying to ascertain." She pointed up at one corner of the hallway. "All the video feed has been compromised. From about zero three hundred to zero three thirty, every manned monitoring station showed an empty corridor, just like it's supposed to. A wellness check was performed every hour on the hour, or thereabouts," she amended.

"No one heard or saw anything. The tech guys are on it, but I think the answer has to be somehow the feed was put on a loop to hide whoever broke in here." She flicked her hand toward the door. "How they managed to do that is a real mystery, too. But," she added with a frown, "it was someone from the outside. No way one of my people did this. I'll stake my career on it."

Trey nodded. "I agree. Nothing in my report is going to suggest otherwise. I mean, look at the state the prisoner is in. He obviously knew his killer or he would have screamed the house down."

The women smiled grimly. "That's my take, too."

Of course, he didn't point out that a gun would have kept the kid quiet, as well. There was no use in raising that obvious point. He knew once the tech guys did their thing that they would confirm the tampering angle. No sense is stressing anyone else out more than necessary. He was doing a sufficient amount of freaking out for all of them.

And just when he thought his morning was as shitty as possible, he caught sight of someone striding down the hall who tweaked his misery up another notch.

"Duncan, I heard about what happened." Craig was dressed in jeans and a long-sleeved T, obviously having a day off.

Before he could respond, they all had to step away farther to give the morgue people access to the room and body. It gave Trey a few extra seconds to marshal his response. His first thought was to hand Craig a polite 'fuck off'. On reflection, he decided that wasn't a great idea.

He strove to hide his emotions — all of them, from his guilt and misery over how he'd made a complete hash of things with Demi, to his guilt and frustration over how he'd failed to get the dead kid to talk. His fuck-ups were going to hurt a lot of people, including a good chunk of the humans who had no idea what their world was dealing with.

"Yeah," he finally said, "it sucks. And it looks like someone breached our security, which is going to bring the brass down on everyone's head." It needed to be said because while that aspect of things didn't rate high on his lists of worries, he had to at least act like a regular cop in this situation.

Craig's eyes popped. "Wait! So this wasn't a suicide?" He whistled. "Damn, I thought it was bad, but this is shit-your-pants kind of bad. I suppose that's better than one of our own going rogue."

"We appreciate the moral support and all that, Jefferson," Karl added, "but this isn't your worry."

"Isn't it?" They watched the body bag being wheeled out. Craig pointed at it. "That was one of mine, even if I never had a chance to help him. This is vice related, so I want in."

Trey scrubbed at his face, realizing for the first time that he hadn't had a chance to shave. That thought led to Demi, however, so he quickly dropped both his hand and that line of thinking. "Like Karl said, we appreciate it, but how can you help?"

"Assuming this was done on the orders of my Dark Knight, I can start tracking down his boys, rattle them to maybe get more information about who and where he is."

Trey nodded. "That might help. Do you know a boy named Mateo?"

Craig nodded. "Yup. I know who you mean."

"We were chasing him down as a lead when this dead kid popped up riding Father Ted's bike. We dropped Mateo because this was obviously a better line to tug. If you can corral Mateo, it would free us to pursue what happened here."

While he hated asking Craig for a favor, neutralizing the current alien threat mattered too much for his hurt feelings to get in the way.

"I can do that. I'll get on it right now."

"Thanks. Sorry about ruining your day off."

Craig shrugged. "It's the job, right? Not like I had any big plans anyway." For a moment, he looked kind of sad, wistful even, which was ridiculous. Craig had never needed anyone to make his life meaningful. "I'll get back to you."

"Thanks," Trey said again and watched Craig walk away. He tried not to stare at the perfect bubble butt the man's jeans accented. Then when he failed, was surprised by how much that muscular ass didn't matter to him. He only wanted one type now, and it was attached to a smaller, more winsome body.

He shook at the force of that desire. "Christ, I need coffee — and maybe a lobotomy." He took off with Karl at his side.

"Okay, maybe now would be a good time for you to explain how a spectacular night turned into a crappy morning. Did he, ah, not appreciate your performance, or something?"

He couldn't look his partner in the eye. "Actually, he loved it far too much and wanted a lifetime of encores. That's the problem."

"I'm not following."

"Forget it. I'm sure as hell trying to. We've got work to do."

Even as he said the words, he knew he was lying to Karl and fooling himself. He wasn't making any real effort to put thoughts of Demi out his mind. The boy was firmly lodged in all parts of his brain, the thinking ones and the emotional ones. His body ached with the memory of what they'd done together. His worn-out dick was trying to rally at the mere mention of the boy. No matter what he'd insisted that morning as he'd eviscerated Demi's hopes and dreams, Trey knew that this whole thing would end with his heart broken far more than the half-alien's could ever be.

Because he *was* in love with Demetrius Stelalux.

* * * *

Whatever the other boys saw on Demi's face when he entered the dance floor, they immediately shut up and asked no uncomfortable questions. He'd successfully avoided both his fathers all morning, letting them believe that he'd crept into his bed to sleep in after his busy night. Undoubtedly, they were feeling conflicted about seeing him too, knowing what they did. How many parents could say they knew the exact night when their kid lost their virginity? So yeah, that human squeamishness was keeping both Dad and Papa at bay. Fine by him.

He wasn't prepared to talk about anything at the moment. The idea of relaying his horrible dumping by Trey was more terrible than he could bear. What he needed was to work off some of his anger and misery. Although it was a Saturday afternoon, and not normally a busy time for the club, the many months of closure had led to a surge in interest, apparently. As he sauntered through the main room, many pairs of eyes followed him.

Good. At least some men understood his worth. He would gladly capitalize on that. By the laws of Papa's people, he was now fully grown. While his fathers might not agree with that assessment, he wasn't above appealing to Alex, if necessary, to gain some freedom. He wasn't looking to leave, of course. He valued his family and, frankly, the money at his disposal. It was simply a matter of wanting more autonomy, including the right to hook up with club members if he so chose.

Screw Trey. What he thought didn't matter. Demi was through being a good boy or a brat. He was going to just be himself. With a nod to Kitty, he took a position in the middle of the dance floor. When the song playing ended, the opening strains of Evanescence's *Bring Me to Life* filled the room. The sound effects of wind blowing and sirens wrapped around him, struck chords in his psyche that perfectly called up everything that he was feeling. The reminder of what the man he'd loved did for a living was helpful, not debilitating.

He twisted his body slowly in sync with the building speed of the haunting notes. He wore only yoga pants and a crop-top white T. Every line of his body was on full display. When the guitar strumming kicked in, he flipped his way over to the nearest stage. The boy that had been humping against it, leaped out off with a stunned look on his face.

Demi grabbed the pole and swung around it before climbing up to the top. He spread his arms out wide as he anchored himself by hooking one knee then he turned upside-down. But he wasn't reaching out to anyone to save him. He needed only himself. Letting go, he tumbled onto the stage. Gasps reached his ears, making him grin because, of course, he landed on his feet then flitted away to the next stage.

He pirouetted across the dance floor in a whirling blur that was just this side of human. When he reached the next pole, he shimmied up and twirled around frontward and backward. He contorted his body in provocative poses, showing what he had to give to the right man, one who would appreciate his flexibility, strength and devotion.

Men gathered around the sides, clapping and whistling but not getting in his way when he once again moved on. He hugged the third pole, undulating against it in what he hoped was a sexy parody of fucking. With each snap of his hips, he flipped his hair and pouted. His focus became fixed on his movements, the way in which he was expressing his misery without words—and, all without the one person he really wanted to see and understand even being there. It was all he had, and yet he feared it wasn't nearly enough, regardless.

As the music reached its crescendo, he back-flipped his way from one end of the dance floor to the other. Then he launched himself at the final pole, climbed all the way to the top and paused to fling his arms out once more before taking off in a swan dive. He somersaulted in a tight ball to yells that overtook the music before landing in a split. With his mouth popped open in a provocative O, he tore his shirt in two. He tossed the remnants just as he'd done a week ago, only this time, he had no man to aim for.

The room went deathly silent for the span of a few rapid heartbeats, then pandemonium broke out. The club members and go-go boys alike, including Mackie,

Quinn and Jase, rushed forward to encircle him. He could see the leers as well as the concerns. He soaked up the former and ignored the latter. Just when his adoring audience arrived, they got shoved aside by a whole lot of pissed-off Val. The bouncer scooped Demi up with one arm latched around his middle like a steel vise.

Demi shrieked and struggled for about two seconds with futile effort before changing tactics. There was no way he'd get loose, so instead he blew kisses to the men left behind, treating his being carted away as part of the act. By the reaction of the men, he figured he'd succeeded. Now, all he had to do was weather the coming storm. Fortunately, his friends chased after them. He wouldn't be alone in facing the music, as it were. Plus, he was sufficiently mad himself to not be concerned about his fate.

Once they'd all entered the elevator, he pushed at Val's arm. "You can let me down now."

"Hah, fat chance. I'll release you once you're with your fathers." Val did, however, lower him so that his feet touched the floor.

No one said anything, not even Mackie. Demi was too upset to look at his friends. He didn't want to see concern or worse, pity. In fact, as he stood there fuming, he realized he'd changed his mind. He didn't want them around at all. They all had the men they loved. Petty as it might have been, he couldn't stand their hearing how he'd been rejected by Trey—not yet, although they obviously knew something was up. He'd confide in them later.

When the elevator doors opened, he said, "Please, everyone, I don't want an entourage right now."

"We want to help," Mackie pressed.

Quinn held him back. "It's okay. We understand. You know we're on your side, no matter what, right?"

Demi nodded as Val dragged him down to his family suite. Dad opened the door, because, of course, the one he hated disappointing the most *would be* front and center. Not that it mattered. Papa along with Alex popped over from the stairs a moment later.

"Demi, what is going on?" Papa demanded.

Dad put up his hand. "Come inside, all of you."

It was so rare for the man to issue anything like an order to the others that no one balked at complying. Releasing his hold, Val gave Demi a nudge. He needn't have bothered. While Demi wasn't interested in having the conversation now, it was inevitable. He had to take a stand about the course of his life. His fathers stood side-by-side in the middle of the living room and patiently waited for someone to explain.

When no one else did, Demi sucked it up. "I was only dancing."

Val snorted. "Is that your story? You were performing sex acts in the middle of the fucking dance floor."

Demi rounded on the man. "Oh, that's so not true! I was expressing my feelings with movement. And, I was killing it," he added with a toss of his head.

"If visually jerking off every club member there is your definition of doing a good job, then yeah, I agree." Val turned to Demi's fathers. "Sorry to be blunt, guys."

"Demi, what were you thinking?" Papa demanded.

"I wasn't…thinking. I was trying *not* to think, actually. It was working, too, until this big ape came and spoiled everything."

Alex stepped forward. "Demi, remember your place. That was neither respectful nor biologically accurate."

Their family leader rarely rebuked Demi directly, leaving that up to his fathers. And while the man was usually quite patient and kind with him, when he was angry, he could be very scary.

Demi coughed. "I'm sorry, sir."

"Besides," Val added, "I was only doing what Duncan would have if he'd been here."

The mention of his former lover made Demi gasp. He couldn't help himself, nor could he resist rubbing his hand over his heart. "You're wrong. He wouldn't have cared. He doesn't want me."

Val snorted again. Alex rolled his eyes and turned away. Papa simply blinked back at him. It was Dad who stepped up and reached out to place his hand on Demi's arm.

"I'm sure that's not true."

Demi shook off the hold and backed away. "It is! He told me himself. What he did last night was a *favor*." He put as much venom as he could in the word. "He doesn't want anything more to do with me—recommended, in fact, that I pursue other men to find out if he was actually a good lay or not. No reviews yet on *my* performance in bed."

Dad flinched and Papa came up to hug him. "Demi!"

He threw out his arms. "What? What do you want me to say, Papa? I'm telling you the truth, whether you can handle it or not. You handed me off to the man I love, loved," he amended because he wasn't going to wear his heart on his sleeve anymore, "and he's tossed me back."

"Jesus, does this mean I have to kill Duncan?" Val mused. "I was really getting to like the human."

Papa's turned his head. "This is no time for levity, Val."

"Who's making a joke?"

"Stop!" Holding out his hands, Demi pleaded. "None of this is helping. I don't want to talk about it anymore. It's done, and this isn't making me or the situation better." He swiped at the tears leaking out. "I'm sorry if my dancing upsets you, but I'm grown now, right? I have to make my own decisions about the path I'm going to take. And, I can't stay here." He turned and ran. "Sorry!" he tossed over his shoulder and raced toward the stairs, half expecting to be followed and hauled back.

No one did, and, half-blind with his despair, he sought a place of refuge.

Chapter Nine

Dafydd woke with a start, certain the sound of a baby had woken him. But no, that had surely been only a dream. He sat slouched in the large chair by the window, where he'd apparently fallen asleep while peering out at the world. There was so much to see and most of it new to him. He'd rarely left the castle in the hundreds of years during his captivity. All he knew of modern times had come from television and the Internet. Seeing people going about their business made him wonder if he could perhaps join them sometime, a thought both intriguing and frightening.

There was a scratching at his door that was not in his head. Before he could decide what to do, it opened and a figure slipped inside.

"Demi?"

The boy uttered a wounded sound before closing the door again and sliding down to sit against it. "I'm sorry. I didn't know where else to go. This is the only room in the club that the others won't breach. Please, can I stay? It won't be for long."

Because he could hear both misery and fear in Demi's voice, Dafydd could only bring himself to do one thing. "Sure you can, mun." It felt strange to give anyone permission to do anything, let alone control who got to come and stay in the room.

He found he liked having even a minor, fleeting power.

Getting up, he crossed over in the gloom. He hadn't opened the curtain much and feared doing so now would only upset Demi further. He turned on the lamp by the side of his bed and sat on the edge. Demi was clearly visible now, shirtless for some reason, his face crumpled and covered in silent tears.

"What's happened, then?" He wasn't certain he had any right to ask.

Demi swiped at his face and sniffled loudly. "It's all gone to shit."

Dafydd hesitated, still unsure that he should get involved, especially as he had nothing of use to offer. He'd gone from one prison to another, this second one of his own making if his 'hosts' could be believed. Who was he to help solve Demi's problems when he was such a pathetic, scared man himself? And yet, he owed the boy something, didn't he? Demi had risked his own life to see Dafydd through his delivery.

"Tell me. I can't say it will do any good, but if you want to talk, I'll listen."

Demi pressed the heel of his palms against his eyes, and for long seconds, it seemed as if he wasn't going to speak. That was okay. He could stay as long as he liked. It wasn't as if he was interrupting anything.

"I had my manhood ceremony last night. Um, you know, I guess maybe something like that was done for your sons."

Dafydd immediately started shutting down at the mention of his horror twins. He shook himself out of it before it went too far. The time when Dracul and his seed could hurt him was past.

He cleared his throat. "I remember when they reached an age where Dracul threw a couple of slaves at them to brutalize." He swallowed back the lump that formed in his throat. "I suppose it was something of a milestone in their lives."

"Oh, I'm sorry. I should have assumed that, given what I know about the asshole. It was different for me. My fathers handed me over to the man I love. Loved. I don't feel that way anymore."

"Don't you now?" There was something in Demi's tone that made Dafydd skeptical.

Demi shook his head violently. "No. It didn't mean anything to him. Taking my virginity was like a job or something. A 'favor' was how he put it."

Dafydd winced. "That's harsh, mun." Something clicked in his brain in the next instant. "Are you talking about the man who came to rescue you? The one who killed Kronid and fed you his vein while you gave me a transfusion?"

"That's him, the rat bastard."

Dafydd laughed. He couldn't help it. The sound bubbled up of its own accord, and it was so foreign sounding to his own ears, he almost didn't recognize it. Clamping his hand over his mouth, he pushed the mirth back down. Now was not the time for him to rediscover his sense of humor. Demi was shooting daggers out of his eyes.

"I'm that sorry, Demi. I don't mean to make light of your unhappiness, but there's no way that man doesn't love you."

"Shows how much you know" — the boy crossed his arms — "because you're wrong. He doesn't."

"Demi, I was staring at him when he shot Kronid. I didn't think I had any more fear left in me, but the look in his eyes was *that* fierce. He wanted to kill him, and what reason could he have to hate the fucker other than knowing he was preying on you? And, I know how scary it is to be fed upon. He offered you his blood out of love. There is no other explanation."

"Then, why doesn't he want me?" The question came out in a heartbreaking wail, and yes, Dafydd was surprised he still had enough of the organ to be capable of feeling another's pain.

Hopping off the bed, Dafydd went to sit cross-legged in front of Demi. "Did he say as much? Did he use those words?"

Demi sniffed. "Not exactly." When Dafydd simply sat and stared, the boy elaborated. "He said I was too young to make a commitment to anyone, that I should get more experience and come back to him in ten years if I still wanted him."

"Ah."

"Ah, what?"

"He's trying to be noble, mun. Can't you see that?"

Demi leaned forward. "I don't want that of him. I love him and told him as much. I had assumed we'd get married. Pathetic, dumb shit that I am."

Dafydd sat back on his hands. "Long ago, when I was a bit of a lad, I used to spy on the lord's men as they bathed in the river. I was ever so worried I'd get caught and flogged — or worse."

Funny how he hadn't thought of his youth in so long — hadn't dared, given that it was so far removed from his reality. "There was one in particular that caught my fancy. He wasn't the biggest or brawniest for the lot, but he was wicked with a blade, quick on his feet. I used to weave fantasies of what it would be like to be his."

He took in a shuddery breath and let it out slowly. "You know how my story ends, then, heh? Dracul gave me no choice and dragged my dreams through the mud. For a long time, I thought God was punishing me for my unnatural desires. That is, back when I believed in such a thing as God."

"I'm sorry, Dafydd." Demi stared back at him with wide eyes. "I wish that hadn't happened to you."

Dafydd quirked his lips. "Me, as well. It did, though, and my point is that after the shock of it wore off, I started plotting my escape. I gave it a few tries then stopped because the punishment was too great. Still, I bided my time, pretended to be cowed. For a while, I managed to keep from getting pregnant again. And when that plan failed, I schemed some more.

"I only truly lost hope in the last few months. Dracul had taken Brenin. I saw in him myself, only he wasn't going to survive the brutality for long. That, plus my cumbersome belly, left me with little choice. I tried to save him while giving up on myself. I could also see my eventual death in the monster's eyes every time he looked at me. I had hesitated too long."

"You lived, though, because freeing Brenin proved pivotal in the assault on the castle. You saved yourself in the end."

"Hmm, I suppose that's one way of looking at it." It hadn't occurred to him that his helping Brenin had eventually helped himself. Up until that point, he hadn't wanted to discuss any of it. "Thanks for that."

"You're welcome, except, I'm sorry this isn't making me feel better." The boy made a face that reminded Dafydd how young he actually was.

"Oh, well then, I guess what I truly mean is don't give up. What you want isn't gone simply because it hasn't worked in the short term. There's always hope, so long as there is another day to try again. Funny hearing me say it, I know, given that I hide in this room."

"No, I get it. You're more than just some ghost guest. You have experience and you're not wrong. I just don't have much time to get Trey to change his mind."

"What's your hurry, then?"

Demi raised his eyebrows. "He's human, remember? And not a very young one at that. If we're going to make a life together, we need to get a move on. Plus, I'm not sure I'm that patient, and I for sure don't want to sleep around with other men. Trey's all I want and has been since the moment I saw him."

"Huh. You think if you fed him your blood that would prolong his life? That would solve one problem. His stubbornness, not so much, I'm thinking." That got a smile out of Demi, and seeing it lifted Dafydd's spirits a little.

"I honestly don't know. He's too old to, you know, change."

Dafydd instinctively palmed his abdomen. "I understand. You should ask the doctor, though. He might have an idea."

"You mean my papa?"

"No, I was thinking of the other one." The human man with the warm brown eyes and the gentle touch.

"Oh, Dr. Paz. I doubt he'd know. But I should ask Papa." He sighed. "If I hadn't just told him and my dad and everyone else to fuck off."

Dafydd's widened his eyes. "You never?"

"Not in so many words. But that was the gist of it. Everyone thinks they know what's best for me. I'm sick of it, and I'm hiding out here because I can't face them again yet." Demi dropped his head in his hands. "I don't know what to do!"

"Sure you do. You got him to love you, make no mistake on that. Now, all you need to do is figure out how to get him to admit it. It can't be that hard. He's only a man, and men are stupid."

Demi looked up and frowned. "*We're* men."

"Exactly. And look at us, sitting in a gloomy room, fretting over things we could change if only we'd get our bottle up."

"Huh?"

"Courage, Demi. It means having the guts to do what you need to. It may be too late for me. I honestly don't know. But we will fix your problem. We only have to come up with a plan."

The way Demi beamed at him, trust shining through, made Dafydd feel better than he had in longer than he could remember. Perhaps he was fooling them both into thinking he had something left to give. Regardless, as he sat on the floor looking at that expression of hope on Demi's face, he knew he had to try.

* * * *

"What's with all this cloak and dagger stuff anyway?" Karl grumbled.

Trey drained the last of his takeout coffee and sighed. "Beats me. This is how Craig wants to play it and we've got jack shit after a day with our thumbs up our asses."

No autopsy results had come in yet—or they hadn't reached him. The higher-ups were, as predicted, having fits over this security breach. Paz hadn't sent him any unofficial information, either. The tech guys so far had come up empty on the sabotage to the video feeds, no surprise there. Every lead on the Father Ted murder had dead-ended. If Craig had worked some magic to produce useful information, Trey was willing to play any game his former lover wanted.

Crushing his paper cup, he tossed it into the back of his car. Tidiness had gone out the window hours ago. He was sitting there in the same clothes he'd put on almost twenty-four hours ago, with his shirt half-buttoned and the scent of Demi somehow clinging to the material—or maybe that was only his imagination. God knew thoughts of the boy crept into his mind at every opportunity.

"We'll give him another ten minutes before I text him to see what's going on."

"Fine by me. I've got nowhere else to be." Karl gave him the side-eye. "I take it you don't, either."

Trey's nostrils flared at the pointed question. He had to work at not snapping at his partner. "What's that supposed to mean?" And failed.

"I'm just saying you've been acting like a baited bear all day. And you've given me shit-all to explain it. Great night, crappy morning. You rocked it between the sheets, leaving your lover wanting more, yet somehow that's a problem? I need details, Trey, if I'm going to have to put up with you much longer."

"Why? You have just succinctly summed it all up already. There's nothing more I can add that's going to make either of us happier at the moment."

Karl snorted. "I beg to differ. Come on, unload on your old Uncle Karl. Who else can you talk to about this? What's eating at you?"

"Nothing." He really didn't want to get into with anyone. It felt like a personal failure. He should have expected Demi to take a night of sex and turn it into forever. He'd known that kid was infatuated with him, and hybrid though he might be, Demi was very much like any other teenager. His emotions ran high and leaned toward the romantic. It should have been no surprise the kid was hearing wedding bells that morning.

"Look, Trey, if you don't want to tell me for personal reasons, do it for the case. We need to be on our game here. This murder is almost certainly part of the alien war, albeit in wind-down phase, I hope. If we fuck up, people die. You're not good to anyone if you're distracted. Spill."

"Once again, I hate it when you're right." He tapped on the steering wheel a few times before relenting. "It's not about having sex, last night or again. The thing is while I was feeding my lust in the guise of doing a good deed, Demi was picking out china patterns."

Karl whistled. "Who could have seen that one coming? Oh wait, everyone."

Trey turned his head slowly to look at the man. "Fuck. You."

"Come on, Trey. The kid's had a mega crush on you since forever. You had to know that regardless of how this whole thing was being dressed up, he saw as the start of the rest of your lives together."

Trey was stunned. "Is that what you thought?"

Karl shrugged. "Sure. I assumed you'd finally given in to what you obviously wanted, too, and being an honorable man, would also do the right thing."

"Christ, this isn't the fifties. I don't have to marry him just because I slept with him."

"No, but it's a good excuse for you do so, given that you love him."

"I—" He'd intended to deny it, but somehow the words got stuck in his throat.

Karl clucked his tongue. "Don't bullshit me, Trey. Don't bullshit yourself. You love that boy, and everyone knows he loves you. I'm on Team Demi with this one."

"There are no teams," he stressed. *Dammit, where is Craig?* He checked his phone and ground his molars when there was still no text.

They sat in silence for a minute. "He's too young for that kind of commitment." Apparently, he couldn't let the topic go himself. "It's exactly like what's happening between Alex and Quinn. Both boys have so many years ahead of them to settle down. They need to have a chance to explore what life has to offer before doing something that they can't change later on if they realize they've made a mistake."

"Okay, first of all, Quinn changing his physical nature is way different than Demi marrying you. Divorce is always an option. I don't think Quinn can ever go back to the way he was once that blood gives him lady parts. Although I don't know... That Dafydd guy seems to be doing okay."

Ah logic. Such a practical way of looking at things. He could marry Demi then watch him waltz back out again once he realized being tied to a decrepit human was no longer any fun. Sure, that could work so long as Trey didn't care about having his heart ripped out and immolated right in front of his eyes.

"I don't think I could stand that," he confessed in a low voice. He shifted to look at Karl squarely. "I do love Demi. I don't want to. It's inappropriate, for one thing. It doesn't matter how many years he's been alive, I can only see him as the teenager he appears to be. And if I can get past that emotional block, there's this deep well of fear that he truly is merely infatuated with me. Eventually, I figure he's going to wake up the fact that he can do better. Maybe that happens in a few weeks or a few years. Regardless, if I let myself plan forever with him, it will kill me when I lose him."

"Ah, shit, Trey. I got nothing for you on that, other than I don't think that kid is ever going to change his mind where you're concerned."

Trey winced. "Referring to him as that doesn't help."

Before Karl could respond, a dark SUV pulled up to park in front of them. A split second later, a text came through. "That's him," he said before opening his door.

Trust Craig to drive some monster of a vehicle that was both conspicuous and private with its tinted windows. He could only hope that something useful was going to come out of this clandestine meeting. He held some optimism as he and Karl approached the SUV from opposite sides. While Craig was untrustworthy in his personal life, he was a top-shelf cop. And they needed a break in this case.

In unspoken agreement, he and Karl each opened a back-seat door and climbed in. Craig sat in the driver's seat, naturally. A familiar-looking kid slouched down beside him hunched in a hoodie that obscured most of his face.

Craig turned to greet them. "Sorry I'm late. I had trouble convincing Mateo here that cooperating was in his best interest."

"You didn't have to show me those pics of Umi, dude. They nearly made me puke." The boy hunched in his shoulders more.

Trey raised his eyebrows. "Is that the name our dead prisoner went by?"

Craig nodded. "That's all we got, so he gets buried in an unmarked grave, his poor mother probably never knowing what became of him."

Mateo snorted. "Dude, his mother was a fucking crack whore who rented him out to pervs since he was a baby. I don't think she'll care."

"Is that how it was with your mother, Mateo?" Trey asked, trying to establish a report with the kid and silently grateful that Craig had tracked him down. Trey hadn't liked exposing Damien, and for sure not Demi, to another effort at ferreting out info.

"What do you care?"

Trey strove for patience. "I was only thinking that you wouldn't want to end up the same way because it would hurt your family."

Mateo snorted again. "Fuck my family. I don't want to end up dead for my own sake, bro. That's why I don't want to be sitting in this mother-fucking SUV spilling to cops, yo."

"I told you that it's safer here for you than down at the station. Your boss has no qualms about silencing people, whether it's a priest or his latest boo."

"Oh, dude, you are too old and too straight to talk like that." He shook his head. "Besides, the boss doesn't do relationships. He's all about which hole makes his dick happiest. Guess Umi had a real tight one. Didn't do him any good when the boss thought he'd squeal."

Trey leaned forward. "Is he the one who beat and raped you that night Father Ted brought you to the emergency department?"

Even in the gloom for the vehicle, Mateo's shudder was visible. "You can put that down to a job interview, one I was convinced to take." He shook his head. "That is not a man you cross. I tried to warn Father Ted to let it go, but he only laughed and said God would protect him. Dumbass got his throat slit."

Because there was emotion underlying the indifference the words conveyed, Trey took a soft approach. "You liked Father Ted, didn't you?"

"He was okay. Thought he might be just another guy looking for something, but he seemed on the level."

"Don't you want your involuntary 'boss' to get what he deserves for what he's done to both Father Ted and Umi?"

Mateo shifted enough to eye him. "What I want, dude, is to keep from having my throat slit or my neck broke."

"I promise you that I can protect you, Mateo," Craig interjected. "I have safe houses where you can be kept until we get the fucker. I'm not taking you into custody if you can help us here and now."

Mateo shook his head. "I don't know." He swiped at his nose. "You don't know this guy. He's the biggest motherfucker I've ever seen and mean as a snake. It's like he's a total psycho."

Trey shared a look with Karl before saying, "Tell us more about what he looks like."

"Okay, yeah…he's big, muscular, you know? Long, black hair, darker than mine. Shaved on the sides. But his skin's pale like he never goes outside during the day, which I've never seen him do. And it's kind of cold to the touch. He's got an accent, too."

"What kind?" Trey asked, although he already knew the answer.

"I dunno, English maybe. Anyway, he's got pretty eyes — purple, except they turn black when he's sticking it in you. They're snack eyes, too. Dead, like nothing human going on behind them." Mateo took a deep breath and let it out in a rush. "I know Umi, and some of the other boys, think he's good looking, even with the scars down the side of his face."

The penny dropped all the way down for Trey. A vision flashed of an underground room for the T where Val tore a chunk out of the face of Dracul's son.

"You know who he's talking about," Craig remarked in an almost accusatory tone.

Trey tried to school his face to a more neutral expression. "I might."

"You want to let me in on the secret?" His former boyfriend gave him a familiar look that was part cajoling and part demanding.

Trey ignored it. "Mateo, I heard that this guy operates from somewhere underground. Do you know where?" Could it be that having used the vacant part of the subway system before with his brother, Dracul's whelp might be doing it again?

"Nah, I don't know. I've only seen him outside a few times at night where we hang for clients. The one time I was, um, brought to him, I was blindfolded." He grunted. "Seemed funny, like in a movie, until he, ah…did what he did. Nice crib, though. Uptown, you know."

So not some unused storage room of the subway system. *Where, though?* They'd have to do some research and guesswork or find another boy willing and able to tell them more.

The boy shook his head. "I don't want to die."

Putting his hand on the boy's shoulder, Craig said, "I'll keep you safe. Now, is that all you've got?" When Mateo nodded, Craig turned to Trey. "That's it, then. Hope it's helpful."

Trey nodded as he reached for the door handle. "It was. Really. Thanks, I owe you one."

"I want to be kept in the loop, Trey, maybe be there when you move in."

"I'll see what I can do." A necessary lie. No way in hell he would risk Craig learning more than he should now that it was confirmed they were dealing with Dracul's son.

Craig's eyes narrowed. All he said, though, was "Thanks."

Trey and Karl returned to their car and Trey started it up. "Do me a favor and text Val. Let him know we're coming over with info."

"Sure thing. You know who we're looking for?"

"Yup. One of Dracul's evil twins. Not sure which, not that it matters."

"Fuck!"

"My sentiments, exactly."

* * * *

By the time they reached the club, more news had come through confirming what they already knew. Paz had managed to text Trey an unofficial autopsy report that said there were healing puncture wounds around the boy's groin area. Trey couldn't help tracing his own faintly scabbed points at the base of his throat. That moment when Demi had struck and sunk his fangs deep into Trey's jugular had been intensely erotic and not the least bit frightening. Odd that. He'd been dreading it most of all, even though he'd experienced the feeding process back in Wales. There was something more fear-inducing about having your neck sucked.

In any event, he could well understand why the doomed Umi had seemingly been unbothered by it enough to want the alien vampire who'd ultimately killed him. *Poor bastard.*

He felt a disturbing flutter in his stomach and pressure at his temples, like a nascent hangover trying to break out. Returning to the club he'd honestly fled from that morning wasn't setting well with him. It was a cowardly fear of running into Demi or facing his fathers after crushing their precious boy's heart, driving these physical reactions. He hated himself for being so weak.

He hated himself, period.

"I asked Val to meet us by the side door so that we can go directly into Alex's office without running into anyone," Karl remarked as they got out.

The sense of relief didn't better Trey's mood, but he was grateful to his partner's thoughtfulness. "Thanks, man, I appreciate it."

And there stood the bouncer in the doorway in his usual stance of legs braced and arms folded. He didn't look pissed off as he watched them approach. Perhaps Demi hadn't been vocal in his unhappiness. Either that or the family was fine with Trey getting the job done, then booking out in a cloud of dust. Who knew what these aliens were thinking? He didn't, most of the time.

Val nodded to them before stepping aside to usher them in. "Gentlemen."

Trey led the way to their destination, having made the journey many times and never for good reasons. Alex's office contained not only the man himself, but Emil, Harry and Logan, the woman set apart as usual next to the doorway. Quinn was also there, curled up on one end of the couch instead of perching on Alex's lap, as was normally both their wants. *Interesting.* Trey could only assume their fight over Quinn's immediate future was ongoing. It couldn't have been too heated, though, or the boy wouldn't have been hanging out there at all.

Alex rocked forward in his chair. "I take it you have news that we're not going to like."

"Got it in one." Trey's weary tone was obvious to his own ears.

"I bet you've been running on nothing other than coffee for hours," Emil observed. "I have sandwiches here." He waved his hand at a side table laden with food."

Karl headed straight for the minor feast, muttering something about 'lifesaver'. Because he couldn't imagine putting anything in his jittery stomach, Trey threw himself into a vacant chair. He relayed the information he had without preamble.

The room went quiet for the span of a few breaths before Val broke the silence. "Fuck, that's Cadoc."

Trey eyed him. "Is that the twin you took a bite out of?" When Val nodded in confirmation, Trey mused out loud. "Why would he bother to come to Boston simply to start pimping? It's so almost normal in a sick way. No world domination plans start this way that I can see. And it has the added risk of attracting your attention."

"Because he's as arrogant as his sire with an unfortunately large dose of stupidity," Alex replied. "I'm sure Dracul was very disappointed in how his first efforts at fatherhood turned out."

"Lucky for us, though," Emil interjected. "Makes it easier to deal with him once and for all. At least we know where he is and what he's doing. As harmful as he's been to those boys under his thumb, he isn't plotting something that could have wider consequences."

Karl weighed in. "He killed Father Ted and that wretched boy we took into custody. That's bad enough for me." He looked up from his plate. "The fucker waltzed right into our house and killed a prisoner under our noses. It doesn't get any more personal to a cop."

Emil nodded. "I understand. Forgive me if I seemed to make light of the situation."

Karl waved away the apology. "No, it's fine. I get what you meant. After centuries of dealing with mass destruction wreaked by that fucker, a couple of humans don't rate quite so high." He chewed, shaking his head. "I can't let go of that image of the kid lying on his stomach with his neck broken." Tossing what was left of his sandwich on the plate, he added, "Puts me off my food, actually. And that's saying something."

Karl's stark reminder of Umi made Trey's stomach roil even more. Although it was only superficial, he couldn't shake the eerie way the dead kid had reminded him of Demi. It would have been Demi's fate if they hadn't rescued him in time or at all. Trey had to fight down a shudder that threatened to send him flying out of his seat.

"There's nothing to be done about either of them, except get some measure of justice," he said. "Our biggest problem is finding this asshole, Cadoc. I would have thought he'd gone back to the T, given how we've been told from multiple sources that he lives underground. Except this latest information claims it's somewhere nice. More than. And that's not some used storage room, I'm thinking."

Alex looked over at Logan. "Can you be of assistance in this matter?"

She snorted. "I don't do swanky. Sorry."

He shot her a smile. "Not to worry." He tapped one finger on his chin, glanced at Quinn, shifted a bit in his chair. If Trey didn't know the man better, he'd swear Alex was fidgeting.

Maybe because he's missing his lap anchor.

"Well, as the owner of the club, I have contacts of my own — members, other club owners. I'll see what I can dig out. What's your next move, Sergeant, if I might ask?"

Trey opened his mouth to answer, then shut it with a painful click of his teeth when Demi came sauntering in.

Chapter Ten

Even though he knew already via the club's grapevine that Trey was there, Demi still had trouble keeping his expression cheery. As he breezed into Alex's office uninvited, he stuck with the plan he and Dafydd had hashed out during the day. He fixed his gaze on their leader first and gave Trey no more than a passing glance. He thought he caught a flashing of eyes and stiffening of the man in reaction to his coming in. Having that possible effect on the object of both his fervent desire and volcanic ire helped him keep his own emotions in check.

"Sorry to bother you, sir. May I come in?"

Alex gave shot him an indulgent look. "You already are, dearest boy. And as our business is more or less concluded, how may I help?"

Demi stood just inside the door with his hands behind his back, mostly to hide how much he was twisting his fingers. "Oh well, I don't want to bore everyone. I was hoping to talk to Papa and you about my plans." He gave his most ingratiating smile.

"What are you talking about, son?" Papa leaned forward.

Turning to keep him in his line of sight gave Demi a better side view of Trey. The guy's jaw appeared clenched and there was a rapid heartbeat audible. It wasn't necessarily Trey's, but Demi would have bet anything it was.

"First, I'm sorry about my earlier outburst." He was careful to include Val in his apology, as well as Alex and Papa.

Trey's mouth opened then slammed shut again. *You're dying to know what I'm talking about, aren't you?* He took satisfaction in that.

"We understand the strain you're under," Alex replied. "Think no more of it."

"Except you need to take this apology to Dad directly," Papa admonished.

"I will. I promise. I figured I'd give you and Alex the rundown of what I have in mind first." When Papa nodded, Demi continued, taking a deep and obvious breath. "So, I'm thinking I need to get my driver's license. I'm certainly old enough by human standards, and it will make my getting around easier. Then, I should get my GED. Obviously my home schooling has been sufficient for that. I'm going to maybe take some summer classes at community college, but I'll definitely enroll in the fall full-time. It should be easier for me to go that route rather than apply to a four-year college straight away, given that humans perceive me as being younger than I am."

He waited a few beats to let that information sink in.

"Um." Alex looked at Papa.

Papa cleared his throat. "Those are excellent ideas, Demi. I'm not sure we need to trouble Alex with all of this, though."

"I was actually thinking that maybe Quinn could take some classes, too. It would make me more comfortable, given how little time I've spent out in the real world with humans. We could carpool, and well," he added with a shrug, "it could be fun."

Alex perked up. "What an even more excellent idea."

"What do you think, Quinn?" Demi asked quickly, before Alex could railroad his boy into something. Demi felt a little bad incorporating Quinn into his scheme without his prior approval, except he'd meant what he'd said. He really would like Quinn to join him. If it helped ease the strain between the guy and Alex, all the better.

Quinn frowned. "I suppose that would be okay. I mean, if you really want to go and it helps to have me along, then sure. I'm willing to take a few classes. I guess." Something in his gaze told Demi that he was going to have a lot of explaining to do later.

"Marvelous." Demi had never seen Alex quite so happy. The man stared at Quinn with a naked look of love that was almost painful for Demi to see. He wanted so badly for Trey to show him such devotion.

Saying nothing more, Alex held his hand out to Quinn. The risk he was taking in front of all of them was impressively brave. What if Quinn rejected the upspoken request? He didn't, though. No more than two seconds passed before Quinn got up, took the proffered hand and allowed Alex to twirl him onto his lap. They both sighed in utter contentment as Alex wrapped his arms around Quinn, who sank into the embrace.

Now it did hurt, deep inside his chest. Demi had to clench his fingers in order to keep from rubbing at the spot. "I'm not quite done," he said, and now everyone turned their attention from Alex and Quinn to him.

"The rest impacts the family, and I think is going to require Alex's permission. You see, I also want to get a job, earn my own money. While I appreciate the family's generosity, I can't be a leech. It will take years for me to qualify as a doctor. I should really get a part-time regular job like any boy would."

"Not as a go-go boy!" That command burst out of Trey's mouth, filling the room at the same time it sucked all the air out.

Demi turned slowly to look at him, eyes wide and acting as if he'd barely realized the man was in the room. "Oh, hello, Trey." He blinked at him a few times, slowly before saying, "Um, no, not as a dancer. While I love it, I can appreciate how much that bothers my fathers."

He said nothing about how Trey must feel, because the man's wants where Demi was concerned didn't matter—not unless the idiot was ready to do something about it. "I was thinking of working at a clothing store. It is something that I both love and know a lot about. Then, I can get an apartment of my own."

Papa raised his eyebrows and glanced at Alex, who shrugged. "I suppose in a couple of years."

Trey made a strangled sound. "Are you crazy, Harry? It's not safe out there for him."

"Isn't it?" Demi asked wide-eyed. "Dracul is dead and what's left of his men don't seem much interested in us."

Trey popped to a standing position, his eyes blazing. "I've just confirmed his psycho son is out in the city running boy whores and killing anyone who gets in his way."

"Father Ted?"

"And the kid you fished out of the Charles for us. Cadoc somehow broke into the station and snapped that boy's neck."

Demi flinched at Trey's vehemence and at the news. He'd missed a lot hanging out in Dafydd's room and not heard enough during the few minutes he'd listened outside of Alex's office door. "Oh, that poor thing." His well-crafted agenda faltered in his distress. Only for a moment, though. He couldn't let Trey send him off track.

His lifted his chin. "Anyway, it has nothing to do with my finding my own place. It won't be for at least a year, and I'm sure you all will deal with Dracul's son. In the meantime, I'm equally sure he has no interest in me. It's not like I'm planning on selling myself out on the street. Plus, I'll need a place to bring my dates. The club is hardly appropriate."

Trey's eyes practically popped out. "Dates?"

Demi folded his arms. "That's right. You know, young men of my own supposed age with whom I'll want to have sex."

Trey let loose a string of curses that were so inventive, Demi wasn't sure what most of it meant. In the next instant, he stopped trying because Trey closed the distance and grabbed his arm.

"With your permission, Harry, I'd like a word with your son." Trey spoke through a clenched jaw.

Demi was delighted his efforts were yielding results already. He gave a token resistance with a tug of his arm. "Really, Trey, there's nothing we need to talk about."

Trey paid him no mind and Papa merely nodded in approval. The next thing Demi knew, Trey was dragging him out of Alex's office and, after opening the first door he came to, he tugged him inside.

"This is a storage room, Trey." It was filled with chairs and other bits used by Kitty in the bar area. It all became visible when Trey turned on the light.

"Like I care." The livid man shut the door and pressed Demi against it. "What do you think you're doing?"

Demi hid his glee. "I have no idea what you're talking about. I was merely telling my family about my sensible plans for the future. You, of all people, should understand that. Didn't you urge me to do that only this morning, after you informed me of what my life *wasn't* going to be like? At least, not for the next ten years."

"You told your father your plan included having sex."

"Naturally. Our species isn't as hung up about that stuff you know? Now that you've ushered me into manhood, Papa and the others would expect me to have sex whenever I want, although obviously not with the club members. That would be hitting a little too close to home. Plus, it would bother my dad. He's human, after all. I really need a place of my own for privacy and —"

The rest of his ramble was cut off by Trey's mouth slamming into his. The force of the man's kiss knocked Demi's head against the door. Trey proceeded to mount a full-frontal assault on Demi's lips, all teeth and tongue, and gave him no time to muster a defense, not that he wanted to. After the initial shock, he dived right in with his man, matching his fervor and welcoming every touch. Every part of Trey's moves was a demand, a claiming. It thrilled Demi.

Trey's hard cock tried to bore a hole into Demi's pelvis. Because he still wore his yoga pants and a borrowed shirt from Dafydd that didn't quite reach his waist, the pressure felt like a brand on his exposed skin. And he wasn't the only one with openings available. Trey's shirt gaped where buttons had come off. *Because he was so eager to fuck me.* Wiggling his hand between their bodies, he skimmed his fingers along the flesh stretched tight over Trey's ribs. The touch caused Trey to inhale his breath sharp enough that he sucked hard on Demi's lips. Fine tremors ran through Trey. *Or am I the one who's shaking?*

Demi didn't care. Any sign of vulnerability was fine with him. He wanted Trey to know how much he loved him. He ached for some indication that the feeling was reciprocated. His own dick lay twisted and trapped — and demanding release. He slipped his free hand past the waistband, only to have it knocked away. Instead, Trey yanked the pants down, exposing Demi's cock to the rasping of Trey's clothing. Not for long, though. With a few more fumbling moves, Trey had freed his dick, as well. Then Trey mashed the two hard shafts together in his big, warm fist.

Demi gasped and bucked his hips forward. He wrapped his arm fully around Trey's waist, one arm trapped inside the shirt, the other under his jacket. Trey jerked the cocks together, sliding dry skin until pre-cum added a bit of lubricant. The pleasure shooting up from Demi's balls and along his shaft elicited a hiss and a moan. His fangs punched down, whether he'd willed it or not. With that came a blinding thirst. He whined at the effort to keep himself in check.

Trey broke the kiss with a tug of his teeth along Demi's bottom lip. "Do it," Trey gasped and ground the cocks together even harder.

Demi forced his eyes open. Trey had already tilted his head to one side. The quick pulse at the base of his throat was tantalizing. *Irresistible*. Demi struck without another moment of hesitation. He sank his fangs into Trey's tasty flesh with ease, then the blood flowed in to fill his mouth and coat his tongue. He tugged at the vein, syncing the rhythm of his pulls to the way Trey worked their dicks.

The orgasm caught him by surprise, rising and cresting before he'd sucked Trey's blood for more than a few seconds. Trey followed a moment later, his movements becoming clumsier, his body squishing Demi against the door as Trey essentially collapsed into him. Demi clutched at Trey's back to hold him up and have something to keep himself from sliding to the floor. Reluctantly he retracted his fangs and licked the puncture wounds closed. He dropped his head onto Trey's shoulder while the aftershocks of the climax ran through him.

Then the room tilted as they both ended up dropping in a collapse controlled by Trey's impressive strength. They landed in a tangle of limbs and heaving chests. It didn't matter, because it all meant that Demi was holding on to his man. More importantly, Trey was also holding on to him, brushing his face along the top of Demi's head. Trey roamed his hands over Demi's arms and back, rubbing lightly. His warm breath played across Demi's hair. The casual affection told Demi a lot more than the almost brutal sex. The latter was passion and easily triggered. But this? This was a more tender emotion. Demi basked in the attention, savoring what he knew would be short-lived.

And it was. Trey pressed a firm kiss against Demi's temple before releasing him entirely. "Christ, that was not how I intended this visit to go." Looking down his front, he twisted his lips in a wry grin. "I've lost a couple more buttons."

Demi couldn't hide his smile. He'd done that. "Sorry. I wanted to touch as much of you as I could."

"Yeah." Trey sighed. "I get it." He spent the next few seconds righting what he could of his clothing, including tucking his dick into his underwear and zipping up his pants.

Demi's spent cock flopped on his hip, still half-hard. Pulling his waistband back up, he stuffed it in, not wanting to highlight how easily he'd recovered from orgasming compared to Trey. That was one of the things that had been flung in his face that morning. The scent of Trey's cum mixed with his own lingered on his fingers. He stole a few licks.

Trey sighed heavily and banged the back of his head on the door. "How much of that show you put on in Alex's office was for my benefit?"

"All of it." Although he wasn't above manipulating the man, he intended to be honest as well.

"Figured. Congratulations, it worked."

"Thanks." Demi fluttered his lashes. "But it also happens to be all true. I'm going to do each and every one of those things."

Trey narrowed his gaze. "Oh, yeah?"

Demi nodded once. "Yup. Why? Which ones do you think I shouldn't? There's nothing on that list that doesn't match what you insisted on this morning. That includes dating."

"Touché, kid." Trey barked out a laugh and shook his head. "You've got me right by the short hairs. Just what you want."

Demi folded his arms and glared. "What I want is for us to make a life together. You're the one who has a problem with that plan. So, I have no choice but to play it your way. That means working and school and having sex with other men in order to be *sure* I want your old man body forever and ever."

"Jesus!" With a pained look, Trey turned away. "I had that coming." He closed his eyes and banged his head again. "I don't know what to do. I can't believe I reacted the way I did. I really can't believe we're both going to be coming out of a fucking storage room reeking of sex. Your father is only a few feet away, for God's sake."

"I've told you... They don't care about that. They aren't hung up about sex the way you humans are."

"Fine. I can be the one to die from embarrassment and Harry can resuscitate me."

By unspoken agreement, they fell silent for a while. Demi used the time to try to figure out a way to keep Trey from castigating himself and not hate Demi for playing him. He really hadn't expected such an outburst. The way he and Dafydd had envisioned it, the relentless compliance with what Trey had demanded of Demi was supposed to slowly drive the man crazy — and right into Demi's arms. Eventually. Honestly, he hadn't expected Trey to crack within the first five minutes of the plan's execution.

"I'm sorry," he said in a quiet voice. "I didn't mean for this to happen. I don't want you to be upset or mad at yourself for losing control."

Trey reached out and ran a hand down Demi's arm. "You don't have to apologize. I'm the one giving mixed signals here. You've always worn your heart on your sleeve. I knew what I was getting into when I agreed to usher you into manhood. I was simply fooling myself."

"Really?" Demi tried not to get too optimistic.

"Yeah, but...everything I said this morning still stands."

Demi's heart sank. "Oh. I understand." *Not.*

"Come here." Trey tugged him onto his lap. Demi gave only a token resistance. "I need time, Demi. This is hard for me. I like everything about your plan except the dating other guys part."

"You said—"

"Forget that. I'm stupid. There is no way I can handle you having sex with other men, not simply because I think you need to experience it. If you decide that's what you want... If *you* decide," he emphasized, "I promise I won't stand in your way."

"I won't."

"We'll see. Anyway, please give me the space to deal with my own demons, not to mention that I have to help deal with this Cadoc asshole."

"Oh, right. Honestly, I was listening at the doorway before I came in and caught that he's behind everything. I know what you're up against." Sitting there in Trey's arms, it was hard to remember that there were problems in the world other than their personal ones. He rested his head against Trey's broad chest. "I promise to be good, so long as I know you haven't shut the door on us."

Trey sighed deeply. "Nope. I am apparently incapable of doing that."

"Good." He smiled. "Can we stay like this for a little while longer?"

Trey hugged him tight. "Sure. If we wait long enough, maybe the others will forget we're here and I can leave without taking the biggest walk of shame ever."

* * * *

"Hi there. Can I buy you a drink?"

Ric shook his head at the guy offering. "Thanks, but I'm afraid I wouldn't be very good company right now."

His pursuer, a nice-looking blond, didn't give up. Instead, he slid onto the stool next to the one where Ric sat. "Bad day at work, huh?"

"The worst." He took a sip of his beer as if that would both discourage the guy and somehow wash away the memories of cutting open that kid, Umi. He twirled the glass in his hand. "And given what I do, you wouldn't be that interested in socializing with me afterward." It was a cheap shot, testament to how he really wanted to chase the man away as firmly as possible.

"I don't know. Someone as hot as you warrants the effort."

Ric smiled, appreciating the compliment as much as the next person. It was always flattering to be told he was attractive, and normally he would use his looks to get laid without compunction. Not this night, though. Besides, for the last couple of months, he'd found that he'd become picky when it came to whom he wanted. Pale beauty accented with long black hair seemed to be his type now, which was so fucked up, yet nevertheless true.

He stared into his drink. "I'm a coroner." A bit of a stretch. Quicker than explaining his medical residency, though. He lifted up his hands. "These were sunk deep in a kid's chest cavity only hours ago."

The guy's eyes widened a second before he stood. "Okay then, have a nice night."

Ric almost felt bad. The relief at being left alone again overruled his natural inclination to playing nice with other boys. He really was in a mood and had to wonder if he'd be having the same reaction after helping in the autopsy of that boy if he hadn't known about the aliens and their war. His life had taken an unfathomable turn in the months since Emil had pushed him against a hospital wall to keep him from interfering in Val's feeding Mackie. At the time, he'd known only heart-stopping fear. Then, he'd convinced himself that it was all about the cool science he had access to. Now?

He mentally shrugged and drank some more. His adventure in Wales had been surreal, so much so that he'd still managed to box his experience with the aliens into the clinical part of his brain. Cutting open the boy he could only ever think of as Umi, thanks to Trey, he could no longer pretty-up the situation. Umi had lived a short, brutal life, most of that being squarely a human phenomenon. Even the tearing and scar tissue in and around his rectum was an all too common form of abusive damage. But there was something about how the boy's neck had been snapped cleanly in two that really got to Ric. A loop kept playing in his head of Umi's last moments, of being fucked right as his head was violently twisted.

It could have been Dafydd. Yeah, that was another problem. He saw the Welshman in the same role. There was a superficial likeness, perhaps because the alien went for boys who looked like him. And he'd bet that if he examined Dafydd, he'd find similar signs of abuse.

The thought made him shudder when it shouldn't. He was a doctor and had seen horrific suffering in the emergency department. Horrible accidents, gun shot and stab wounds, children beaten by parents, women raped by intimate partners. Nothing should faze him now. Yet, here he sat, haunted by Dafydd and Umi alike.

Shoving his beer aside, he signaled to the bartender. "Can I get a shot of tequila, please? Beer isn't cutting it tonight."

The handsome guy smiled at him. "Sure thing. I get a lot of that in here."

As he waited, Ric glanced around the room by way of looking in the long mirror behind the bar. He'd come in to check the place out as well as drown his sorrows. A couple of his friends had raved about it as a new gay-friendly pub that was fast becoming a nice pick-up place. It was pretty packed with mostly men.

The bartender came to pour him the shot. "Checking out the prospects?" he asked with a wink.

"Not tonight." Ric downed the liquor, winced and nodded for another. "Right now, I'm looking for numbness. Maybe another night. I heard this was a great new hang-out."

"Well, it's under new management, but it's been in business for about a hundred years."

"Really?" Ric tossed back the next shot and after a half-second's worth of deliberation, gave the signal for one more.

"Yeah." The bartender tossed his head to one side. "See that corner over there with the big guy standing like a gargoyle?"

Picking up the shot glass, Ric turned his head to look.

The bartender leaned in. "That's a secret entrance to the club beneath us. The bookcase actually has a door built in that swings open when he pulls a hidden latch. Back during prohibition, it was a speakeasy. Pretty cool, huh?"

Ric slammed down the tequila and stared at the spot and the man through the mirror so as not to be obvious about it. The hairs on the back of his neck stood up, not that the man in question was anything other than human. He was African-American, for one thing, and he knew the aliens were monochrome in all respects. But he was a scary motherfucker and there was something about him that screamed criminal, as well. Perhaps it was the dark, wraparound sunglasses that he wore indoors.

Waving off a fourth shot, he asked, "What's down there now?"

The bartender shrugged. "Some private club of the owner." He turned to put the bottle away.

"How does one join?"

"Sorry, dude. I have no idea. I've never met the boss, but the manager says that it's strictly off limits. Pretty cool, though, still, huh?"

Ric nodded as the man headed down the bar to help another customer. He gathered his glass of beer in front of him and kept his gaze on the mirror and the corner with the bookcase. He nursed his drink because now it was about killing time, not getting drunk enough to forget his life for a while. It took nearly thirty minutes before anything of note happened. An older man, nicely dressed in an expensive suit and, like the gatekeeper, wearing sunglasses inside what was already a fairly dark room approached the entrance to the hidden downstairs. There was some kind of card produced discreetly, a nod from the doorman-slash-bouncer dude, then a section of the bookcase opened only wide enough for the man to slip through.

Ric's grip on his glass tightened spasmodically, as if his body recognized something that his brain was still processing. His first thought was *Nope, you've been hanging around blood-sucking aliens too long.* Because really, what were the odds that he'd stumbled upon something useful to Duncan's investigation into Father Ted's and Umi's murders? He was being ridiculous. On the other hand, the math wasn't that outrageous. There were only so many places in Boston catering to a gay clientele, even fewer ones that were the more upscale spots he liked now that he had some money in his pocket. Add to that, anything new got spread around the community and attracted attention. So no, not a long shot after all that he might have walked into the monster's lair.

He nursed his beer and one more for another hour, keeping tabs on the bookcase. Two more men went through and two came out. Every one of them was middle-aged and well-heeled, a sharp contrast to the younger, hipster crowd that filled the bar area. His bladder finally forced him to pay his tab and leave his seat. The restrooms were on the other side of the room from the speakeasy entrance, so he had no chance to get a closer look. But, a little bit of luck was with him as he started to leave.

One more man came out of the hidden spot, hunched over, eyes shaded and made a beeline for the front door. On a quick and perhaps stupid impulse, Ric raced out, twirled around and flipped on sunglasses that he had in his pocket. Then he deliberately put himself in the man's path.

"Oh, sorry," he said jerking back, as if only seeing him that moment. He put out a hand as if steadying himself and made contact with the guy's shoulder. "I'm in too much of a hurry, I guess." He chuckled, trying for a skeevy sound. "How are things tonight?"

The man quirked his lips. "No apologies necessary. I wasn't looking where I was going, either. And these damn sunglasses don't help. Stupid rules." He smiled broadly. "I'm also wiped out. Barely know my own name. There's some new blood on tap. Tight as a goddamn tick." With a chuckle, the man slapped Ric on the back and ambled off.

And it was that easy. A man spent from his time exploiting a boy, maybe a child, was only too happy to share a convivial moment with a stranger of like tastes. Ric felt sick and elated at the same time. Anything he could do to bring down what was left of Dracul's cabal was cause for celebration. He told himself it was to protect his own people. Humanity was at risk so long as any vestige of the monstrous alien roamed the globe. Really, though, his goal was simpler and more complex at the same time. He wanted to help Dafydd. The man deserved the peace necessary to regain and live his life without fear.

That was difficult to face, however. So, he concentrated on the nobler goal of helping his own species. He also felt suddenly vulnerable, as if his interaction with the man had been observed. As he hurried away, he glanced up and around. There must be security cameras. Even if no one was watching them now, surely the feed was being recorded. It could be routinely reviewed, for all he knew.

He raced through the narrow alley where the entrance stood, past other people heading to their own fun. It wasn't as if he were isolated or anything. It was simply every horror film he'd ever seen playing inside his head, reminding him that this was the part where the nosey secondary character got killed. By the time he hit the nearest street, Tremont, his heart was pounding and sweat coated his skin. With shaking hands, he pulled out his phone and called up a Lyft. He whipped off his glasses and wiped his forehead with his sleeve.

Then, he called Duncan. Because, even now, he worried that he would somehow die before telling someone what he knew.

The cop picked up on the third ring, thank God no voicemail situation cropping up, again like in the movies. "Doc?"

"Duncan, I think I've found something important, maybe the very place you're looking for." He scanned the crowd before continuing. He gave the name of the pub and its location before adding in a few details in a low voice. "It could be nothing," he finished up with.

"No. It sounds promising. Where are you now?"

"Waiting on a corner of Tremont for a car to pick me up."

"Can you come to Lux?"

Ric licked his lips and blinked a few times to clear his head. Damn, all that liquor was hitting him hard. "Sure, no problem."

"Good. I'll call ahead and let them know we're coming." The cop ended the call.

Ric stuffed his phone back in his pants as a car pulled up to the curb amid blaring horns from cars that had to swerve around him.

The driver's side window slid down. "Ric?" the man asked.

"Yeah." He hopped into the car as fast as his suddenly clumsy body would allow. He fumbled, as well, with his seat belt. "Change of destination, though." He gave the address for the club, then collapsed against the back of the seat.

"Hey, dude, you're not going to, like, hurl back there, are you?"

Ric waved the concern away, although his stomach was churning. Not from the booze, though, but from the almost certain knowledge that he'd sunk deeper into the morass that was the secret internecine alien war. He would have been happier never knowing, except he couldn't bring himself to truly regret anything, because anytime his thoughts strayed in that direction, the image of Dafydd intruded. Whatever else this journey did to him, he couldn't shake the belief that it would someday be worth it.

Chapter Eleven

"I'm beginning to think I should rent a room at the club," Karl griped. "Kitty told me that Alex has acquired the building next door. He intends to turn it into more space for the members to play and hang out in on an extended basis for an extra fee. She's also planning on taking one of the suites herself and giving up her apartment in the West End."

"Well, there's a good reason to move that has nothing to do with the never-ending shitshow of a war."

It was also interesting intel. He hadn't known about Alex's expansion plans. Maybe he could do the same. Alex would likely be reasonable about the rent, given Trey's less-than stellar income. And it would put him closer to Demi, which would be both a blessing and a curse. *God.* He'd been such a weak bastard, taking the boy like that, roughly against a door. In a storage room no less. Demi deserved silk sheets and tender kisses, not splinters in his ass and bruises on his lips.

Mixed messages? What a fucking understatement that had been. And, boy, did Demi have his number, all that talk of moving out and sleeping with other men. He'd known exactly where Trey's buttons were and had methodically, brutally and gleefully pushed each and every one. Even understanding what he was doing, Trey had been helpless to keep from reacting with unbridled fury and possessiveness. He'd been, if not proud, then content with how he'd handled Demi's frightening and unrealistic expectations of what their having sex meant. In the span of less than twelve hours, he'd torched his own accomplishment.

"What's eating at you, Trey?"

He gave his partner the side-eye. "Nothing."

"Oh, no, can we not get on this ride of denial again?"

Trey blew out a noisy breath. "Fair point. It's Demi."

Karl snorted. "I already know that. I meant what's new about Demi that's bothering you?"

"I'm sorry. Were you *not* in the room when I dragged him out and… *You know.*"

"Not all the details, and I like it better that way. I take it you've been castigating yourself over your lapse ever since. I figured as much. That's why I was nowhere to be seen before you and the kid reappeared. I take it the conflicting feelings weren't improved by whatever it was that happened between you."

"No, they weren't. The only thing we managed to do was agree he wouldn't date other men."

"You mean fuck them."

Trey took his eyes off the road long enough to glare at his partner. "Yes," he bit out.

"That doesn't seem fair, Trey, given that you aren't willing to commit."

"Because it isn't!" he roared and instantly regretted his outburst.

Karl, damn him, merely chuckled. "God, that kid has you by the short hairs."

"My point, exactly, but I don't know what to do about it. I only know what I can't stand at the moment and that includes making a commitment to Demi and not wanting any other man to have him."

"Poor bastard," Karl muttered.

"Thanks. That helps a lot," Trey snapped, then shut his mouth because he was only making a fool out of himself the more he talked.

By the time, they entered Alex's office, Paz was already there, nursing a giant mug of what smelled like coffee. He looked a little worse for wear and accented that impression by giving Trey and Karl a brief nod before practically sinking his face into his drink. The usual gang was ensembled, minus all the boys. Trey almost sighed in relief. That last thing he wanted was another encounter with Demi before he'd had a chance to remotely consider how he was going to handle everything. He was even happier when Alex asked him to close and lock the door.

He raised his eyebrows when he turned to face the room. "Is there someone in particular you're keeping out?" The answer was kind of obvious, except Alex surprised him.

"Quinn. He's out dancing and I don't want him to hear any of this. I don't think my nerves can take another instance of his being in the middle of a fight. And," he added, pinching the bridge of his nose, "I don't want to have a new argument, having just ended the previous one."

"I agree," Emil chimed in. "Jase is a sweet boy, but nothing gets him steamed more than thinking I'm heading into trouble without him by my side."

From where he sat with a laptop, Val snorted. "Sucks to be you. When I want Mackie to stick in one place, I simply lock him up."

Emil scowled. "Unless he safewords, then you're just as stuck as the rest of us." He turned to Trey and Karl. "I've got cookies and coffee here if you want."

"No, thanks." Trey went over to the couch and slouched down. He nodded in greeting at Harry, then skittered his gaze away because he couldn't face Demi's father yet.

Karl, of course, headed straight for the food. But Alex was starting the meeting, asking Paz to run through his experience at the bar. It made as much sense as it had the first time Trey had heard it, and everyone in the room agreed that the doctor had stumbled upon useful information, thank fuck. Because Trey and Karl had racked their brains for hours trying to figure out where Cadoc might have set up his lair.

"I've run a search on that place," Val said, taking over the conversation. "It changed hands within two weeks after what went down in Wales. The former owner wasn't making a go of it, apparently, and sold the whole set-up, including the building. There was a general notice to creditors, as well as a filing at the registry of deeds."

He tapped the computer keys. "The buyer is a Massachusetts limited liability company formed right before the sale." He glanced up. "There's only one name listed for manager and registered agent, a lawyer in Boston named Seth Murphy."

Trey jerked his chin toward his partner. "I know what we're going to be doing first thing tomorrow — unless you think that's a bad idea, Alex. If we rattle the lawyer, he's bound to report back to Cadoc."

"He will indeed." Alex drummed his fingers on his arm rest. "We can only risk it if we can do more than ask him questions. I suppose it's too much to hope that we can find some leverage over him."

"Hm-m." Trey mulled over that idea. "How did Cadoc find him?" he asked the room at large. "Human criminals usually hire shifty attorneys, guys as lawless as they are. I have to assume that Dracul did the same and taught that lesson to his sons. I can't believe this Murphy character is ignorant of what goes on in the private club area."

"If he is," Karl interjected, "we could interview him without concern. Once he learns what his client is up to, he'd want to distance himself from it and help with the investigation."

Trey nodded. "Yeah, right, except how do we know which way he swings? Unless…" He leaned forward as the idea snapped into place. "On the theory that any lawyer a pimp would use might be also a customer, someone he came across while running boys, maybe this Murphy is known to the boys."

"You're thinking Mateo," Karl said, right before stuffing a cookie into his mouth.

"Right. That's the kid who gave us the description of Cadoc," he explained to the others, because he hadn't actually bothered to name him before.

"Yes, the one your vice cop friend is holding somewhere safe," Alex offered. "That would be convenient if he recognizes this lawyer. Can you print out a picture of him, Val?"

"On it." A few seconds later, Alex's printer whirred. Val got up to take the picture off and handed it to Trey.

Murphy was middle-aged and non-descript, not that it mattered. Trey had learned a long time ago that some of the worst criminals looked like your typical mild-mannered uncle. He folded the paper and tucked it into his inner breast pocket. Then he glanced at his watch. It was late, but not too late. So, after pulling out his phone, he called Craig. The fucker's number was still in his contacts.

"Trey, this is a surprise." The guy hadn't lost his silky phone voice, either.

"I need to see the kid," he said without preamble. "I have something to show him."

Craig blew out a breath over the line. "It's hardly the shank of the evening, but I suppose you wouldn't be asking if you didn't have a hot lead."

"We hope so." This is where it got tricky. No way he could allow Craig in on the kill. The last thing they needed was yet one more person in on the big secret. "Tell us where the kid is and Karl and I will meet you there."

"Sorry. I'm not giving that out over an unsecure connection. I'll meet you and drive you there."

Trey mulled that over. He didn't want to have to explain why he was at the club. "How about we meet in front of the station instead?"

"Fine. Thirty minutes?"

"Sure. See you." Hanging up, he spoke to the room. "We'll go meet Craig and speak with Mateo."

"We heard," Val said.

Of course, alien hearing. "Right. Let's go, Karl."

His partner slurped up the rest of his coffee before going to wrap a fistful of cookies. At Trey's look, he said, "What? I figured it wouldn't hurt to bribe the kid with something sweet."

"I'll call you later, Alex."

"We'll be waiting with bated breath, Sergeant. And, in the meantime, we'll plan the assault on the pub. We'll only get one shot at it, so we must take our best one. Cadoc never had his father's intelligence but he has a cunning for survival that makes him less than an easy target."

"Awesome. At least it's not a fucking castle," he said as he walked out of the door.

* * * *

Mateo munched on his cookie as he stared at the grainy photograph. The kid was clearly more interested in his treat than in helping the investigation. Still, he could hardly refuse, given that the police were all that stood between him and a murderous pimp. The boy's eyes shifted to one side before going back to stare at the picture. It was all the 'tell' Trey needed.

"Who is he?" he asked before Mateo could try to weasel out of the truth.

"Um-m."

"Come on, Mateo," Craig urged from where he stood over the boy's shoulder. "You know our deal. We need the truth, and the faster we get this guy off the streets, the safer you'll be."

Mateo crunched noisily on his cookie. "Yeah, okay. I recognize him," he added, handing the piece of paper back to Trey. "He's a customer."

"You're sure?" Trey pressed.

The boy nodded. "He's kind of a mean dude, you know?" He made a face. "Makes you cry sometimes." His gaze flitted up to Trey's. "I think he wants the boys not to like what he's doing. Gets off on playing at rape."

"Charming," Karl observed.

Just Cadoc's type. Trey almost said it out loud before remembering that he wasn't with the in-the-know crowd. *Christ, I'm tired.*

He rubbed his eyes. "Okay, anything else?"

The boy shrugged. "Not really. I don't know his name or anything."

"That's okay. We do." He motioned to Karl that it was time to go.

Craig stepped forward. "Give me the name."

Trey shook his head. "Sorry. This is still a murder investigation. The vice element is peripheral at best."

"Don't be an asshole, Trey. However you might feel about me, we're cops. I'm protecting what is currently your only source of information. The least you can do is keep me in the loop."

Karl moved on ahead, leaving Trey to deal with the awkward mess. "All I can tell you is that an informant of mine led us to this guy." He rattled the paper. "We think he's the legal side of the prostitution ring, but we needed leverage, and your boy here just gave it to us. If it leads anywhere, I'll let you know."

There...some truth with a lie slid in. When Murphy rolled—and he would—Trey and his alien friends would shut Cadoc down and make up some excuse as to why there was no body to pick over when he brought Craig in to deal with the trafficking victims.

Craig stared at him suspiciously, knowing him too well. Trey kept his expression as open and blank as he could. Finally, Craig nodded. "Okay, fine. Do it your way. Give me a minute with Mateo then I'll drive you back to the station."

Relieved and trying not to show it, Trey followed his partner out.

* * * *

"I'm sorry," the young man huffed out, "Mr. Murphy can't be disturbed."

Trey bared his teeth at the receptionist. "My badge says otherwise. Either you buzz him or we go straight in."

Of course, Trey intended for both to happen. The moment the flustered guy pushed the intercom button, Trey surged forward and opened the door to Murphy's office. It took no more than a few strides. This wasn't some swanky office in the financial district. Murphy obviously didn't have well-heeled clients. *No surprise there.* Cadoc went with someone both vulnerable to blackmail and easily co-opted with the lure of illegal sex.

The lawyer sputtered in outrage, the phone in one hand, as they entered. He stood from behind his desk. "What is the meaning—"

"Mr. Murphy, sir. I'm Detective Sergeant Duncan and this is my partner, Detective Anderson. Please sit down, because we have a lot to discuss."

"I have no idea what I could possibly have to say to you. If this is about one of my clients, I have to claim attorney-client privilege. You have no right to that information."

As Karl shut the door firmly behind them, Trey approached the desk. "Very true, sir. Fortunately for us, we're here about something that isn't protected."

Murphy sucked in his chest and stood straighter, not that anything was going to make the man taller. The picture hadn't shown how short the slender man was. *What did Mateo say about this guy liking to hurt the boys?*

Bet it strokes all sorts of inferiority complexes in you, doesn't it, fucker?

Out loud, he said, "We have some questions for you regarding soliciting boys for sex, some of whom are undoubtedly underage. That really adds to the charges and the prison sentence, doesn't it, Karl?"

"Yes, sir." Karl grinned evilly as he said it.

Murphy sputtered. Trey cut him off. "Fortunately for you, Mr. Murphy, we come with a solution that should please us all. Why don't we sit down and discuss it?"

Murphy flapped his lips a few times and swallowed noticeably hard before doing as told. Then, Trey and Karl did the same. The plan had been worked out over the past day with Alex et al. They were going to strike fast, that night. All they needed to do was put the fear of God in this asshole and keep him under control until it was time to move. He hoped like hell it would go smoothly. At least the boys they loved would be out of the fray this time. That one bit of news made Trey happy enough that he was able to put aside the problem of what to do with Demi in the future.

"So, Mr. Murphy," he began, "here's what you have to do to keep from spending the rest of your life in a cage."

* * * *

Demi uttered a squeak as he was grabbed by the arm, a sound quickly muffled by someone's hand over his mouth. Mackie's, as it turned out. The boy dragged him into the very storage room where Trey had delightfully ravaged him. They weren't alone, however. Quinn and Jase were also there, the first one standing on top of an old high-top table that Jase was holding steady. When Mackie shut the door, he released his hold.

Demi frowned. "What are you doing?"

"Sh-h-h," the others admonished him in unison.

Demi asked again in pantomime, spreading his arms out and popping his eyes.

"We're trying to listen in on the meeting in Alex's office," Mackie said in a whisper.

That's when Demi noticed that Quinn had his ear to a vent on the wall. He opened his mouth in a silent O, even as he realized that if sound could travel that easily between the rooms, it was entirely possible that Papa and the others had had an earful of what he and Trey had done in there. *Oops. Better for Trey to never learn about that.*

"I didn't know there was a meeting," he whispered back.

Quinn climbed down with Jase's help and the two came over to huddle in a tight circle. "That's because Alex and the others have decided to keep us in the dark."

"Seriously?"

Quinn nodded. "Ever since I agreed to take classes at community college with you, Alex and I have reconciled, as you know."

Demi did. Quinn had gone back to sleeping in Alex's bed, and Demi was surprised to find that he missed the company. With his virginity gone, that overwhelming need to come every five minutes had left.

"So, I didn't find it too weird that he encouraged me to dance more over the last couple of days until I realized that there were closed-door meetings going on. That got my suspicions going. Even during our epic fight, he still insisted I stick close. He's never shut me out of his office before. When I asked him about it, he distracted me by fucking me silly." He rolled his eyes and shook his head.

Now, Demi understood how that could happen. He was able to join in with the others with playful sympathy.

"Anyway," Mackie picked up the thread, "Quinn told Jase and me and we've both tried to ply information out of our men. Val strapped me to the Saint Andrew's Cross and that was that." He looked at Jase.

"Emil baked me my favorite cake, Black Forest. I forget my own name with that inside me. Oh, then I had Emil inside me."

Everyone sighed in appreciation. Demi wished he'd known, except he hadn't seen Trey since their time in this very room. "Is my man in there now?" he asked, liking that he could refer to the cop that way, at least among this group.

"He is," Mackie confirmed. "We've been trying to hear what's going on, but none of us can, not even me with my enhanced senses. We're hoping you'll have better luck."

Without any further coaxing, Demi broke away and leaped onto the table. He pressed his ear against the vent and opened up his hearing to the maximum. Murmuring came through that got clearer the more he concentrated. While full sentences were allusive, he heard enough to get the gist — Cadoc, the name of some place and that there was going to be a raid later that night. He listened until the topics turned to fueling and arming up for the fight, then he jumped back down.

Once more, he and the other boys huddled. "It's on for tonight. I know the time and the place and basics about what they're going to do."

He licked his lips as he thought about it. "I know the natural inclination is to follow them, but I propose we leave before instead. We tell them we're having a boy's night out. That will hopefully cause them to put their guard down, because it plays right into their misguided attempt at keeping us safe."

He shook his head. "Those dopes. Haven't we proved that we can take care of ourselves and help?"

The was a general murmur of righteous agreement before Mackie said, "That is diabolical, Demi."

He grinned. "Thanks. I agree, even if I do say so myself."

"Right," Quinn echoed. "Now, we have to plan it out. We need somewhere that the men can't possible overhear us." He peered up at the vent. "The problem is that none of has a private space."

"No," Demi added, "we don't. But there is a place in the building that we can be sure the men won't disturb us—or think about at all, really." He hated doing it. Dafydd's domain was his for a reason. Demi had already breached it and had been lucky to be welcomed. Would the Welshman do the same for the others and help to plan a way to bring down the man's son?

He explained to the others what he meant. "Give me a few minutes. I need to see if it's okay with him."

Surprisingly, Dafydd didn't bat an eye over it. He'd sanctioned the use of his room as a staging area for their machinations. He stood by his window, staring out through a crack in the drapes at the world below. It was only when the boys had finished and were heading out to change into nicer clothing to make their story more believable that Dafydd brought the hammer down.

"I'm coming with you, then."

Startled, everyone froze and turned to stare at him.

It was up to Demi to say what they were all thinking. "That's probably not such a great idea."

Dafydd pulled back from the curtains. "You think so? Why? To protect me the way the men here are doing for you?"

Ouch, hoisted on my own petard. "Well, um…it's kind of different, isn't it? You've been so isolated and to go out for this? Plus," Demi added dropping his gaze. "You know how this is going to end for your son."

"Cadoc is Dracul's in every way. He is a monster who will do monstrous things until he's stopped. Please don't worry on my account. I-I need to do this for my own sanity. I won't interfere." He huffed out a laugh. "It's not like I'm going to try to save him or anything."

That actually hadn't occurred to Demi. It did now, except he'd come to know Dafydd quite well first in Wales, then in this very room. He couldn't imagine that this damaged man would really do anything to perpetuate the misery Dracul had started.

"No, of course you won't. And you have as much right as any of us to come." He didn't dare look at the others as he spoke for them all. No one disputed him, however.

In fact, Mackie said, "You know, in a way, it gives us more cover. What's better than us helping Dafydd go out in the world?"

Dafydd's lips quirked. "That settles it, then." He looked down his front. "I don't think I'm dressed right for it, though."

"That's okay. I have something you can borrow from when I was younger and shorter. Come back to my room with me." Dafydd hesitated, and it took Demi a moment to realize why he might not want to do that. "Or, I can bring it to you."

Dafydd shook his head. "No, it's fine. I'll come."

And that was that. None of the others said anything other than hasty goodbyes and promises to meet down in the garage in an hour. Mackie was taking them out in his vehicle so that they would have maximum flexibility of going where and when they wanted. And, they really did need to go out and eat, given how early they were leaving. Demi could only hope that Dafydd wouldn't freak out during what was likely his first experience in a restaurant.

They all scattered, once in the hall, Demi electing to take the stairs up to his family suite, Dafydd on his heels. When they entered, their luck turned because there was Dad pacing the living room with a fretting Idris. He stopped the second he spied them and rocked side-to-side.

"Hello, Dafydd. It's good to see you. Have you come...?"

"He's here to try on clothes, Dad," Demi jumped in because he could see the color rising on Dafydd's cheeks. The man was flustered and getting upset. They didn't need the extra drama.

The man surprised him. "Is he...? Is he all right, then?" he asked with a nod toward the baby.

Dad gave him a gentle smile. "He's teething. That's all."

"Oh."

Demi thought Dafydd might actually go to the child, but no, he stood there, not looking at his son anymore or saying anything.

"All right, let's go look in my closet." Taking Dafydd by the elbow, he steered him around the living room and into his bedroom.

He swung the doors to the walk-in wide and stepped into the jungle of clothing. "Let's see what might fit." He went farther in to where his older stuff was tucked away.

Dafydd didn't follow him immediately, however. He stood staring in the direction of the living room, as though he could see through the walls. Demi thought he might go back, but then with a slight shudder, he turned in Demi's direction and joined him.

* * * *

"This is a fire lane, Mackie," Quinn said from the back seat. "You can't park here."

"I'm not. We're merely sitting."

"I don't think a cop will appreciate that distinction."

"It's a risk we have to take. This is the only spot where we can see the entrance to that pub without also being easily seen by our men. We don't want to fuck up their plans because they abort to get us back to 'safety', like the overprotective jerks that they are."

Mackie was right. It was still risky given that it was late and the crowds in the area had thinned significantly. They had had hours to kill while waiting, lingering over their dinner. They had chosen seafood, at Demi's suggestion. It was food Dafydd was familiar with, and the guy had weathered his first time in a restaurant with surprising ease. Maybe centuries of keeping up with Dracul's capriciousness had left him quick to adapt to any situation. Regardless, he seemed to enjoy himself, albeit in an almost silent way. He sat quite still between Quinn and Jase.

A familiar figure approached the pub, catching Demi's attention. He leaned forward to stare out of the windshield. "Hey, it's Dr. Paz."

Mackie hummed. "So it is. Was he supposed to be part of the plan?"

"I didn't hear anything about him, but then again, I came into the middle of the conversation. He must be, though. No way it's a coincidence, and he's on our side, isn't he?"

"Of course he is, mun." Dafydd's voice brooked no argument. "He's a good man, make no mistake, and he shouldn't be in harm's way. Not again. What are they thinking?"

And just like that, Demi understood how much Dafydd was one of them.

* * * *

Trey checked his watch. It had been ten minutes since Paz had entered the pub. Trey turned to glare at a sweaty Murphy, who sat in the back seat with Karl. "You're up. I'm sure I don't have to remind you how important it is for you not to fuck up. It's the difference between seeing the light of day again as a free man before you die and not."

The lawyer tugged at his collar. "I understand. No need to be vicious about it."

Trey bared his teeth. "And there was no need for you to brutalize vulnerable boys, but here we are, heh?"

"Come on," Karl said, opening the door and dragging Murphy by the arm.

The moment they left the car, Trey hopped out and sprinted over to the SUV where the Stelalux men were positioned. When he opened the door, he could hear Karl's voice over the monitoring device Val had rigged him with. The sunglasses dress code worked in their favor. Val had already had a pair rigged for this kind of surveillance. Once inside the vehicle, Trey could see the video feed on the dashboard screen, as well.

Karl, bless his little heart, was reinforcing the rules on Murphy as they headed into the pub. It was nearly closing time, except that the private club could stay open as long as it liked. That would give them a chance to conduct the raid with as few humans around as possible. The place was already fairly empty, from what Trey could see. Karl positioned himself to catch sight of Paz. The doctor sat at the bar, sipping a beer. He nodded in a particular direction, confirming that Murphy was leading Karl to the right spot.

Trey and the others watched intently as Karl followed over to a bookcase in the corner where a large man wearing a dark suit and sporting sunglasses stood at parade rest. This was another bit of luck. According to Murphy, this was the man who had engaged him. As far as the lawyer knew, it was this mere human named Kevin Fuchs, who ran the show. And Fuchs had a long list of arrests and convictions for vice-related activities and violent offenses. It made him the perfect fall guy.

Cadoc had helped them in being smarter than they'd anticipated. Because he'd kept to the shadows, when they turned him to dust, no one would worry about the lack of a body. Everyone would accept that Fuchs was their guy, at least where the prostitution ring was concerned. The scary man with the scarred face had been the dupe who fronted the operation and acted as the enforcer who ran the boys and even killed when needed. Too bad he'd gotten away, but at least the head man would be behind bars. That story wrote itself, thank fuck.

Of course, there would never be legal closure for the murders of Father Ted and Umi. Although everyone would accept that the guy who'd escaped was the killer, he wouldn't be caught. The cases would stay open, a mark against all concerned. Yet, Trey couldn't bring himself to frame even a fucker like Fuchs for crimes he hadn't committed.

Karl and Murphy stopped in front of Fuchs. "Good evening." The lawyer's voice sounded almost normal. "This is, ah…a good friend of mine. He's here as my guest."

Fuchs' expression remained stony, although it was hard to tell his expression with those glasses hiding half his face. "I see. He understands the rules."

"Naturally." This was where Murphy's natural defensiveness helped their cause. His indignant tone sealed the deal.

Without further comment, Fuchs activated a hidden device and a narrow section of the bookcase opened. Then the men descended a narrow, winding staircase into an underground world decorated like an eighteenth-century brothel. At least, that was Trey's impression. There was a lot of red velvet and black lace, plus disturbingly young and pretty boys scantily dressed. Some wore frilly girl-type lingerie, others were more obviously masculine. It was like something out of a movie, an echo of Club Lux, except there boys were all of legal age and anything they did with the members was purely voluntary and entirely of their own making.

Plus, however alien Alex and his 'family' were, they weren't monsters. The same couldn't be said about the hulking figure sitting in a large, high-backed and overstuffed chair in the corner. Like a gargoyle, Cadoc presided over the large room with a boy sprawled on his lap. No, impaled on the creature's dick. The boy's eyes were at half-mast, probably high on something. He reminded Trey of Umi, who then reminded him of Demi. Cadoc had a type, apparently.

Those thoughts caused him to mutter his concerns out loud. "Are we sure the boys are safe tonight?" He hadn't liked learning that they had all gone out for the evening.

"Relax, Duncan," Val said from the passenger seat up front. "They're on a mission to help Dafydd adjust to society. They're probably back at the club by now."

"They are going to be very pissed off when they find out what we did," Emil observed.

"They'll get over it," Alex replied.

Trey wasn't convinced about that. He had a feeling the men were going to have some lonely nights in their future. As did he, but that was nothing new. And once this was over, he could take the time to figure out how he wanted to handle the Demi situation.

A moment later, all thoughts of the boy fled when Cadoc turned his dead-eye stare in Karl's direction. This was the risk they had to take. After the fight in the underground T storage room, the hybrid would know Trey. The hope was that he'd never had the chance to see Karl in any setting that would out Karl as a cop.

"That's the bouncer," Murphy said in a low voice. "Good luck with him. He makes Fuchs look like a pussy cat."

"You let us worry about that," Karl replied. A boy came up to flirt with him. Trey could only imagine how hard it was for Karl to keep in character. "Sure," he said, "I'm up for a party, but my friend and I want to stick together. You know, a foursome?"

"Anything you want, big guy," the boy cooed. "Right this way."

Karl allowed himself to be tugged away but managed to keep his camera positioned so that they could watch Cadoc. Then Paz left the pub and came over as the rest of them were piling out.

"I count twenty or so people, including the staff, still inside the bar and restaurant area," the doctor said as he took the seat vacated by Emil. "I have no idea what the kitchen situation is, though."

"That's my job," Emil assured him before shutting the door.

"Thank you, doctor, for you excellent help this evening. Please wait here and lock up." Alex got out to join the others.

Trey popped his head back inside before shutting the door. "Hey, doc, I thought you might want to know that Dafydd went out tonight with the boys. They had dinner or something. Good sign, huh?"

Paz's face lit up. "Yes, very. Thanks."

Now, Trey really put everything out of his mind except checking one final time that his gun was loaded. He palmed his badge and, letting the aliens enter first, followed them into the pub. They'd planned out their movements carefully. Alex and Val raced straight toward Fuchs, restraining him before he could activate any warning system in place. Emil headed for the kitchen, while Harry positioned himself in the dining area.

Trey held up his badge. "Everyone, if I could please have your attention. This is a police raid. I need everyone to leave the premises now, please, patrons and employees alike. No need to run, but don't dawdle. Forget your bills and tabs, too. It's all on the house tonight."

No one moved at first, surprise causing them to hesitate. And in the age of the Internet, they might have even thought it was some kind of prank. "Now!" he repeated in a louder and sterner voice.

A herd of employees fled the kitchen, as well, courtesy of Emil, who was shooing them from behind as if they were a gaggle of geese. That also helped get everyone moving, and Harry was guiding them along like a flight attendant, as if finding the door would be too hard for the humans. Satisfied that those men had the evacuation under control, Trey pocketed his badge and pulled out his gun. He followed Alex and Val as they frog-marched Fuchs down the stairs.

There were screams now from the boys and cries of alarm from the patrons. Unlike the legitimate pub customers, these guys knew what a raid meant to them. Trey planted himself at the foot of the stairs to stop any escaping. Across the room, Karl disentangled himself from a boy and pulled out his own badge and gun.

Trey took the whole room in a glance. He saw a short hallway at the far end. "Karl, check whatever rooms might be down there and flush out the occupants."

Then he turned his attention to the main show. Having knocked out Fuchs, Alex and Val had Cadoc cornered. They couldn't take a shot, however, because the fucker had the boy from his lap held up in front of him by his armpits. The kid was so strung out, he didn't even struggle—or maybe he'd learned not to fight back.

Regardless, he made an effective shield as Cadoc kept the boy between him and his enemies' fatal bullets.

Trey ran to join them, hoping to find an opening. Cadoc was quick, his movements almost a blur as he backed away to a spot behind his chair. Then, in the blink of an eye, he tossed the boy at them and disappeared.

It was Val who caught the kid and gently lay him on the floor before the three of them took off after Cadoc. No surprise there was a secret escape route. As Trey followed the aliens into the dark, mustiness and mildew assailed his nostrils. He stumbled in everyone's wake, his human eyes at a disadvantage until he thought to take out his phone and turn on the light. The others were already out of sight around a bend in the old brick tunnel. He pressed forward as fast as he could.

Chapter Twelve

Demi watched the humans flee the club, his heart in this throat now that the assault on Cadoc's lair had begun. He hated not knowing what was happening to Trey. He was so vulnerable compared to the rest of them. As much as he trusted Alex and the others to keep his man safe, he also knew that their first priority would always be ridding the world of Dracul's evil son.

"I wish we could go inside," Demi lamented to no one in particular.

"Why don't we?" Jase asked. When they all turned to look at him, he shrugged. "We could help with the boys, just like we did in Wales. Right? There must be some. That's the whole point, isn't it?"

Demi shared a look with Mackie before they broke out into a grin. "Brilliant! Why didn't we think of that?" he asked Mackie.

The boy shrugged. "And here I thought Jase was the quiet one. You go, girl," he teased before getting out. Quinn and Jase also jumped out, and the three of them sprinted toward the pub's front door.

Before joining him, Demi looked at Dafydd. "You should probably wait here."

The Welshman nodded, his expression unreadable. "Yes, all right. Be careful, like."

"I will."

Demi started after the others when a flash of movement caught his eye. Out of a narrow back alley charged a large, dark figure. Although he'd never seen Cadoc before, a hybrid knew his own kind. It took no time for the import of the situation to assemble in his mind. There had been an escape route and Cadoc had managed to use it before the others could stop him. Demi refused to believe it meant that Trey was somehow incapacitated. He couldn't allow himself to think that or he'd end up curled in a ball of fear.

So, he did the only thing that made sense to him. He abruptly changed direction and ran headlong at the beast.

* * * *

As the pub patrons hurried out and away, Ric sat drumming his fingers on his thigh and feeling useless. He hadn't wanted to get involved in another fight between these alien factions, yet he was in too deep to ignore what was going on. It had been easy, as well, to simply sit and nurse a beer until Anderson came in with that sleaze-ball lawyer. With a nod to confirm that they were heading in the right direction, and not into a trap, his job had been done. No one would fault him if he got out and simply went home.

No one other than himself. *What if someone gets hurt?* Those abused boys downstairs might need immediate medical help, and sure, Harry was in there, but he could only do so much at once. He had to stay, except the SUV was too small to contain his nervous energy. Stepping out, he stretched and scanned the area.

That's when he saw Dafydd. The Welshman had come out, as Duncan had said, but he wasn't at a restaurant or any other place that was safe. No, he was running toward the back of the building.

Ric didn't even question himself as he took off after him.

* * * *

Although he was going at a speed faster than he should for a human, Demi felt as if he were in slow motion. He could almost see his own death in the hulking form he was on a collision course with, not that Demi had any intention of dying, nor did he think he could overpower Cadoc.

Slow him down until the others arrive.

That was his goal. He merely had to turn into an immovable object, keeping Cadoc from escaping. It was hard to keep going, however. Seeing him, the fucker twisted his scarred face into a sneer and seemed to pick up his pace.

Demi's heart skipped a beat, but he continued. Visions of Trey wounded and in need of help egged him forward. He put his head down and poured on a burst of speed at the last moment. It was like hitting a brick wall. He knew it would be, although the shock of it nevertheless scrambled his brain. Fortunately, all he needed was his muscle and he used it to impede Cadoc.

The asshole barely grunted at the contact. He grabbed Demi's arms with his meaty fingers, digging into the flesh with sufficient force to cause Demi to cry out.

When Cadoc tried to swing him out of the way, Demi leaped up and wrapped his legs around the guy's waist. He hung on like a rhesus monkey, no matter how fast or hard Cadoc moved to toss him off.

That was until the guy pushed him against the alley wall, causing Demi's head to hit the hard surface. His vision winked out and his limbs went limp. He fell off his enemy and slid down to the ground. He managed to pry open his eyes in time to see the muzzle of a gun pointed at him.

"Trey." He whispered his lover's name one more time, knowing that he'd failed his man because Trey would never forgive himself for this ending.

* * * *

Dafydd's steps faltered at the sight of his son slamming Demi against a wall. The boy, who had been so kind to him at the risk of his own life, fell like a ragdoll onto the ground. That wasn't enough for Cadoc, though. Like his viciously cruel father, he wasn't content with defeating his enemy. He had to annihilate him.

He watched him raise his gun, saw him aim it at Demi's head and acted without thought. After months of proper food and care, Dafydd was able to tap into a strength he hadn't really understood he possessed. Dracul's blood and done more than make him ready to bear children. It made everything about his body better and faster. He was upon his son before the monster could pull the trigger.

Uttering the battle cry of his youth, he slammed into Cadoc's arm. The surprise attack did the trick. His son let go of the weapon, and it went flying away. Cadoc countered by shoving Dafydd aside. He landed face-forward, scraping his hands and knees against the pavement. He ignored the bite of pain and lunged for the gun that had landed a few feet away. He grabbed it and rolled up to a kneeling position.

Cadoc stood sneering down at him. "Why, father, what a surprise! You survived my brother's birth, I see. I hope you killed the brat. There's really no room in this world for more of Dracul's sons. Bran is a thorn in my side, as it is."

He cocked his head and took a step forward. "Are you Alex's slut now? You never were good for anything more than taking a strong man's cock." He laughed as Dafydd raised the gun. "You'd better give me that before you hurt yourself." He held out his hand.

Dafydd had to use both of his to steady the weapon. A well of painful emotion overtook him, making his shake. There was no choice, though. There was only one thing that he could do. He had to be strong, for Demi and the others. For all of humanity — and even for Idris.

"If there is a God, I hope He can forgive me."

Then he pulled the trigger.

* * * *

"Jesus, fucking Christ," Trey fumed, "find the damn lever."

"Not helping," Alex retorted as he felt along what looked like a solid wall at the end of the tunnel. Val threw his weight against it in the meantime. "That's not helping, either. Even you can't force bricks and mortar to move."

There was nowhere to pace in the narrow space, so Trey stood there, slowly losing his mind. Cadoc was getting away. Maybe they could track him by scent, but in this part of town, there were still cabs and private cars for Cadoc to escape in. Why hadn't they waited and scoped out the area more? They might have realized there was a back exit to the place. They'd been too anxious to move against Cadoc before he brutalized more boys and possibly ramped up his criminal acts. And this was the price they were paying for their haste. After so many centuries of fighting, the aliens could be forgiven their desperate efforts to end it. Trey couldn't be so easy on himself.

There was a click. "Got it."

Alex and Val went out ahead of him, but when the shot rang out, Trey shoved them aside. If there was to be a confrontation out in the open, he wanted to be front and center. He was still a cop and this was his city. When he rounded the corner, he tripped to a stop from the shocking sight.

Dafydd knelt beside a pile of clothing, weeping uncontrollably and raking ashes through his fingers. Paz stood behind him, his hands on Dafydd's shoulders, giving silent comfort. But it was the crumpled form against the wall that finally had him racing forward again.

He shoved his gun in his holster as he yelled. "Demi!" He skidded against the wall before dropping beside the boy.

Demi blinked back at him and smiled. "You're all right?"

"Of course the fuck I am. *You're* not." As carefully as he could, he pulled Demi into his arms and felt for wounds. His hand came back bloody when he touched the boy's head.

Trey's heart skipped a beat. "You're hurt."

Demi winced. "I hit my head when Cadoc shoved me into the wall."

"Paz, Demi needs you."

The doctor looked at him with a conflicted expression.

"No," Demi insisted. "Dafydd needs him more. He, um, killed Cadoc. He's the one who shot him. His own son. I can't imagine how he feels."

Neither could Trey. The Welshman was obviously distressed, his sobs quieter now, yet still heartbreaking. He stood with Demi in his arms. "I'll take you to your father."

"Good God," Alex exclaimed. "Don't tell me all of the boys are here."

Demi curled into Trey's embrace. "Okay, I won't."

"It's fine. Don't worry about it." Trey hugged him closer. "You can berate him later, Alex. He needs tending to."

"I'll leave that chore to you, Duncan. I have my own boy to deal with. Val, clean this up, if you will. I need to go back inside and see what kind of mess we've made. Join me when you can."

"Sure thing, boss. Do me a favor and find some rope in that place and tie Mackie up in a nice bow for me."

"It will be my pleasure. Dr. Paz," he said, turning directions, "would you please take Dafydd to our vehicle? Remaining here isn't going to do him or the situation any good."

"Certainly." He tugged at Dafydd's shoulders. "Come with me now. There's nothing more for you to do."

After a slight resistance, Dafydd stumbled to his feet. Ash fell from his grasp to litter the ground. Then the man slid into Paz's embrace and allowed the doctor to take him away.

"I think they're falling in love," Demi murmured.

"Yeah, I think that, too. Come on. Let's find your father."

"I'm fine."

"You damn well better be." He huffed out his frustration and his fear. "What am I going to do with you, Demi?"

"Marry me and make yours forever and ever."

Trey chuckled, surprised he had any mirth inside him at the moment. "Yeah, that might be what I'm going to have to do."

* * * *

"I can walk on my own, Papa, really." Demi tried to slip from under his father's embrace as they entered the elevator.

"Let me be the judge of that. I promised Sergeant Duncan I would take good care of you."

"I wish I could have stayed with him."

"Now, now, you know that wasn't possible. None of us could. With Cadoc dead, this has become a purely human operation. Our continued presence will only make matters harder for him and Detective Anderson."

"I suppose."

Papa chuckled as they arrived at their floor and got off. "If you intend to make a life with this man, you must accept what that entails. I suspect you will have to get used to spending many nights waiting for him to come home."

"I don't like the idea of how vulnerable he is. Do you think it's possible that if I feed him my blood, he might change a little? Not to have babies or anything, but perhaps to be stronger and live longer."

"It's possible. I will look into it, if you wish."

He pressed his head onto his father's shoulder. "Thank you, Papa. For everything—rescuing Dad, giving me to Trey, trusting that when I said I wanted him, I meant it."

"There are no thanks necessary, my son. I love your father with all my heart and I have always known you were smart enough to make up your own mind. I could see through the brat you pretended to be."

His past behavior hadn't been an act, exactly, but there was no point in saying so. He wasn't anymore, and that was all that mattered.

Before they reached their door, Dafydd stepped out from the stairwell, Dr. Paz hovering by his side. Both of them looked whipped, Dafydd's eyes still red from crying his heart out. So were his hands where he'd skidded across the pavement, although they had already started to heal, thanks to the residual effect of Dracul's blood.

"I'm sorry to intrude," Dafydd said in a soft voice. "I was wondering if it would be all right if I...if I see Idris," he finished after Paz gave him an encouraging smile.

Papa paused then smiled. "Of course. Come in."

As Papa ushered their guest into the suite, Demi felt him stiffen, on alert. That made Demi do so as well. Having killed one son, why did Dafydd want to see another one? After rejecting his baby for so long, what was he going to do? Surely, he wasn't going to try to hurt him. Demi couldn't imagine such a thing, yet he'd been surprised as well when Dafydd had pulled the trigger back in the alley.

Dad was sitting on the couch with Idris, a bottle in his hand. He focused on Demi first, frowning and shaking his head, yet saying nothing. Then he turned his attention onto Dafydd and Paz.

"Welcome. Please come in and have a seat. Can I get you anything to drink?"

"No, thank you," Paz replied.

"I'm fine as I am, thank you," Dafydd said, and approached the couch slowly. Paz hovered beside him the whole way. Dafydd sat next to Dad. "I was wondering, if you don't mind. I would like to hold him."

"Idris?" Dad glanced over at Papa, who nodded once. "Certainly. He's your son, after all."

As Dad passed the baby over, Papa led Demi to a chair and sat him down. He remained standing, though, just in case he needed to move quickly. He needn't have bothered.

Dafydd held his son as if he were made of glass. At first anyway, before slowly easing back with the baby on his lap. They stared at one another.

"I'm your *tad*," Dafydd said, "but we're in America now so I suppose you should call me 'dad' instead." He said a few more things in Welsh, Demi assumed, all those weird-sounding twisting consonants.

"Here." Dad passed over the bottle. "He was about to eat."

Dafydd smiled and cuddled Idris in the crook of his arm while feeding him. "You're going to be different," he told his son, "not like the other ones." He looked over at Demi. "You don't have to be evil if you're raised right."

Thank you, Demi mouthed and sat back to watch the happy scene and dream of one day having his own family.

* * * *

"Duncan, you fucker."

Trey winced as he turned to face a furious Craig striding down the hall. "Hey, Craig, I was about to call you."

"The hell you were."

"The hell I was. This is your case now. My killer got away, so this is purely a vice operation."

That took a little of the wind out of his sails. "You were supposed to keep me in the loop."

"Yeah, about that, sorry. Things took off all of a sudden." He nodded at the interview room he'd left. "I had to act quickly, and like I said, the boss of the prostitution ring, Fuchs, is inside there while the guy who killed Father Ted and the kid, Umi, got out via a back route to the building they were using."

The lack of a collar on the murder was going to bite him and Karl hard in the ass. Couldn't be helped. It wasn't possible to book a pile of ashes. "The asshole insists that the guy who got away was the boss, but the lawyer says otherwise, and this Fuchs has a compelling record."

He sighed. "Look... Anderson is writing up his report and will email it to you shortly. I'll do the same. Any questions, you know how to get a hold of me. In the meantime, I have to keep searching for my killer."

Craig blew out a breath. "Yeah, okay. Thanks, I guess. I hear it was a high-class place with more than a few prominent members going down."

"Start practicing your smile for the cameras, buddy." He started to walk away. Craig stopped him.

"Hey, Trey?"

"Yeah?"

"I was a moron to chase you away. I should have known what I had."

"That's okay. Really. If you hadn't, I wouldn't have realized what I was missing."

"You've found the right man, have you?"

Boy. No, Demi was a man. Man-boy, maybe. God, it's complicated. "I've found love."

"Good, I'm glad."

"Me, too." As he walked away, he saw his path forward clearly for the first time. It wasn't going to be easy, but then again, Demi was worth any effort.

* * * *

"Here it is." Trey stepped aside to let Demi pass and enter his half of the duplex.

He'd spent most of his first day off since the raid cleaning his apartment to within an inch of its life. His mother would be so proud if she were to see it, which she wasn't, not while Trey courted Demi. It was too soon for family introductions.

"It's not much," he said, closing the door.

Demi made the circuit of the open space that served as dining and living room. The scent of the lasagna Trey had put into the oven before going to pick up Demi lent a homey air to the place. It was still a far cry from the luxury Demi had grown up with.

"It's lovely." Demi shot him a shy smile.

Trey tugged at his ear. "Yeah well, it's mostly second-hand stuff. I'm not exactly the decorating type."

"Oh, Trey!" Demi flitted over and threw his arms around him. He pressed a sweet kiss on his lips. "You don't have to impress me. I love your home because it's where you are. I don't need much, really."

"Says the kid wearing clothing worth my one month's salary."

"I will gladly donate all of my things to Goodwill."

Trey shook his head. "No, I don't want you to change for me. I know how much you love dressing up. I just can't afford to give those things to you, but your family can for now. Eventually, if you want, you can earn a high salary as a doctor. I'm not so pig-headed and macho that it will bother me if you make more money."

Demi's eyes went wide. "Why, Trey, is that a proposal?"

He squirmed under the scrutiny. "That's me taking baby steps, Demi. I'm just saying that I don't want you to worry about my ego."

Demi couldn't hide his disappointment. "Oh, okay. What's for dinner?" he asked, letting go. "It smells wonderful."

Trey resisted the urge to drag him back and kiss him senseless. "Lasagna. Come into the kitchen."

He led him through the open doorway and over to the oven. The timer was about to go off, so he stopped it then, grabbing mittens, took the casserole out. The cheese and tomato sauce bubbled.

Demi leaned over. "Mmm, can't wait to try it. Can I see your bedroom first?" he asked coyly.

Being a mere man, Trey assented without a fight. He made sure to turn off the stove before clasping hands and tugged Demi down the short hallway.

The moment they entered his bedroom, Demi jumped him. He held Trey tight with both arms and legs and attacked his mouth. Trey didn't muster much of a fight as his lover used his lips and tongue. He matched the boy's fervor while carrying him over to the bed. They toppled down and wrestled with flailing body parts.

He inhaled Demi, sweeping every corner of his mouth and lunging his tongue down his throat. As they thrashed, they tugged at each other's clothing. Trey kicked off his trainers and rolled Demi onto his back in order to rip open his shirt. Buttons popped — again — although this time, more expensive ones. He didn't care because it gave him access to all that smooth, tasty skin. He broke the kiss to lick a stripe instead from Demi's belly button to his nipples before latching on to one nub and sucking.

Demi cried out and arched his back. Their hands clashed when each of them worked the other's pants open. Trey got there first, exposing Demi's hard dick. He grabbed it and tugged while scraping his teeth along the nipple. Demi dropped his hands away, fisting the bedding. A few drops of pre-cum dribbled out, easing the movements of Trey's fist.

He lapped back down the flat stomach, flicked the cockhead peeping out from his fingers, before rearing back. He needed both hands to get those tight skinny jeans off his slender boy. Gentleness flew out the window in his rush to get Demi naked. He tossed everything away before diving in to suck Demi's shaft into his mouth.

"Trey!" Demi bucked, sending his cock all the way down. "No fair," he wailed as Trey swallowed convulsively. "I wanted to do that to you first and…" He screamed as he came.

Trey stayed with him through the orgasm, although it wasn't easy. Demi thrashed and rolled, his cum spilling out in warm spurts that filled Trey's mouth faster than he could handle. It dribbled past his lips, even as he licked and sucked. But he kept to it, even when he choked, until Demi lay whimpering and trembling.

Trey pulled up and grinned at the wanton display on his bed. Here was his boy, his lover, boneless with his release from Trey's efforts. He could picture Demi lying in this bed for the rest of their life together. That image and thought didn't scare him so much anymore.

Already, though, Demi's cock was hardening to stiff mast again. Trey tore off his own clothing, freeing himself and taking a few strokes to appease his dick. When he knelt naked over Demi, he clasped the boy's rod and slowly jerked it. He wiggled two fingers of his free hand under Demi's firm ass. They slid into his hole with ease.

Natural lubrication. Amazing. It would make their sex life delightfully easy. He thrust the fingers in a few times, crooking them on the way out to tease Demi's prostate. How wonderful that the aliens had one. Demi stared up at him with pupils that had turned black as night. His puffy lips were parted as he panted and moaned.

"Fuck me, Trey."

The demand made his cock jerk. He squeezed Demi's hard enough to make him squeak before letting him go to rearrange their legs. Then he had Demi's pushed wide with knees bent, leaving space for Trey to slide into. Grabbing Demi's cock again, he lined up his own against the puckered hole. He pushed shallowly so that only his head was gripped by that tight ring. He stayed still, savoring the feel of the tightness against the sensitive nerves of his glans.

Demi clenched him. "Come on. All the way in."

Trey groaned loud and long as he slid balls-deep into his lover. The exquisitely snug channel welcomed him with undulating waves. He dropped down to brace himself with one hand, while still working Demi's shaft with the other. Then he did what only a short time ago would have been inconceivable, but now felt perfectly normal—he bent his head to offer his jugular.

Demi struck with lightning speed.

It was better than before. Demi would have expected that nothing could top that first night together. But as Trey drilled his ass and Demi tugged at his vein, the pleasure topped anything he'd experienced. This was love, not duty or even animal need. His man was claiming his body while feeding him his life's blood. Demi's heart soared with the intensity of his emotions and his mind floated blissfully from the blood sliding down his throat.

He came again in a longer, slower ride than the urgent climax from before. He wormed his body up against Trey's, pressing their chests together. Then he encircled Trey's ass with his legs and kicked him into higher gear. Always a smart man, his lover picked up speed, driving his cock deeper into Demi's still-demanding channel. When Trey stiffened and flooded Demi's ass with hot cum, he joined him with a quick third climax that nevertheless left him huffing against Trey's skin.

He retracted his fangs just in time before Trey collapsed on top of him. Demi reveled at the feel of the dead weight pressing him into the soft bedding. It was typically Trey, a simple blue color, utilitarian like the rest of the apartment. As he lay there wrapped around his man, he wondered how quickly he could steer Trey into blinging the place up a little.

Eventually, Trey rolled away. "Sorry, kid. I don't mean to squash you, but you do wear an old man out."

Demi swatted him on the chest. "Don't say that. You aren't old, and maybe there's a way of helping things slow down, actually." He hadn't intended to bring this topic up yet, but Trey had given him an opportunity.

Trey opened one eye. "Yeah?"

Demi slid onto his side, laying his head on one palm. "Um, yes. I mean, I spoke with Papa about it. He says it's possible that drinking my blood could help make you stronger and healthier. It might extend your life, too. If you want, that is. I totally get it if you don't."

He couldn't look Trey in the eye afterward, fearing he'd pushed too far too soon. He busied himself tracing invisible patterns on the man's chest with a fingertip. "I like the contrast between our skin tones," he remarked when the silence dragged on.

Trey placed his hand over Demi's. "So do I. You know that my mother is black and my father is white?"

"I guess. I haven't really thought about it. It makes no difference to me, except," he added with wide eyes, "does this mean I'm going to meet your family?"

"Eventually. I'm going to tell you all about them, and me, because really, Demi, you know next to nothing."

"I know all I need to." He started to sit up. Grabbing him, Trey tumbled him onto his chest. With a smile, Demi allowed himself to be captured and held.

"Not by human standards. We need time to get to really know each other. That means dating, meals like tonight, movies, museums even. It's not all about sex, you know?"

"Hm-m. But this is such an awesome part of it." He kissed one pec before swirling his tongue around Trey's nipple the way the cop had done to Demi. Trey's sharp inhale of breath made it worth doing again.

"I need time, Demi." Trey was beginning to sound breathless.

"Uh-huh." He wiggled out of the embrace to press opened-mouthed kisses all along Trey's chest.

"A good two years. My, uh, family will still see you as too young, but I figure it will help." He grunted when Demi scraped his teeth down the ridges on Trey's six pack.

"I understand," Demi assured him, because he could wait that long and also figured if he could get Trey down from ten to two, the two was negotiable as well.

"Good." Trey grunted again and his torso lifted up enough to make Demi's head bounce. He followed that thin trail of dark hair down to the man's spent cock. "I'm not going to be ready for a while for another round. Sorry. Perhaps we should eat."

"Okay."

Demi didn't pull away, however. Instead, he kept going, running his tongue around the sticky head. He tasted what must be himself and didn't care. He placed more open-mouthed kisses down the shaft. He sucked on Trey's big balls while tracing his hole with one finger.

"Stick it in," Trey commanded and lifted his ass a little, as if there were any doubt of what he meant.

Demi was careful to wet his finger first before sliding it into a tight heat that gobbled him up. He kept playing with the dick, fucking Trey's hole, scratching at his prostate until the cock rallied to a nice stiffness. Pulling out and letting go, he straddled Trey's wide pelvis and sat on his dick. He didn't even try to hide the breathy moan as he filled himself with his lover's cock.

"What were you saying about eating dinner?" He smirked down at his man.

Trey growled. "Never mind. Get that pretty ass moving."

Demi happily complied, using his extraterrestrial speed to rip another orgasm out of Trey. He flung out his hands and came in great spurts over Trey's stomach from the fucking alone. He felt like he did when he was dancing on the pole, free and happy, and putting on a show, only now it was for an audience of one. It would be that way for the rest of their lives together.

He sprawled down with a laugh. "Oh God, Trey, I love you so much."

Trey held him tightly before tugging up his head for a slow, yet passionate kiss. "I love you, too, Demi," he said when it ended. "It scares me silly how much."

"There's nothing to be afraid of. I may be half alien, but my love and devotion is as human as yours."

"I don't doubt you, baby. It's me I worry about." Trey closed his eyes briefly. "And I want as much time with you as possible. If your father thinks my drinking your blood will give me more, then I'm willing to try it."

"You don't have to for me."

"I have to for myself, baby." He eased Demi off, breaking the connection of his deflated cock with Demi's ass. "Hold on a minute."

He scooted off the bed and went over to his dresser. Demi stretched wide while he lay there watching. Trey returned with a little box in his hand. Demi's heart tripped when he recognized that it was for a ring.

Trey knelt beside him and opened it up. Inside was an oval swirled with purple, turquoise and gold and set in a silver-colored metal. Demi rocketed to a sitting position.

"This is heather set in white gold. Nothing expensive, but I'd be pleased if you would wear it."

"Oh, Trey!" He placed his right hand over his heart while extending his left.

Before he slipped it onto Demi's ring finger, Trey said, "Now, understand this is a sort of friendship ring. I'm a little too old for this kind of thing, but you're not, at least by my estimation." He slipped it on. "It's a promise from me to you that in two years' time, if you haven't changed your mind, I'm going to be replacing this with an engagement ring."

He searched Demi's face. "Okay?"

In way of an answer, Demi shrieked and pulled him down. "I love it!" He held up his hand above Trey's shoulder and admired how it looked on him. "And I will not be changing my mind. I will be changing my name, though."

He pushed Trey onto his back. "Demetrius Duncan. I love the alliteration. Can we get monogrammed towels?"

With a laugh, Trey pulled him in for a kiss. "Baby steps, Demi. School first, then dating — and you know the rest."

"Right." He nodded firmly. "Whatever you say."

"Good, because that includes bowing out of the family fight. No more haring off to confront what's left of Dracul's rebellion. Seeing you in that alley after hearing a gunshot nearly stopped my heart. None of that. Understand?"

Demi gave him an adoring smile, putting all his emotions into that one look. Then, he dropped his gaze. "Yes, sir." Because he didn't want to lie to his almost-fiancé. Love the man as he did, he really had no intention of standing on the side while Trey risked his life.

But there was no reason to even think about that now. Cadoc was dead, and if the others were smart, they'd hide away forever.

"Let's go eat," he said, bouncing off the bed and heading for the door.

"Demi, we're naked."

"I know. Isn't it great?" He raced away, certain his man would chase after him.

And he did.

Epilogue

"My dear, what is going on?"

Lucien turned at the sound of his husband's voice and bowed. He was wearing traditional Thai clothing in a Raj style, although he'd opted for a red jacket to honor Harry's culture, along with black pants, but no socks or shoes. He preferred to be barefooted. It was also reminiscent of their first meeting.

He twirled in a single circle on the dance floor. "Do I please you, husband?"

"Always," Harry replied, glancing around the room as he approached.

"There are no members or boys about. Only the two of us are out here and I'd like to dance, if you please." He nodded at Kitty, who put on his chosen song, *Why* by Shawn Mendes.

Harry gave him that smile that assured Lucien he was treasured. He opened his arms, letting Lucien into his familiar embrace.

He followed his husband's lead, because that had always been their way. Lucien didn't want it differently. From the first moment he'd laid eyes on the man who wasn't human, he'd known that his destiny was to belong to him. Unlike any other man who'd taken Lucien's body without his consent to his constant repulsion, Harry had only ever given him the freedom to choose to be his.

"What is all of this about, my dear? We rarely dance and you hate being in the club."

Lucien nodded in agreement. "That's true. I don't like it down here, but that's only because of its patrons. The space itself is lovely. And after all we've been through lately, I wanted to give us a little time to ourselves. I'm selfish that way."

"You are anything but that. You have always put others before yourself."

With a shrug, Lucien rested his head on Harry's chest. "Perhaps I simply find myself with more time on my hands than I know what to do with now that Demi is learning outside of home and Dafydd is caring for Idris. And, I miss being with only you."

Harry gathered him closer, moving him around the floor in time to the music. "We are classic empty-nesters. You are right. We should take some time for each other. We could go on a trip, if you would like."

"Anything, so long as I'm with you."

He gave them a minute more, enjoying the song and the slow turn around and around. "You know that I love you, do you not, husband?"

Harry held them in place and leaned back to stare at him. "What makes you ask that now, after so long?"

Lucien frowned at finding the right words. "I think perhaps it comes from seeing Dafydd, knowing how he was abused, and also watching Trey struggle with his feelings for Demi, believing him to be too young. I worry, have for all our time together, that you think I gave myself to you out of obligation, not desire."

Harry turned his head away, not looking him in the eye as he answered. "It has been a concern of mine." He did gaze down at him now. "After all that you'd been through, how could I ever be sure you truly wanted me? I would cut out my own heart rather than force you into my bed."

"Hush." Lucien placed his palm against Harry's cheek. "That is exactly what I feared. But you needn't worry over it. I gave myself to you because I fell in love with you."

"Is it love or gratitude, my dear?"

Lucien had to stand on his toes to reach Harry's mouth. "Can't it be both? It started out as one and slipped into the other by the time you claimed me. I schemed for years to make it so. You were very stubborn about it."

Harry turned his head to place a kiss on Lucien's palm. "I had to be sure, and even then, I wasn't fully. I am weak where you are concerned. As much as you submit to me, you have the power to kill me with a single word—no."

"I will never say it," he rushed to reassure his husband. "I love you, Harry. You must never think otherwise. Never doubt how utterly perfect we are for each other. That is what would cause me to die."

Harry's grip tightened in that show of raw power that should have frightened him, yet only served to make him feel cherished and safe. "That won't happen for a long time to come."

"Good, that will leave us plenty of time for sex."

Harry's eyes widened. "Lucien, my dear, how uncharacteristically naughty of you."

"Some of Demi must have rubbed off on me. What are you going to do about it?"

Without saying another word, Harry swooped Lucien up into his arms, as he'd done over a hundred years ago, and carried him away to a place of promise and hope.

Want to see more from this author? Here's a taster for you to enjoy!

Alien Slave Masters: The Captive Pet
Samantha Cayto

Excerpt

"How much is the buy-in?" Rone kept his face neutral, cool and disinterested, as if the answer made no difference to him. He'd been watching his quarry fleece idiots from their credits all evening by cheating at quaz.

The privateer, a male going by the name of Arpell, took his time to respond. Arrogance radiated off him like a stench. While most others in the disreputable male-only relaxation center set in the middle of a far-flung minor space station were likely impressed by the gambler's name, Rone wasn't. He doubted the male truly came from the caste his name implied. Out here, no one really looked too closely at someone's pedigree. You could be anyone you wanted to be, pretend as much as you liked. Rone counted on that ability.

"Five hundred credits," the guy finally barked out. He trained his beady eyes on Rone.

Mother, the male disgusted him and not only because of the cheating and the dubious work the male did. He was also layered in fat, an almost unheard of condition among males of their species and a testament to how

261

much time the gambler spent sitting in his dirty clothes in the rank corner of the place. On a female, extra weight would have been lush and alluring. On a male, it spoke of slovenliness. If Rone weren't so sure of the intel he'd gleaned through contacts around the Empire, he would never have suspected this guy was part of a sophisticated arms smuggling operation.

It didn't matter what the cost of playing was. Rone had credits to spare, courtesy of the government. He waved his wrist unit over the credit register on the wall and sat down on the less than clean pillow across from his opponent. Like the other male, Rone had a role to play in front of everyone else. He'd cultivated his own persona of a privateer out only for himself, no one to fuck around with. As he sat, the leash attached to his belt tugged tight, forcing Preen to follow and sit on its haunches next to Rone.

Rone hated treating his companion with such blatant disregard, but that was also part of the game he played. Preen understood. It hadn't taken long for Rone and the former pet of his mating sister to form an alliance born of loneliness and, on Rone's part, grief. They communicated through mostly hand signals that, again, they'd developed themselves, although Preen understood much of what Rone spoke. The noises that Preen made didn't translate into Travian at all, yet, after a while, the meaning of each sound had also become clear to Rone. Their hand signals allowed more sophisticated communication, however, with the added advantage that no one else understood their meaning.

Before the game began, Rone glanced to the far side of Arpell. Sitting in a tight ball was the male's own pet. Rone recognized the species immediately — a human, a male one at that. Had to be. Even in this backwater place, no one would allow a female pet to be kept openly. With its face hidden within its arms, Rone couldn't see the creature much at all. A curtain of long hair the color of bright starlight covered its head and fell over the arms wrapped tightly around small knees. Rone knew from his experience with his former house brother's pet that humans didn't tolerate Travian temperatures very well. Poor beast. Life with Arpell must be a misery, not that Rone had time to dwell on any sympathy he might feel for the human. He had a job to do.

Grabbing up the quaz pieces strewn before him, he nodded to Arpell. "First move to the dealer."

The male regarded him with barely bridled glee, expecting Rone to be the next easy victim. For a time, Rone allowed himself to be just that, losing a few games and lots of credits. He pretended not to see the sleight of hand, moving pieces out of turn and substituting them with better ones. The effort, while impressive, was not hidden from his keen vision. The other players had either been stupid or chemically compromised — or likely both.

He shook his head over his latest loss and swiped in more credits, as if the large amount he'd already wasted didn't concern him in the least. It got the attention of others in the place, one of the points to the game he played. Whoever supplied arms to the rebellion that still percolated within the Empire needed to notice him.

"You are a worthier opponent than I typically encounter," Arpell said, leaning back. His meaty hand pawed at his pet's head. A barely visible tremor ran through the boy's body.

Rone hardened his heart to the sight and concentrated on his mission. "I'm new to this station." He glanced around dismissively. "So far, this game is the most interesting thing I've encountered here."

Arpell huffed out a laugh and made the next play. As with before, Rone let himself be cheated time and again. Then, having sufficiently lulled his quarry, he made his move. Arpell might be very good at cheating, but Rone was better. The look of surprise on his opponent's face when Rone outmaneuvered him gave Rone the most satisfaction he'd felt in a very long time — since his mate had died, except he wouldn't think of her or of the child she'd lost, along with her life. He didn't allow any emotion to show in his expression. He simply continued his campaign of winning.

Arpell knew Rone had cheated. He could see it in Arpell's eyes, yet what could he do? If he called Rone out on it, he'd open himself up to the same accusation. With so many others avidly watching their game, a quiet confrontation would be impossible. Rone didn't want one, anyway. What he wanted was a pissed-off Arpell, in the hopes that he could leverage that into information when Arpell made a move against Rone. He would, too. All of Rone's intel on the guy said that he was a smuggler, privateer, outright thief and a killer when crossed. Rone certainly hoped so. Physical fights had become a handy outlet for his anger and grief.

The crowd around them grew larger the more Rone won. He made sure to lose a few, as well, so that his winning streak wasn't completely unbelievable. Eventually, though, he'd gained all that he'd lost and so much more. Arpell sneered down at the game pieces when Rone placed the winning one yet again. The male grasped the strands of his pet's hair once more, the only sign of his distress. A small sound reached Rone's ears, a whimper perhaps, although it was so faint that he almost thought he'd imagined it. Almost. He couldn't afford to be distracted, however.

Picking up his pieces, he raised an eyebrow at Arpell. "Another round?"

Arpell licked his lips. "Your luck has certainly changed."

Rone leaned back on one hand while he rolled the pieces in the other. "It has. I seem to have stolen yours from you." The threat hung between them. If Arpell entertained the idea of calling Rone a cheat, he'd be on the receiving end of the same accusation. "If you wish to end the game..." He moved, as if intending to stand.

"No," Arpell barked out. "I feel my luck will return. It's only that you have temporarily cleaned me out of credits."

Rone was willing to bet he'd taken just about all of them. "Then we can't continue," he replied, lacing his tone with a modicum of regret for the benefit of the onlookers. Once more, he began to rise.

"Wait. I have something I can bid." When Rone merely stared back at him, Arpell shifted his gaze briefly to his pet. As he did so, he also tugged the boy's head up by its hair.

A delicate face came into view, young and so beautiful that for a moment Rone believed he'd been wrong about Arpell keeping a female pet. But no, this was a boy with skin as pale as any Travian. When it... No, when he raised downcast eyes for just a moment, Rone caught a glimpse of ice blue ringed with white — and fear, before it was quickly banked and the gaze dropped again. Arpell's brutal grip kept the human's face up, though, on display. There were murmurs in the crowd and some lewd remarks.

"I don't understand," Rone said slowly. "Are you intending to offer your pet as a wager? If so, I'm not interested. I already have a pet." He gestured toward Preen, who still sat quietly by his side. The little alien had endless patience.

Arpell's expression turned nasty. "Ah, but mine is better. You can fuck it, and it knows how to suck cock. I've trained it very well, if I say so myself."

Laughter broke out and more rude observations were made. Rone ignored it all, as he did Preen's hiss. Rone knew that sound, and it meant his companion was pissed off. Small as it was, Preen could be dangerous when provoked. Rone entreated it to silence with a subtle gesture. He needed to consider this turn of events. His simple plan to provoke Arpell and gain notoriety hinged on beating him soundly and taking as many of his credits as possible. If Rone didn't continue to play, another male would take his place. He could already see the speculation in some of those around them. The idea of owning such an exotic and enticing pet would prove too tempting. No one would win the boy, of course. Arpell would see to that. He'd rack up more winnings, and all of Rone's efforts would have been for naught.

"Very well. I suppose it's pretty enough. If nothing else, I could sell it. Your move first."

Arpell released the boy then leaned forward. "No, I insist the first round is to you."

Idiot. He thought to gain an advantage by seeing Rone's opening gambit and reacting accordingly. Rone could already see the extra pieces moving their way down the male's sleeve. Really, Arpell's cheating was amateurish compared to others — compared to Rone's. The male was too full of himself to even realize Rone had maneuvered his extra pieces where he needed them while they'd talked. Winning would be easy. He just had to make it look hard.

* * * *

"No!"

Frey tried not to quiver at the angry sound of his master's voice. He didn't have to lift his head to see what had happened, either. He knew. His master had gambled him away. The vicious creature who prided himself on cheating others so well and often had met his match and lost. There was no suppressing the violent shudder that overtook Frey's body as he absorbed the awful truth that, as bad as his life had been, it had just become infinitely worse. He'd glimpsed the Travian who'd just won him and had seen a depth of hell in that moment that had surpassed all others. Not since his ship had been boarded and its crew slaughtered right in front of his eyes had he been gripped by such mind-numbing terror.

"You have lost." That low voice held more menace than any loud one would.

"We'll play another round."

"I think not. You have nothing left to gamble with, and, in any event, I grow weary of the game. I'll take my winnings now."

For a few tense seconds, there was silence. Frey didn't dare look up, but he wondered if there would be a fight. What happened when one cheater lost to another? He had no doubt that the other alien had, in fact, cheated. How else could he have won? Finally, Arpell, whom Frey had always thought of as Jabba the Hut in an effort to find some humor in his predicament, tugged angrily on Frey's leash. Choking against the sudden tightness, he tried to move quickly to his feet to ease the strain. The Travian gave him no consideration, as usual, and yanked so hard that he sent Frey stumbling into his new master.

Where Arpell had carried soft, doughy flesh over muscle, this new alien was like a wall of rock. Frey couldn't help but cry out when he hit that unyielding tower. He cringed, expecting a blow. None came. Instead, a large hand grabbed his shoulder and steadied him. The grip was firm, yet not as painful as it could have been. Frey forced himself to remain still, not to shy away. Resisting would only earn him a beating, and he'd had plenty of those. Besides, he wasn't sure he would survive one meted out by this creature. Taller and broader than Arpell, with a coldness far more frightening than anything else Frey had encountered, his new master looked like death on two legs.

In the early days of his capture, when Arpell had brutalized and humiliated him, Frey had prayed for death. He'd fought hard, too, every step of the way. Eventually, though, he'd realized that resistance only led to unimaginable pain that wouldn't be alleviated by something as merciful as death. And he'd decided that he wasn't ready to die. He could withstand the dehumanizing life as an alien's pet and fuck toy. If he held on, there might be a way to get back home. Maybe he'd fooled himself with pointless hope. If he had, this new alien master would be the one to kill any dreams he had of a better future. For now, he'd be a good boy, give him no reason to hurt. No more than necessary, of course.

"Thank you for a most entertaining evening." That cool, clipped tone held a note of derision, even to Frey's human ears. Did the guy want to goad Arpell into violence?

If so, Arpell turned out to be brighter than Frey imagined. He didn't react, simply handed over Frey's leash and stomped away. The crowd of Travian males parted for him. In all the places Arpell had dragged

Frey, no one seemed to be the cream of Travian society. Although what did Frey know, other than that they were a ruthless species that occupied New World Colony Seven? If the rumors were true, Frey wasn't the only human boy to have been forced into sexual slavery, either. As far as Frey could tell, the entire species was populated by murderous thieves.

Which brought him to his current master. With more timidity that he would have wished for in himself, he glanced at the creature from under his lashes. It was like looking at a mile of grim, all-black leather, with nothing soft or colorful to break it up. Other than the monkeyish pet with the purple hair. That creature stood almost casually on the end of another leash hooked into the master's belt. It peered around the master's massive legs and grinned at Frey. At least it appeared to be grinning. Was that even possible? Frey hadn't seen much of other aliens besides Travians and nothing so almost-cute.

"Come." The command, sharp and curt, reclaimed Frey's attention.

He dutifully fell into step behind his new master as they wove through the crowd of onlookers. One of the males dared to grab Frey's ass when he passed by. That was nothing new. It happened all the time. He was an oddity on these stations, he knew. Arpell had seemed to enjoy the attention and had even lent Frey out to business associates from time to time. That's how Frey knew for sure that not a Travian alive would treat him with anything other than brutality. This time, however, things unfolded differently.

As if he had eyes in the back of his head, Frey's new master stopped, turned and growled at the offender. He actually bared his teeth, scaring Frey so badly that he couldn't hold back a whimper. He hated showing such fear, yet he was beaten down, hurting and starving, as always. But the master's ire wasn't directed at him, so really he was being a baby. It was the male who'd groped him that was in trouble. The guy's eyes went wide then he turned to push his way through the crowd to get away. With that show of force, everyone else found something new to take their attention, dispersing rapidly.

No one bothered them further on their journey into the sleeping quarters. Where Arpell had always taken meager accommodations, this master had more means — or at least a taste for a bit of luxury. He led Frey into a large chamber with a bed that promised far more room than Frey was used to. That was assuming he wasn't kicked onto the floor when the creature finished fucking him. Then again, he might just shove his dick in Frey and keep it there for the rest of the night. It would be painful, but at least Frey would be warm and lying on something relatively soft.

His master surprised him by immediately taking the leash and the choke collar it was attached to off Frey. Once again, he couldn't hold back his reaction to the sudden and looming hands. He flinched and shied away before remembering to be still. Be good. The alien didn't seem to notice the reaction or care. He merely did the same for the other pet and tossed everything onto a table. Then, walking farther into the room, he started removing his clothing.

"Seek your bed, Preen. We've accomplished all we can for now."

It took a moment to understand that the master spoke to the monkeyish creature. It had a name, apparently, and the master was inclined to use it. That alone was something new. Arpell had always called Frey 'boy,' 'pet,' or 'slut.' He'd never bothered to learn Frey's name. Preen let out a series of chattering sounds that stumped the translator that had been forced inside Frey's head soon after capture. Weird. Frey had just assumed it could allow any being to communicate with any other. Obviously not, although just as obviously, the master somehow understood what Preen had said.

The Travian held up his hand. "I know. It can't be helped." He eyed Frey briefly, making Frey want to hunch in on himself and become invisible. "Just go to your own room, please. I'll see you tomorrow."

With a final screech, Preen scampered toward a door at the far side of the room, then through it. Even weirder. The other pet had a room of its own? And did Frey hear his master right? Did he say 'please' to the pet? Maybe Preen wasn't a pet at all, but if that were the case, why the leash? Nothing made sense to him anymore, and given how hungry and thirsty he was, maybe he was starting to hallucinate.

"Take off your clothes."

Frey started at the brisk command. No 'please' this time. Before his mind even registered the order, his fingers had already started to comply. He had precious little of his uniform left, only his pants and T-shirt. Everything else had been ripped off him and tossed away. It might not be much, but the worn material helped with the never-ending cold of Travian domains. It gave him a modicum of privacy, as well. He removed it quickly, then carefully folded it. The cleaning treatment he'd given it before leaving for space still lingered enough to keep it from smelling. That would change soon, not that Arpell had cared about something like a bad odor. The guy had reeked, at least to Frey's sensibilities. The new master didn't, however, so maybe he'd be inclined to let Frey bathe himself more, then also wash his clothing when the time came.

After placing his meager pile on the same table as the leashes and collars, Frey turned to his master and waited for the next command. The Travian already stood naked himself — and aroused. Frey kept his gaze firmly on the ground, not wanting to see the thing that would soon invade his body and make him hurt. There was no avoiding it entirely, of course. He caught enough of a glimpse to know that this new master was hung even bigger than the last. Not so surprising. Everything else on the guy was bigger, so why not his cock, too? Another shudder ran down his spine, and he ruthlessly beat it back. He couldn't let fear rule him now. He needed to stay sharp and obey, so he could eat. God, he was so hungry his stomach had given up growling about it.

"Get on," his new master said, pointing to the bed.

Again, Frey moved to comply quickly. His master sounded annoyed with him already. How had he screwed up? Probably it didn't matter what he did. This master would find fault with him, regardless. Nevertheless, he went straight to the bed and lay face down. He pillowed his head on his folded arms, raised his ass, bent his knees and widened his legs. He always thought he must look like a frog in this position, but Arpell had liked it. He hoped this master would, too. It might be demeaning, yet it was far better than being forced to ride his rapist. He closed his eyes and kept his breathing steady.

The bed depressed with the heavy weight of the Travian joining him. Frey tensed at the approach before making himself relax. He could do this. He'd learned how to make his body go slack in order to accept the invasion with as little pain as possible. If he was very good, his master might not do anything more than fuck him once. No beating, no being made to dine on alien cock instead of real food. That was his goal for the evening. Pathetic, but that was his life now and crying about it wouldn't get him anywhere except in a worse situation.

A warm hand landed on his back, the touch startling in its lack of force. It was almost a gentle caress as the palm slid down Frey's bony spine. Always thin, he'd become gaunt from lack of regular meals. He wondered idly whether his master even found him appealing. An inward snort brought him back to reality. He was no longer the pretty boy that men, women and girls gave sideways looks. He was just two holes to be used.

That hand moved onto his ass while his master positioned himself between Frey's opened legs. The heat of Travian skin chased away the chill of the room. That was something, at least—a small comfort to help offset the misery to come. And there it was, the blunt, wet thing sliding up Frey's cleft, then rubbing against his tiny hole—pressing, breaching, stretching. Oh, God, the burn of it. How could something so big fit inside his small channel? Each time a Travian fucked him, he marveled anew that the act didn't simply tear him apart. Sometimes he did bleed—never enough to kill him, only enough to make walking and sitting cause a special hurt.

He bit back the cry. Crying wasn't allowed, not unless the master wanted him to, then he'd find a way to wrench the sound from Frey's throat. He made his lungs breathe in and out to the rhythm of the thrusting. He made his muscles melt into the bed, become totally pliant to the invasion. In his mind, he played out the best memories he had—the ones where he and his mom had first arrived on the fertile plains of New World Colony Five and finally had clean air to breathe and endless space to grow food, run and be free. His mother had been so beautiful. Everyone had said so. And she'd been happy and hopeful, even when she had gotten sick. The doctors had shaken their heads and said that the only real hope for her had stayed back on Earth, a place they couldn't return to. Memories of her, the sound of her voice urging him to make something of his life, to take the gift of a new start and be whatever he wanted… That's what really kept him going in the face of this horror.

With a muted grunt, his master came. The hated sticky wetness spurted deep up inside Frey, marking him as the property of this new Travian. Frey understood how it worked. Arpell had taunted him with it. Everyone would smell his new master on him and know him for the thing — the *nothing* — he'd become. The thick rod slid down Frey's channel as his master pulled out. Frey could feel every tug and pull of his delicate flesh as it emptied. He turned his face into his arms and grimaced with revulsion. At least it was out for now.

The master heaved a breath and tossed himself onto his back next to Frey. Silence reigned. The Travian didn't move, didn't speak, didn't give Frey leave to go scrounge up food and water for himself. Oh, God. He wasn't going to be allowed to eat or drink still. After the seemingly interminable amount of time that Travians marked as a day, Frey was still going to be denied. It wasn't fair! He'd been a good boy, no struggling and no whining. He was supposed to be rewarded for that, wasn't he? Then he remembered that fairness wasn't part of the devil's bargain he'd struck by default in order to live. His head already swam and his stomach clenched for the first time in a long time with the knowledge that, after being so patient, it was still going to be denied. He quickly shoved his fist in his mouth to silence the groan.

Not fast enough.

"What is it?"

Frey forced his eyes open. He didn't dare look at his master's face, of course. He stared instead at the creature's massive chest. "Sorry, master." His apology came out in a strangled whisper. Another cramp chose to strike him at that moment, too, and he flinched with the pain.

His master raised himself up on one arm. "What is the matter with you?"

For a few frantic seconds, Frey weighed his options. Complaining always earned him a beating, but so did lying. He went with the truth. "I'm sorry, master. I'm" — he swallowed back the bile threatening to erupt — "I'm hungry."

With alarming abruptness, the Travian sat up. Frey cringed when he saw him raise a hand and move it forward. Frey remained in his froggy position because he hadn't been given permission to move. He knew he was vulnerable to all manner of torture. He whimpered and closed his eyes as the hand got closer. He flinched and shook, as well, when that hand touched his exposed side. Fingers, feather-light, fluttered down Frey's ribcage.

No blow came, nor an admonishment. Instead, his master left the bed and returned moments later. Frey didn't dare open his eyes, but he could smell something, something delicious, actually. His stomach cramped a third time in response, making him curl up.

That hand returned, resting on his shoulder. "Easy now. Sit up."

His master pulled Frey up to a sitting position, manipulating Frey's smaller body like a doll. Frey didn't mind, so long as there was no pain. Pride had flown out of the airlock the first time he'd been beaten and raped. He opened his eyes gingerly and saw that the master had brought a container of water and a plate of something that looked like bread and maybe a soy type of protein. He had no idea. Anything, no matter how horrible-looking, smelling or tasting, that Arpell had allowed him to consume had been good enough. As desperate as he was to grab everything and shove it into his mouth, he knew better. He sat cross-legged with his head down, waiting for orders.

His master picked up the water and held it up to Frey's lips. "Drink."

Frey didn't hesitate, he opened his mouth and lifted his hands to hold the container himself, but his master pushed his hands down. Understanding the silent command, if not the reasoning behind it, Frey clenched his fingers together and drank greedily. The water was blessedly cool, a rare treat. It slid down his dry throat and into his empty belly. A cramp tore through his middle again, and he choked a bit in response. The container instantly disappeared from his mouth, making Frey whine. He bit his tongue to stop the noise and bitterly cursed his own stupidity. It hadn't been enough to quench his thirst, which was worse now that he'd had a taste.

"Easy," his master admonished. "I'll give you more soon. You'll make yourself sick if you drink too much so fast."

Frey looked up at him, blinking, before remembering to lower his gaze again. The alien was right, of course. Why he would care eluded Frey's food-starved brain. It didn't matter. Next, the alien held out a piece of the bread in his large, blunt fingers, wrapped around a bit of the other stuff. They hovered near Frey's lips in an unspoken order. Frey obeyed, opening up sufficiently wide for the morsel to be slipped into his mouth. His eyelids dropped involuntarily and a moan escaped. He couldn't help himself. It tasted that good.

His master regarded him intently, that weird Travian smile on his face — the one that looked more like a grimace of pain than happiness. Arpell had looked at him like that often, although with that creature the expression held menace. This one looked more like curiosity. Another bite followed the first one, then more water. His master alternated the drinking and the feeding with slow, measured movements. He kept his gaze on Frey the whole while, probably to make sure Frey didn't boot all of it back up. No need to worry. Frey had suppressed his gag reflex already. Not only had it been necessary in order to swallow alien dick, but the one time he'd thrown up with Arpell, the asshole had forced him to eat it again.

Finally, his stomach felt comfortably full. His master seemed to know that even without Frey saying so. The alien disposed of the remnants of the meal then returned to the bed. Frey instinctively started to move back into position, assuming his master would fuck him again. With his needs met, Frey was only too happy to oblige.

"No. On your side."

Frey instantly complied, rolling over to give his back to his master. He always felt especially vulnerable this way, even though it was no worse than being on his stomach or on his knees. The alien wrapped his arm around Frey's waist while slowly feeding his newly erect cock inside Frey's pliant ass. Jesus, these creatures were quick to arousal, going from zero to sixty in a millisecond. Frey didn't care. With his stomach full and his body hydrated, he felt sleepy. The warmth of the body pressed against him helped, as well. As his master rocked into him, Frey closed his eyes and dropped off.

Sign up for our newsletter and find out about all our romance book releases, eBook sales and promotions, sneak peeks and FREE romance eBooks!

https://totallyentwinedgroup.us7.list-manage.com/subscribe/post

About the Author

Samantha Cayto is a Boston-area native who practices as a business lawyer by day while writing erotic romance at night—the steamier the better. She likes to push the envelope when it comes to writing about passion and is delighted other women agree that guy-on-guy sex is the hottest ever.

She lives a typical suburban life with her husband, three kids and four dogs. Her children don't understand why they can't read what she writes, but her husband is always willing to lend her a hand—and anything else—when she needs to choreograph a scene.

Samantha loves to hear from readers. You can find her contact information, website details and author profile page at https://www.pride-publishing.com